BY JOHN P. STANLEY

TANGLEWOOD • TERRE HAUTE, IN

Published by Tanglewood Publishing, Inc., September, 2013
© 2013 John P. Stanley

Cover by Robert Crawford
Interior illustrations by Paul Forsyth
Design by Amy Alick Perich

Tanglewood Publishing, Inc.
4400 Hulman St.
Terre Haute, IN 47803
www.tanglewoodbooks.com

Printed in U.S.A.
10 9 8 7 6 5 4 3 2 1

ISBN 1-933718-88-9
ISBN 978-1-933718-88-0

Library of Congress Cataloging-in-Publication Data

Stanley, John P.
 Mickey Price : journey to oblivion / by John P. Stanley.
    pages cm.
 Summary: In 1977, three years past the last Apollo mission to the moon, Orlando orphan Mickey Price, Nevada go-cart champion Trace Daniels, and Illinois scientist-in-the-making Jonah Jones are invited to a NASA training camp for a mission they could never have imagined.
 ISBN-13: 978-1-933718-88-0 (hardback)
 ISBN-10: 1-933718-88-9
 [1. Adventure and adventurers–Fiction. 2. Astronauts–Fiction. 3. United States. National Aeronautics and Space Administration–Fiction. 4. Moon--Exploration–Fiction. 5. Extraterrestrial beings–Fiction.] I. Title. II. Title: Journey to oblivion.
 PZ7.S78913Mic 2013
 [Fic]–dc23
                              2012045311

DEDICATED TO SARA
AND TO POSSIBILITIES

CONTENTS

CHAPTER 1
Operation Breakout

Every great adventure starts with a moment. The fleeting moment when you take a deep breath and convince your feet to step off the high-dive board into the empty air. The split second before the roller coaster lurches forward from a standstill. The still silence in the house before the phone rings with news that will change your life.

I guess you could say this adventure started when I convinced my two best friends to jump out of a third-story window.

Getting Big Linus and Taco excited about my plan to sneak out of the house during afternoon reading time actually had been easy. Hooking the tire swing with my fishing rod had seemed like an impossible task, but I snagged it on the third try. And reeling the heavy tractor tire up to my bedroom window almost broke the fishing line, but in the end it only took about two minutes. I'd barely broken a sweat.

But then the crazy plan collided with reality. Somebody needed to find out if it was humanly possible to launch himself from the window and survive the three-story fall without major injury or death.

There was only one kid crazy enough to go first. I took a deep breath. "This stage of Operation Breakout will take a whole lot of skill," I said in an urgent but hushed tone, like a TV sportscaster. "Real athletic skill. We need a leader to demonstrate how to ride this thing." I looked sideways at the others. "Taco, Big Linus, stand back. I'll show you how it's done." I gripped the tire and pulled it toward me.

"Whoa, Mickey. Not so fast," protested Big Linus. "You need an athlete for this? Who are you kidding? I'm the athlete here. Watch and learn."

Got him, I thought, fighting back a grin.

I gave Big Linus my most serious expression and said gravely, "Yeah, what was I thinking? If anyone can do it, you can, Linus." I breathed a huge sigh of relief.

Big Linus put his legs through the tire swing, and Taco and I backed off, letting him scoot to the center of the windowsill.

"Um, Linus?" said Taco. "This will probably be a painful death, but at least it should be quick. Kinda. Anyway, it's been nice knowing you. So after you're gone, can I have your bedroom? And your Miami Dolphins jersey?"

A shade of doubt passed across Linus' face, like a cloud blotting the sun. As he pondered Taco's prediction, he looked nervously from the tire-swing rope, to the giant cypress tree, to the ground, to Taco.

Rope, tree, ground, Taco. Rope, tree, ground, Taco.

I could feel his confidence draining away at exactly the wrong time.

I groaned to myself as my plan started to unravel. Don't get me wrong. Taco was my roommate and best friend at the Orlando Home for Boys. But this was classic Taco, the walking disaster. One time, when we were lighting the jack-o-lantern at Halloween, he actually set his shirt on fire and then ran inside and managed to set the living room curtains on fire. He would have burned down the entire house if quick-thinking Jimmy Reilly hadn't thrown the bowl of orange Halloween punch on him and extinguished the flames.

By opening his mouth, Taco was about to set fire to Operation Breakout.

"Taco, zip it!" I said, kicking him sharply in the shin. "Linus, you're the mission commander. You can let some rookie like Taco steal your glory and go first, but I don't think that's your style." I could see Big Linus' expression change from uncertainty back to determination. "And besides, I'll get the Dolphins jersey, but Taco can have your bed. It smells like butt."

"That's enough, pipsqueaks," said Big Linus. His tone declared the conversation over. "I'm gonna be buried in my Dolphins jersey when I die, so nobody gets it. And nobody gets my bed, either. They'll send it to a museum in Washington D.C., and people will line up for hours just to see it. So get outta my way, I'm going."

"WAIT!" I yelled, grabbing the back of Linus' shorts. "Some advice before you go." I put my head next to his and pointed out into the yard. Both of us looked out along my outstretched arm. "If you jump straight, you'll swing into the tree, right? Horribly, directly, smack-tastically into the fattest part of the trunk?"

Linus squinted down along his flight path, his eyes getting big as he pictured himself hurtling headfirst into the enormous tree.

"Here's what you do, though," I explained. "Jump out sideways. Put your feet on the ledge and shove off as hard as you can to the right, off toward the road. That should spin you out in a circle. Instead of swinging straight at the trunk, you'll go out over the grass, curve around the tree, and end up . . . right . . . over . . . the sandbox."

Linus followed my index finger, turning his head to the right and tracing the big, swooping path. He grinned when his eyes finally landed on the giant sandbox.

"Remember," I said, "if you land safely . . ." I caught an angry glare from Linus. "Okay, *when* you land safely, I'll cast the hook back down, and you can attach it to the tire. Try to do this from the other side of the tree, though. Keep out of sight. Mrs. Finley is on guard duty. She might be old and feeble, but she's not *completely* blind and deaf. If she catches us, this is all for nothing. And we'll get in huge trouble. And we won't get our ice cream. And that's not … going … to … happen," I added, poking my friend in the shoulder with each word.

Mrs. Finley lived next door to the Orlando Home for Boys and often came over when Sister Rinaldi had to leave the house on an errand. Sister Rinaldi was in charge of the house and was the closest thing to a parent any of us had—which made Mrs. Finley like our mean old grandmother.

Right now, Mrs. Finley was sitting guard at the foot of the stairs in the front hall as all the boys were supposed to be reading in their rooms for an hour. This gave the three of us just enough time to execute Operation Breakout, walk a mile to the Dairy Queen, get a Deluxe Banana Split Supreme, and make it back to our rooms before the good Sister came home.

With that, Taco and I started the countdown. "Mission Control," said Taco, "we're clear for launch of Meatball One."

Linus shot him another one of his classic dirty looks, but Taco didn't notice. Or didn't care.

"Ten, nine, eight, seven ... lighting main engine ... six, five, four ... digging a grave for this fearless astronaut ... three, two, one, zero ... zero ... zero. Come on, Linus ... I said ZERO!"

And with that, Linus launched himself out into the open air, pushing far right and away from the window. It was a beautiful sight. It seemed like he was sailing in slow motion. He curved down, down, down and out, around the tree to the far side. And with perfect timing, Linus let go of the tire at just the right moment as it zipped low over the sandbox. Linus landed feetfirst and executed a perfect somersault with a spray of dry, white sand.

"Touchdown!" shrieked Taco as I clamped my hand over his mouth to muffle any further celebration.

Linus gave a wave and scrambled off to retrieve the tire as it continued to swing around the tree. I grabbed the fishing rod and cast the hook again down into the yard, where it landed in the short grass just to the right of the tree trunk.

After Linus snagged the hook into the tire, and as I reeled it up for a second time, I started coaching Taco. He was suddenly silent as he eyed the long drop to the ground below.

"Taco, you got it. You saw how Big Linus did it, right? Same thing for you. Dairy Queen is waiting for you."

Taco looked slightly green and was gripping the windowsill so hard his nails were scratching the paint.

I realized this would take more than the promise of ice cream.

"Taco. You see Linus down there? You know what he's thinking? He's not thinking about Operation Breakout. And he's not thinking about his banana split."

Taco gave me a curious look.

"He's thinking about how totally awesome it would be for him to be the only one to do the swing. How totally awesome it would be for you and me to chicken out right after he jumped. You can't give him that satisfaction. You just can't."

I could picture it. I think Taco was picturing it, too.

"Be the man, Taco. Be the man. And don't look down."

Taco turned back to face the giant tree and grabbed on to the rope. "Be the man and don't look down," he whispered out loud. "Be the man and don't look down. Be the man and don't look down."

With his eyes tightly shut, he scooted his feet into the tire, curling himself into a ball, holding the rope tightly. The tire tipped gently forward and started to scuff off the ledge.

"And don't forget . . ." I said quickly. But it was too late. "Don't forget to push off to the right." My words floated out after Taco as he plummeted down toward the yard—streaking straight at the giant cypress tree trunk.

The tire hit the tree, dead on, with a deep, echoing "BWOMPPP!" At first, I thought the tire had split into two pieces on impact. Then I realized that the part bouncing far to the right was the tire. It was rubber, after all. The part bouncing to the left was Taco. And he was . . . well, he was kind of rubbery, too. He sailed over a bench and went crashing into the enormous blackberry bush about twenty feet from the base of the tree and disappeared.

It was like the bush had swallowed him whole.

And then the bush talked. "I'm okay," it said. "It'll take a while to get these branches out of my side. But I'll be okay."

Linus was doubled over in silent laughter. I was giggling so hard I could hardly reel up the tire.

By the time I made it out the window and had swung down to the sandbox, Taco had escaped from the blackberry bush, but not without scraping every visible bit of skin. And a large branch was still sticking out of his hair at an angle.

"Operation Breakout, phase three," I said as the three of us crouched behind the tree. We moved silently along the edge of the yard, out toward Pickett Street.

I don't know why I looked back down the street past our house at that exact moment, but I did. And that's when I saw it.

Parked in the sun was a brown, four-door car with a long trunk and an even longer hood, probably a Chevy Impala. Leaning against it were two men wearing neat, white shirts with thin, black ties and black pants. The thing I noticed about those guys most of all wasn't their car and wasn't their clothes. It was their sunglasses. Gold. Gold lenses reflecting the sun, so shiny that they almost looked like they were glowing.

One of them was flipping through a pad of paper held in his left hand.

The other was staring at me.

I stood there frozen in the front yard, meeting his stare, until I felt a sharp tug from Taco snapping me back to reality. At that moment, Operation Breakout was the most important thing in my life. And that moment wasn't going to last long.

CHAPTER 2
The Campfire

"Dad, I pity you," sighed Tom, shaking his head gravely. "If this is the story of your life's greatest adventure . . . well, I'd have to say you don't get out much."

"Tom!" snapped Tess. "Dad made you promise. He was going to tell his story, but no interruptions. You lasted about two minutes! What's wrong with you?"

Dad, jolted suddenly back to present day, glanced at his twins in amusement.

Before he could respond, however, there was a flare of light in the soft glow of the dying campfire. Tom's marshmallow had burst into flames, becoming an intense white fireball with a tapered tongue of yellow flame dancing from the top. Like a comet, it left a trail of light against the black background as Tom jerked the stick up and away from the fire pit.

"Oh, the tragedy!" Tom exclaimed without a trace of regret, his eyes twinkling. "The tiny space capsule passes too close to the sun and is consumed by flames.

The foolish space explorers shouldn't have tried to take a short cut. If only they'd followed instructions from Mission Control!"

"That's your third flamer in a row, Tom," said Tess without taking her eyes off her own marshmallow. It was nearing a golden, toffee-colored perfection, just about the same color as her sun-blonded hair. "No way are you getting a bite of this one."

Tom thought for a minute about knocking his sister's stick, sword-fighter style, into the embers. A sideways glance at his dad, who raised a single eyebrow in warning, changed his mind. Instead, Tom lowered his stick with the now-blackened marshmallow into the fire.

"An offering to the gods," Tom announced dramatically. "I hope they enjoy the taste of charcoal— or else I'm in trouble."

"You're already in trouble with me," said Tess with a mixture of affection and frustration. "Dad, please continue."

Dad took a deep breath to continue, but Tom cut in again.

"Hold on, Dad. Seriously? Your story? We've heard all about how you grew up at the Orlando Home for Boys and the stuff you did there."

"Yeah, Dad," Tess said expectantly. "This is supposed to be the Big One. Your story. THE story. The mysterious adventure you had when you were a kid. The one you and Mom always talk about in some sort of weird code."

"But make it interesting," Tom said with a sly grin. "Feel free to embellish if you have to. You know, add some mystery, a little action, maybe a car chase? You're a pro at making up stories. Just make this a good one."

Dad looked at his twins again, perched on the edge of a large log someone had rolled over to the fire pit several summers ago. The sound of distant laughter filtered through the trees from a campsite a hundred yards down the shoreline of the lake. He shifted his position and leaned back against a tree stump.

"You guys had better get more comfortable. This one's going to take a while. Question time is over. No more interruptions. I need to start at the beginning so you get the whole story. And remember, this one's true. Every word."

Tess grinned and lay down in story-listening position. Her hands were clasped behind her head, and she was looking straight up at the starry sky, a comfortable but expectant look on her face. Tom, still skeptical, unrolled his sleeping bag and flopped down on his belly, his chin propped in his hands and his feet angled upward.

Dad continued. "The year was 1977, and I was just a little older than you are now. I know you think I grew up in a time before technology. Back then, we didn't have cable TV or email or smart phones with a thousand apps. But we did have one thing that you don't have now—"

"Dinosaurs as pets?" Tom jumped in with a grin.

Tess growled. But Dad had not heard Tom. He was staring up through the trees and raised his finger pointing upward.

"We had that. The moon. I know, I know, it's still up there. But it seemed different back then. Some of us thought about it every day and dreamed about it every night. Not just kids—adults, too. We all watched on live TV as astronauts walked on the moon. Sometimes, when we looked up at the moon on nights like this, we knew that astronauts were up there, right at that moment.

"The race to the moon was one of the greatest adventures our country has ever had. Each type of rocket had a different name, and each mission had a different number. First came the Mercury program. Then Gemini: Gemini 1 to Gemini 12. Then—"

"Then came the Apollo program," interrupted Tom. "It was *Apollo 11* that made the first lunar landing in 1969. We learned all about this in school. Mercury, Gemini, and Apollo. And then the space shuttle in the 1980s. We learned about them all."

"Well, Tom . . ." Dad drew a deep breath. "That's where you're wrong. You didn't learn about them all. It didn't go straight from Apollo to the space shuttle. There was another program in between that hardly anybody talked about. One that was shrouded in secrecy. And that's what this story is about."

"Secret?" asked Tess. "Why would the government want to keep it a secret?"

"Good question, Tess. Things were different back then. America and Russia—it was actually called the Soviet Union in those days—were competing in everything: science, technology, military. That all created a sense of urgency and an undercurrent of secrecy. But we'll get to that later."

"Okay, I get it." Tom held up a hand to stop his dad in his tracks. "So, this is the action and embellishment

I asked for?" He narrowed his eyes and put on his best Skeptical Tom look. "But Dad, seriously, you still want us to believe it's a true story? What does this have to do with Operation Breakout? And what does this have to do with you?"

Dad paused as the sound of a barking dog echoed across the glassy surface of the lake. "A fair question," he replied. "It just started with that tire swing ride. And those men with the gold sunglasses? I didn't know who they were. But I had the strangest feeling they had come for me. And as it turned out, I wasn't the only one they were after."

CHAPTER 3
Victory at the Go-Kart Track

The number 14 go-kart shot forward at the drop of the green flag, squeezing through a narrow gap between two other go-karts before the first turn. Trace always got a good jump. But starting at the back, she had a long way to go. And she knew the drivers at the front of the pack would not be as easy to pass.

This was only Trace's fifth race in the KF3 racing series. She finished tenth in the first, eighth in the second, and had won the last two in a row to qualify for the 1977 Junior World Championship in Las Vegas. At age twelve, she was two years shy of the minimum age cutoff. You had to be at least fourteen to compete in the KF3 Cup series. But nobody had asked for her birth certificate at the first race, and as far as everyone was concerned, she was a fourteen-year-old racing whiz. So instead of competing against the other kids her age in the six-lap Speedy Tykes race in the morning, she was driving with the big kids in the fifty-mile main event.

After making some easy passes right at the start, Trace settled into the pack and took it easy for the next few laps. She needed to get a feel for her kart and for the race course. She experimented a little on some of the turns, getting a sense of which ones she could approach with some speed and which ones were too sharp to fool around with.

At the halfway point, after twenty-five miles, she was comfortably in the middle of the pack.

From the start, this race had been different from the others she had driven so far. She was the top driver in Ohio, but this race had drivers from California, North Carolina, Florida, and even one from Brazil. They had arrived at the track in pickup trucks or motor homes pulling shiny trailers with their names on the side— or, even better, the names of big-time sponsors. Trace had met a kid from Hickory, North Carolina, who had posed for photos before the race standing next to his "Jupiter Oil Company" trailer. He even had two people from the Jupiter Oil Company walking around handing out autographed pictures of him. Several of the other kids had big sponsors, too.

But not Trace. She and her best friend had painted on some sponsor names, just so she would not have to race in a blank go-kart. But they were not exactly famous companies. "Joanna's Lemonade Stand" was not even a real company.

But none of that mattered now. With ten laps to go, she was still in ninth place. It was time to make her move. She realized that most of the karts were driving too fast into turn two, meaning they had to steer to the outside and then brake hard in the middle of the turn, losing valuable speed. If she entered the turn a little more slowly, she could stay more to the inside, cut the corner, and hit the gas to accelerate sooner.

The next time through turn two, she passed three karts that way. She held her position, and then again on the next lap, she passed two more. She used the same strategy next time around the track.

This got her all the way up to second place, right behind Jupiter Oil. She soon realized that her trick would not work on this driver. He was too good. Just like her, he held back a little going into the turn, so she couldn't pass him on the inside.

With just one lap remaining, Trace knew there was only one thing left to do. As her mom said, "If you can't pass someone, sometimes you just gotta move them out of the way."

It would happen on turn four, the last turn before the checkered flag.

Trace came down the last straightaway and into the final turn right on Jupiter Oil's back bumper and just a little too fast. She knew she could rely on his go-kart to slow her down, though. She gave his back bumper a tap, slowing herself down just enough to keep her tires gripped to the pavement, but giving his go-kart just a bit more speed at exactly the wrong time. His tires screeched and his back end skidded. For just a split second, he had to ease up on the gas. But not Trace. She pounded the accelerator all the way to the floor, shooting past him.

She could hear him yell "Hey, no fair!" as she zoomed just inches past him on the inside and roared across the finish line in first place.

The surprised track announcer stumbled and fumbled for the right words. "And it's the number . . . the number 14 kart, I think, passing number 1 right at the line! The number 14, driven by Tracy Daniels ... I mean, Trace Daniels. Trace Daniels wins the cup! Newcomer Trace Daniels wins the cup!"

The next few minutes were a dream come true for Trace. As the other go-karts headed to the garage area, she took a victory lap in front of the packed grandstand, and then the race officials waved her into a special winners' circle surrounded by checkered flags.

Her prize was an enormous four-foot trophy and a gift certificate for a year's worth of motor oil. Jupiter motor oil. Take that, Mr. Hickory-North-Carolina, Trace smiled.

She was finally heading back toward the parking area to find her mom when a tall woman carrying a pet Chihuahua and a small tape recorder jumped in front of her.

"Tracy D. Wonder Girl. I'm Lacy McKenzie, editor-in-chief of the *Weekly Tattler* newspaper. And," she said, lowering her shriekingly loud voice to a whisper, "we're going to become best friends."

Trace was not impressed. She narrowed her eyes and looked with disdain at the adult standing in front of her. "First of all, it's Trace. No Y, okay? Second, the *Tattler*? Isn't that the newspaper in the racks by the supermarket checkout counter? The one with fake stories about aliens and ghost ships and five-headed pigs?" As her words hung in the air, Trace reached out to pet the dog—and was promptly bitten.

"Oh, Mr. Poopito, no, no, no, that's *not* how we treat our Wonder Girl." Lacy McKenzie kissed her dog on the head and gave Trace an unconvincing, fake smile.

"Now, Trace," she continued, emphasizing the name as though her mistake was somehow Trace's fault. "The *Tattler* is a very successful newspaper. It just so happens that people *like* reading about aliens and ghost ships and five-headed pigs. But just wait until they read about my Wonder Girl. I'll make you a star."

Her fake smile suddenly disappeared, and her lip curled into a sneer. "But first, we'll have to change your outfit. You should be wearing pink with yellow stars down the sleeves and not . . ." she sighed heavily, "not gray with, oh my gosh, are those oil stains? But that's for later. Right now, tell me, what makes you so fast out there? Did your mommy and daddy buy you a bigger engine so you could beat those boys?"

Trace could not believe what she was hearing. "Uh, noooo. All karts have the same 125 cc, touch-and-go, water-cooled, two-stroke, KF engine. You'd get disqualified if you had anything bigger." Trace paused, looking for any hint of understanding in the reporter's eyes. "You know, under Junior Indy Association rules?"

"Oh honey, you can stop talking like a mechanic. I want to write about something kids can understand. If it's not a bigger engine, then you must be the luckiest little fourteen-year-old girl in the world. That's what I'll write. I mean, come on. Winning three races in a row against all those aggressive boys? Have you got a little rabbit's foot in your pocket? What's your secret?"

Trace stamped her feet, and her mouth turned into

a very thin red line. "Look here, Mrs. Weekly Tattler Newspaper. Maybe I won because I know my kart and I figured out the track. I know the tires don't grip so well until they really warm up in the tenth lap. I know number seven shock springs give too much bounce, so we used the number eights here. And I know they let cars and trucks drive across the track at turn four to get to the infield, which wears down the surface of the pavement and makes it slippery. Meaning, if you enter the turn too fast, or if you . . . maybe . . . get a little bump from the car behind you at just the wrong time, you could lose your grip and spin out. Why don't you go ask the boy driving the number 1 kart about that? Ask him how unlucky he was!"

Trace had expelled that entire outburst without taking a breath, so she sucked in a huge gulp of air. With both fists clenched, panting, red in the face, she looked like she had just run the fifty-mile race rather than driving it.

The reporter took a step backward and held her dog out in front of her like a shield. "Well. Um. So are you telling me you don't have a little rabbit's foot for good luck?"

Trace gave a small, frustrated scream, spun around on her heels, and marched quickly away from Lacy McKenzie and Mr. Poopito.

She was so angry that she did not notice the two men wearing shiny gold sunglasses, with short-sleeved white shirts, thin black ties, and black pants. They had been standing just around the corner of the concession stand building in the shade, listening to the entire conversation with stony expressions.

After Trace stormed past, the shorter one showed the faintest hint of a smile at one corner of his mouth. "Yep," he said to his partner. "Call the director. She's the one."

⭐ ⭐ ⭐ ⭐ ⭐

Trace was still out of breath when she found her mom pushing the number 14 kart over to the flatbed trailer hitched to their old, red pickup truck.

"Oh my gosh, Trace, honey, I swear that trophy is taller than you," she said with a huge smile. "Go set it down on the front seat and then give me a hand pushing this little winner up the ramp, okay?"

"You got it, Mom." Trace had just noticed how hot and sweaty she was in her full-length Nomex racing suit. Oil stains on a racing suit, she thought angrily, I'd like to see that dumb reporter tune up a go-kart before the race without getting covered with oil. She peeled off her racing suit, folding it neatly and placing it on the seat next to her glimmering championship cup.

When she turned to head back to her mom and her kart, she noticed the two men in the neckties and shiny gold sunglasses walking straight toward her. Uh-oh, she thought to herself, this could not be good.

"Ms. Daniels, ma'am? Mrs. Daniels, ma'am? We need a word with both of you for just a minute," said the shorter one. The tall one just stood there expressionless. With his extremely long neck, Trace thought he looked like some kind of awkward bird.

"Absolutely, gentlemen. You look like you might be lost," said Trace's mom. "Where can we send you?" Trace could tell her mother was nervous, too.

"No, we're right where we need to be, ma'am. First of all, Ms. Daniels," said the shorter one, turning to Trace, "congratulations on your victory. You're a remarkable driver." He paused. "Especially considering that you're only twelve."

Trace's heart sank. How could this be happening now? She knew she had to be fourteen to race at this level, but that rule seemed so unfair. Without thinking, she looked back to the truck and could see the sunlight reflecting off the top of the enormous championship cup. Her championship cup. With a sinking feeling, she pictured the two men walking off with this prize . . . or worse, wheeling her kart away, too.

"Now you hold on just one minute!" began Trace's mom. "Maybe you should ask someone who knows a thing or two about how old my daughter is. I think I have a pretty good idea."

"Roger that, ma'am. I don't mean to argue. But I think we all know how old your daughter is."

"Mom, wait. It's okay." Trace paused, enjoying the last seconds of feeling like she was a fourteen-year-old KF3 International Go-Kart Champion. "You're right, I'm twelve. And if that means you have to take away the cup, then take away the cup. But I won," said Trace coolly and calmly. "You can't change the fact that I beat every one of those drivers out there today."

The shorter one looked again like he might smile, but then it faded as quickly as it had come. "You're right, you were the best. And you can keep your trophy. We're not here to talk to you about racing."

Trace tilted her head to the side and shot a look at her mom, who appeared just as confused as Trace felt.

"Truth be told," continued the shorter man, "if you really were fourteen, we wouldn't be talking to you right now."

CHAPTER 4
Smoke and Magnets

Show time! The Griffin Middle School gym had recently hosted an exciting league championship basketball game. And yesterday, it had been the site of a killer dodge ball contest during fourth period gym class. But for Jonah Jones, this was the main event.

This was the first year he was old enough to enter the Tri-County Science Fair, and he knew the top prize was within his grasp.

"A Three-Part Practical Study of Magnetic Force," he proclaimed in a steady, clear voice. He realized it was not exactly an exciting title for his science fair entry. But Jonah thought it was an accurate description of his project, and he believed that accuracy was a highly desirable characteristic.

"Part one, using magnets to perform work," Jonah continued. The small crowd shuffled over toward his experiment area, having just watched Billy Johnson's model volcano explode and shoot flames sideways, setting his entire table on fire. Fortunately for everyone in attendance, the janitor and two teachers had been standing by with fire extinguishers. Which was probably the right call for an experiment called Unpredictable Volcanoes—Nature's Fury.

Jonah cleared his throat and continued. "On the table are three simple coil magnets. Each has an iron core wrapped with boron wire. Lying next to them are three metal donuts. Using only the incredible invisible force of magnets . . ." At this point, he paused dramatically. His mother had been an actress in college and had told him as he was rehearsing the night before that sometimes silence, rather than words or music, produces the biggest dramatic effect.

"Using only the incredible force of magnets . . . I will cause three heavy metal donuts to float in midair." Jonah carefully placed the three metal rings above the magnets, giving each a spin. The audience clapped politely as the metal rings fluttered and spun, floating about four inches above the coil magnets on the table.

"Now, by flipping this switch, I will send an electric charge through each coil magnet. Based on Faraday's Law, the poles of these magnets will be reversed. The metal rings will no longer be repelled. They will be ... attracted!" He flipped the switch, and the three rings came crashing down with a loud *twank* onto the coil magnets.

The applause this time was louder. There were several "oohs," one "aah," and a distinct "Oh my goodness!" from one of the judges.

"And now," said Jonah, the audience's full attention on him. "The *grand finale.*"

He moved to the far end of his table where a strange contraption sat. Bolted to the table was the front wheel from his sister's tricycle. It had a large block of dark gray metal wedged into the spokes. Placed a few inches apart, all around the outside of the wheel, were ten coil magnets. Each one was about the size of a can of soup, just like the kind used in the last experiment. A series of colored wires poked out from the top of these coil magnets, leading back to a block of wood with a single lightbulb attached to it.

"A magnetic field is a force created by electrical current," explained Jonah to the attentive audience. "Through a process called induction, by adding just a bit of motion energy, you can release some of the electrical current produced by the magnets. And if you do it right, you can get enough electricity to power this 100-watt lightbulb.

"Not just any magnet will produce enough electricity for this. Strapped to this wheel is the strongest magnet found on Earth, Neodymium." Jonah looked right at the judges. "I had to order it from a company in Utah. It cost $19.70, and it took six weeks to arrive in the mail."

One of the judges raised his eyebrows and made a note in his book. He was clearly impressed.

"Look," said Jonah, gesturing toward his experiment, "no plugs. No electrical outlet. No batteries. Just a few hunks of metal and wire and a spinning piece of Neodymium will power this lightbulb."

The audience shuffled closer. Some bent over to look under the table for any hidden plugs or wires. People in the back row stood on their tiptoes.

"Okay, young man. Let's see your cure for the energy

crisis," exclaimed one judge, stroking his beard. "If this works, I'll buy one of these contraptions for my house!" A ripple of laughter passed through the crowd.

It was time.

"And now," said Jonah, spinning the tricycle wheel with a small handle attached to one side. "Let there be . . . light!"

All eyes turned to the bulb. All three judges were beaming. But as the wheel spun and spun, their smiles slowly drooped into frowns. The bulb was not lighting.

Jonah spun the wheel faster and faster. Nothing.

The wheel made a *thunketa-thunketa* sound that echoed through the quiet gym.

After a while, the *thunketa-thunketa* started to get slower. Jonah's arm felt like it was going to fall off.

"Well, young man," said the judge with the beard. "You might not have invented a way to make electricity. But you sure invented a humdinger of an exercise machine!"

Jonah stopped spinning the wheel and slumped down into a chair. He felt like a balloon after all the air had just whistled out.

How had that happened? Lighting the bulb was the easy part! It had worked one hundred times in a row at home. And it had worked right before the science fair had started. Aghh!

Jonah's concentration was suddenly shattered when the auditorium lights went off and a single spotlight illuminated the tall girl at the table next to him. She was wearing a white scientist's coat, and her blonde hair was gathered into a high ponytail. Peppy pop music pumped out of the large speakers hanging from the ceiling. The girl's silky English accent cut in above the music, "Okayyyy, who's ready for a spot of science?"

Aghh again! Jonah wanted to throw up.

It was Tiffany Berber Timkins. Everyone called her Princess Tiffie for short. Her parents were both big-shot doctors at the University of Chicago hospital. And from the appearance of her science project, Princess Tiffie had received a lot of help from one of them. Probably both.

Her parents were standing just to one side of her table, beaming at the audience and at the judges. Jonah saw her dad wink at one of the judges and give the thumbs-up sign.

Princess Tiffie tugged a black velvet curtain hanging behind her table, revealing brightly colored posters with sayings like SCIENCE ROCKS! and KOOL KIDZ LUV SCIENCE!

She proceeded to deliver a carefully planned presentation about the awesomeness of science, England, and America. She then explained that she was going to mix some chemicals together in tribute to all three.

Bor-ing, thought Jonah.

Princess Tiffie poured the first two chemicals together. Red smoke. Then two more, making white smoke.

Ooh, what's next, groaned Jonah silently.

"Now the final two chemicals," Tiffie chirped. "The first one is sodium nitrate. And the second one . . . this one in the other jar is um . . . uh . . . um . . ."

Sweet, thought Jonah. Please goof up. Please goof up. Please goof up. Oh, if life is fair, you will totally goof up!

At that exact moment, Tiffie's dad coughed hard. Except it wasn't a real cough. It sounded a lot like the word *chromium*. Then Tiffie's mom gave an explosive sneeze that sounded strangely like *ahhh-carbonate.*

"Oh I remember! Chromium carbonate," said Princess Tiffie brightly. "The second one is chromium carbonate." And this time *she* winked at one of the judges. And the judge actually returned her wink, nodding approvingly.

Princess Tiffie mixed the two chemicals together, and they created a blue mist. Red, white, and blue smoke bubbled out of the three containers, flowing down onto the table and over the edge in a kind of misty, patriotic waterfall.

Jonah had to admit, for just a second, that it looked pretty cool. But it was *not* what he called a science experiment. How hard was it to mix together six tubes of liquid?

"Red, white, and blue! Red, white, and blue!" sang Princess Tiffie. "God bless America and God bless the Queen! Thank you, thank you, thank you!"

Princess Tiffie curtseyed to the crowd. She was getting thunderous applause from her parents and—oh my gosh, thought Jonah—thunderous applause from the judges! One of the judges strode up to Tiffie and took the microphone. "I think we all know who gets first prize here today at the Griffin Middle School science fair! Tiffany, very entertaining. Congratulations!" To Jonah's horror, the judge placed a heavy gold medal around Princess Tiffie's neck.

Boy, that was fast. It was all over. The boy who loved science more than pizza had been beaten by Princess Tiffie Timkins in a science contest.

The overhead lights flashed back on, and a small crowd surged forward to walk around in the smoke still flowing down off of Tiffie's display table.

Jonah turned back to his experiment. Why had it failed this time? He ran through his experiment again in his mind. The Neodymium sample was pure. Everything was set up correctly. The magnets had generated a good charge. The principle of induction was a force of nature that never changes. Why had the bulb not lit up?

Jonah was concentrating so hard, he did not notice the two men making their way toward him through the crowd surrounding the winner's table.

One was tall, the other short. They were wearing white shirts, thin black ties, and black pants. Remarkably, even indoors, they were both wearing sunglasses with reflective gold lenses.

"Don't knock yourself, Jonah," said the shorter of the two men, leaning over to get a closer look at the experiment. "Even the best planned missions can fail because of something completely unexpected."

"Yeah, yeah," Jonah mumbled, without looking up. "Thanks, judge. But I don't want the second-place ribbon."

"I'm not the judge," laughed the man. "And besides," he tipped his head toward the other side of the room. "It looks like they gave second place to the boy who set his table on fire."

"Look," the taller man said as Jonah looked up. "We

don't want to talk to the first- or second-place finishers. They don't interest us. We came to talk to you. You just had some bad luck."

Jonah stood up straighter and looked at the two strangers with suspicion. "I don't believe in luck. There was a reason why the bulb didn't light up. And I'm going to figure it out."

Jonah leaned closer to his experiment for a better view of the lightbulb. He looked closely at the bulb's inner workings. His heart sank. How simple. And how stupid! The lightbulb's filament—the super-thin wire that glows white-hot when electricity passes through it— had broken in half. The lightbulb had simply burned out. His spinning magnets *had* generated enough electricity. It was the light bulb that had failed him.

"Jiminy Christmas!" whispered Jonah, feeling deflated like a limp balloon. "Can you believe *that?*"

Jonah removed the broken bulb and screwed in a replacement. With only two cranks of the tricycle wheel, the bulb flickered to life, giving a bright yellow glow. Jonah stopped spinning the wheel, closed his eyes, and smacked himself squarely in the forehead.

"Very good, Jonah Jones. And why do you think the bulb burned out?" asked the shorter man.

"The spinning bicycle wheel shakes and rattles the table like crazy," groaned Jonah. "But the lightbulb filament is thin and fragile. All the shaking and rattling loosened the filament and ended up breaking it. That's what I get for using a regular grocery store lightbulb. They use tougher bulbs in things like machines or cars or motorcycles. That's what I should have used."

"Very good again," said the taller man. "Not only are you a scientist, you're a detective, too. You know," he continued, quieter now, "if you used an even stronger magnet, you could power one hundred lightbulbs."

"Yeah, right. Stronger magnet," said Jonah, adjusting the wires on his contraption. "I'm using Neodymium, the strongest magnet known to man."

"Oh, it's a strong magnet. The strongest magnet on Earth. But we've seen stronger magnets, Jonah."

Suddenly Jonah stood up straight and looked curiously at the two strange men talking to him. "Wait a minute! What do you mean, you've seen stronger magnets? And how do you know my name?"

CHAPTER 5
The Mysterious Invitation

Walking back from the Dairy Queen, Taco, Big Linus, and I savored the rare feeling of complete freedom. Life at the Home for Boys was always chaotic. Always crowded. Often fun. But never free. It was even sweeter than ice cream to be walking along the road in the hot sun, completely free. And I still couldn't believe we had executed our Operation Breakout escape so perfectly. Well, except for Taco's not-so-perfect swing into the tree.

Peeking from between the branches of the large pine trees lining the road was the moon, sitting pale against the bright, blue sky.

"Hey look, moon's out," I said. "I thought it was Tuesday, but I guess it's Moon-day."

"Ugh, that's awful," said Linus, groaning at my terrible joke.

"No, it's worse than awful," Taco said, stopping dead in his tracks. "It's a bad, bad sign. The moon belongs to the night. It shouldn't be out during the day. What's happening?"

I sighed. How could I explain this? "Taco, the world is not ending, it's just—"

But Taco wasn't listening anymore; he was on a roll. "Moon and sun sharing the same sky. Dogs and cats getting married. Fish walking on the land, cows swimming in the ocean." His hand went to his forehead, and he threw his head back for great dramatic effect. Leaning forward, his voice almost a whisper, he continued, "Peanut butter fighting with jelly."

"The Detroit Lions winning the Super Bowl!!" shouted Linus, feeling the spirit.

"Hold on," said Taco, "that's going too far. Not *that* crazy."

"Come on, Taco," I said, "the sun and moon appearing together isn't crazy at all. Of course they're in the same sky. The moon spins around the Earth." I made a fist with one hand and circled my other fist around it. "And they both move around the sun. You're the sun." I walked in a circle around him, still spinning my fists. "Sometimes the moon is on the back side of the Earth. Sometimes it's on the front side, the side closer to the sun."

Taco looked skeptical.

"Sometimes, the moon actually blocks the sun," I said, setting Taco and my two fists in a straight line. "That's a solar eclipse."

Now Taco looked alarmed.

"Wait. Are you telling me that the moon and the sun are whipping around together out there in the sky?

So they could, like, run into each other?" Taco stepped forward toward me. "Just a little off course, then whoomp!" He bumped his sun-chest into my moon-fist.

"The moon slams into the sun. And there's a giant *sun-splosion*. End of life as we know it! Kiss yourself goodbye!" screamed Taco. "This could be the big one. Impact in ten minutes!"

"Taco," I said, "you are so wrong in so many ways. How did you get this way? Did Sister Rinaldi find you at the dog pound before you came to the Home?" I asked. Taco was laughing too hard to hear me.

That didn't last long, though. We had turned the last corner and were now approaching our house. We stopped talking as we crossed the road, moving quickly and silently across the big, grassy yard.

My plan for reentering the house was simple: We would just wait in the bushes next to the porch until we heard the sound of the other boys coming downstairs at the end of reading time. When they came outside into the yard, we would simply blend in with the crowd. Foolproof.

Or maybe not.

We hadn't counted on the brown Impala, still lurking outside the Home.

As the three of us crouched behind the bushes beside the front porch and listened to the sound of the house coming to life again after reading time, I heard the slam of one car door, followed by another. My heart froze. The two men in white shirts and thin black ties, the ones wearing shiny gold sunglasses, were walking straight toward us.

I stood up as the shorter man with sunglasses reached us.

"Hi there, Tarzan. Nice job with that tire swing. How was the ice cream?"

I was stunned. I had to come up with something fast. "Would you believe, we always have permission to do that if we finish our books early?" I asked, without any real hope of being believed.

"Not even close, Tarzan," said the short sunglasses man. "Why don't you come inside with us. Sister Rinaldi is expecting us at three o'clock, so we're right on time."

Turning to the other two, he said, "Linus, Taco, you're free to go. Believe it or not, that old lady watching the front door had no idea you left, and neither did Sister Rinaldi. Operation Breakout was a success."

Linus and Taco stared at the two men in disbelief.

"But . . . the . . . you . . . how . . . Operation Breakout . . . what the . . . " sputtered Taco, his voice trailing off into nothingness.

I took a deep breath and stood up straighter. "You're not from the Department of Children's Services, are you?"

"Negative," said the two men at exactly the same time, walking past us right into the house.

✪ ✪ ✪ ✪ ✪

My mind was racing as I led the two strange men down the front hall toward Sister Rinaldi's office at the back of the house. Not from Children's Services? But then—where?

The police? Oh, come on. An ice cream run in the middle of the day was not something that would bring out the police. But then—who?

Sister Rinaldi must have heard us coming. As I approached her office, she burst out of her doorway and put her hands on my shoulders, steering me into the room.

"Gentlemen, please come in, come in. I see you've already met Mickey. Let's find you a seat."

The two men did not introduce themselves to Sister Rinaldi, so clearly they must have met her before. Once inside her cluttered office, they both stood rigidly just inside the doorway. They removed their gold sunglasses at exactly the same moment and slipped them into their shirt pockets.

Sister Rinaldi, her hands still protectively on my shoulders, steered me to a chair at the edge of the desk. She gestured the visitors toward two chairs with tall wooden backs on an oriental rug in front of her desk.

The two men paused, waiting for Sister Rinaldi to sit down first.

Sister Rinaldi took a long look at me and pursed her lips before starting. "Mickey," she began, "these two special visitors asked to meet you. They talked to me this morning about a special . . . well . . . a special school . . . or a special opportunity for you. It's a—"

"Ma'am. Ma'am, if I may," said the shorter one. He had buzz-cut hair, just like the other man's. His eyes were cold, steel blue but had friendly wrinkles around the edges.

"Mickey, we need to introduce ourselves. I'm Major Jackson. And this is Major Austen." The taller man nodded his close-cropped head at me without smiling.

"Nice to meet you," I said warily. "Exactly what kind of major are you?"

Jackson looked at me with approval. "Good question. I'm a major in the United States Air Force. But I'm not working for the Air Force right now. I guess you can say I'm on loan to NASA."

I looked at him with surprise. "NASA? The space program? You're an astronaut?"

"I'm an astronaut. And so is Major Austen here. And that's why we're here. We've been sent on behalf of NASA to invite you to the Kennedy Space Center for a camp, an explorers camp, you could say. To learn about the space program, to go through some training exercises—just like a real astronaut does."

I hadn't moved during this entire conversation. Suddenly realizing my mouth was wide open, I closed it.

"You've got to be kidding me," was all I could say. Seriously. It was like the coach of the Miami Dolphins had just dropped by and asked me to be his quarterback. Or like President Carter had strolled in through the front door and invited me to the White House. "Are you kidding me?"

"That's a negative," said Major Jackson. "It's a two- or three-week program. And it's not just you. You'll be joining a class of other kids your age from all around the country."

I thought about that. "So why me? Why was I picked?"

"There are things I need to know, and things I

don't need to know," said Major Jackson. "You asked
about one of the second things. All I know is that a spot
just opened up because a boy from Nebraska dropped
out, and your name is on my list. And the invitation,
the opportunity, is up to you now. The camp starts
tomorrow, so you don't have much time to decide. But
go ahead, talk it over with Mrs. Rinaldi."

"Sister!" she said sharply, correcting the man in
uniform.

"Sorry, ma'am. Talk it over with *Sister* Rinaldi. But
do you want some advice, young man?"

I nodded.

He looked at me hard for about ten seconds
straight. "Say yes."

⭐ ⭐ ⭐ ⭐ ⭐

There was a long silence as Dad got up to put another
log on the dying campfire. Tom and Tess were still
speechless as he flopped back to a sitting position and
took a long drink of water from the Miami Dolphins
cup resting in the pine straw next to him.

Tom finally broke the silence. "Dad. Um, first of all ...
whoa. This is a crazy story. Seriously. Second of all, did
this actually happen?"

"Well, Tom," said Dad, "think about it for a minute.
When I was thirteen, I started going to St. Paul's
School in New Hampshire and spending my summers
in Connecticut. But before that, you remember where
I lived: Orlando. You've seen the pictures of the
Orlando Home for Boys."

Tess sat up excitedly. "And pictures of your friend Taco! Tom, we've seen his picture, right? The funny chubby kid in those pictures with Dad?"

"That's right, Tess. You've seen pictures of him. And pictures of Sister Rinaldi, too."

"But Dad . . ." Tom was nowhere near convinced. "What's up with those other kids, Trace and Jonah? Why are they in the story? I don't understand how they fit in. Wait a minute! Trace, is that supposed to be Trace McGuff, the NASCAR driver?"

"Well, they only made one Trace, that's for sure," said Dad with a grin. "Yeah, that's Trace McGuff. Daniels was her last name before she got married. I haven't seen her in a few years, but we still keep in touch. How d'you think we got the great seats and special tour of the garage last year at the Daytona 500?"

"And the guys in gold sunglasses? And Jonah Jones? And the space camp?" Tess fired off.

"Hey, it's all true. But I'm just getting started. This story is just about to kick into high gear." Dad pulled a camp clock out of his backpack. It was 11:45 P.M.

"Don't. You. Dare. Stop," warned Tess, rising slowly to a standing position on her sleeping bag. "I'm serious. Keep talking and keep telling us about this space camp."

Glancing one more time at the clock, Dad sighed and leaned back against the tree stump. "Okay. Just because it's summer. And just because we're getting to the good part. And," he paused, reflexively looking over his shoulder, "just because Mom's out of town. Don't tell her I kept you up so late, okay?"

The two kids nodded earnestly.

"Okay, in that case I'll keep going."

Tess flopped back down on her sleeping bag. She and her brother were lying on their stomachs, facing their Dad, elbows on the ground, chins in their hands.

"All right," Dad continued. "We came back from the Dairy Queen. The strange men in gold sunglasses gave me a mysterious invitation to some sort of camp at the Kennedy Space Center. And I said yes."

CHAPTER 6
One Small Step

It was a strange feeling, walking into the dining room the next morning at breakfast. Everyone had pretty much left me alone as I packed my clothes, so I was the last one to come downstairs. Instead of being met by the usual happy chaos, it was strangely still, silent, and uncertain.

And everybody was staring at me.

Of course it was Taco who broke the silence. "Hey, space cadet," he called out, "when you pretend to land on the moon at camp, you'll be like Neil Armstrong, except you'll have to say 'That's one small step for a doofus, one giant leap for doofus-kind!'"

With that, it was like a dam burst. Kids started laughing and asking me questions all at once. Plates of pancakes and bacon appeared from the kitchen. This day, spare no expense, we had fried eggs, too, with pitchers of orange Tang to mark the occasion. I felt like I was king of the world—even though I had no idea what was coming next.

The time since the two astronauts left was a blur. Sister Rinaldi made me stay behind in her office to "talk things over." I could hear the other boys whispering loudly outside her office. There were occasional thumps against the door, probably as they jockeyed for a position closest to the keyhole as they tried to catch a stray word coming from Sister Rinaldi or me.

Not that I was saying much. There wasn't anything to say.

Sister Rinaldi kept telling me to think things over carefully, and that I didn't need to go if I didn't want to. But I had already made up my mind to go.

Back in the dining room, I barely had time to gulp down a couple pancakes when Sister Rinaldi came bustling in from the front hall to tell me my ride was here. There was a sudden hush again as all the guys scrambled to the front window. Everybody thought I would be picked up by a helicopter or at least a limousine.

I must say I was a little disappointed to discover that my transportation was far less glamorous. NASA had sent a white van with an enormous driver.

As the driver carried my suitcase from the front porch, Sister Rinaldi pelted him with a hailstorm of questions and information about my bedtime and the importance of adequate fruits and vegetables. This gave me a chance to walk behind her with Taco by my side.

"So Mickey," said Taco, tugging on my sleeve as we walked, "if you don't send me a postcard from rocket camp, I'll be crushed. And you'd better bring back a space helmet or jetpack or something when you're done. Okay?"

"You got it, Taco." He looked like he might cry, and all of a sudden I felt it welling up in me, so I quickly started talking. "Look, you take my bed while I'm gone. It's *way* better than yours because it's right by the window. And you have total control over my comic books. Besides, I'm back in two weeks."

That seemed to boost Taco's spirits. The next thing I knew, the van was backing out of the driveway, and the entire population of the Orlando Home for Boys was in the front yard shouting last-minute advice and waving goodbye.

Taco ran alongside and then behind the van as it picked up speed down Pickett Street. Seconds later, the van turned the corner, and the Home and Taco disappeared from sight. I sometimes think back to that moment and imagine Taco the few moments after I lost sight of him. He probably kept running for a while, then slowed to a jog, and finally stopped in the middle of the road, staring at the empty corner where the van had just turned.

But back then, in the van, I had other things to consider.

"Kennedy Space Center, please," I said to the driver as though I was in a taxi.

"Not so fast, kid," came the reply. "We're heading to Orlando International Airport. We have another pickup."

★ ★ ★ ★ ★

It was barely 15 minutes from my neighborhood in Holden Heights to the airport. The driver bypassed the area clogged with Disney buses and the area for regular passenger pickup, pulling into a small lot filled with some police vehicles and other white vans, at the far end of the terminal. On cue, a woman in a neat, blue uniform opened a door and ushered out a boy with wild black hair, braided in dreadlocks style, carrying an overstuffed green backpack. Right on his heels was a tall, skinny girl with a ponytail wearing a baseball cap and pulling a red bag on wheels.

They both craned their necks to see who was in the van. I decided to sit back and play it cool. The two kids climbed aboard as the driver exchanged some papers with the woman in the uniform and then quickly pulled out toward the highway.

"And then there were three," said the boy. "I'm Jonah from Chicago. This is Trace from Cleveland." The girl nodded her head as she slid into the back seat, while Jonah plunked down next to me. "And you are…?"

"Mickey from Orlando. Nice to meet you."

"*Mickey* from *Orlando?* You've *got* to be kidding me," said Trace. "Does Disney World know you escaped? Where's Minnie?" Her sarcastic look slowly turned to one of embarrassment. "Sorry, you probably hear that all the time."

"Not as much as you'd think," I said, trying my hardest to appear cool and confident. "We usually let the Magic Kingdom crowd do their own thing. We kind of forget they're around after a while."

"So, what's CAMS?" I asked, quickly changing the subject and pointing to the letters on her hat.

"That's what I asked," said Jonah. "Apparently, it stands for Cleveland Area Motor Speedway. Trace and I were on the plane from Chicago together, and she told me all about it. Turns out we're riding with the fastest kid on four wheels, the go-kart champion of Ohio."

"Well, the go-kart champion of the entire USA, actually," said Trace. She said it with pride. But without bragging. I liked her already. "And this guy," she continued, "is some kind of Albert Einstein scientist. Seriously. Mickey, ask him what his favorite magazine is. Go ahead."

"Okay, what's your favorite magazine?" I asked.

"It's a tie between *Modern Robotics Weekly* and the *Journal of Advanced Metal Research*," said Jonah. He was totally bragging. But I found it hard not to like him, too, and had to laugh as Trace rolled her eyes.

"Well then, we have a lot in common, Jonah," I said. "I love robots!"

Jonah perked up and spun in his seat to face me. "You do? Omigosh, how many have you made? Do you have trouble with the transductor circuits and the sonic remote control units? Maybe we can build one together. Did you bring your supply kit?"

Oh boy, I thought. "Um, when I say I love robots, I was thinking more about Rosie from *The Jetsons* or the *Iron Man* comic books. I did bring those along."

Jonah's blank stare told me he wasn't familiar with Doctor Decepto and his Metal Monsters of Doom.

Trace jumped in to change the subject. "So," she asked, "what's your specialty, Mickey from Orlando?"

I paused and wondered what to say. I never thought of myself as having a specialty before. I was just good at being a kid. "Well," I said, "I'm the best pitcher on our Little League baseball team, at least now that Hudson Hooper moved away. I'm a huge fan of the Miami Dolphins. *Huge.* Hate the Tampa Bay Buccaneers, love the fish." No response. "And I can eat more pizza at a single sitting than anybody else in my house, even Big Linus."

I could tell I was losing them.

"Come on, where's the love?" I asked. "I might be skinny, but I can really eat a ton. You guys never had a pizza-eating contest? You've got to follow the rules: If you don't eat the whole piece, crust and all, you don't get credit for the piece."

They both shook their heads.

"Well, I tell you what," I said, undeterred. "We'll have a pizza-eating contest sometime before this camp is over, and I'll show you who's the king."

Jonah's eyes perked up again. "Camp?" he said with a smile. "Is that what you think we're going to? Camp?"

"Um, yeah? Young Explorers Camp? Kennedy Space Center? Didn't they tell you?" I said.

"Oh, they told me all right," said Jonah. He glanced secretively up at the driver, who didn't seem to be paying us the slightest bit of attention. Even so, Jonah lowered his voice. "But do you think you can believe everything they tell you?"

"Oh no, here he goes again. I got this whole theory on the plane, all the way over Tennessee and Georgia,

I think it was," said Trace, rolling her eyes for a second time. "Where's your proof, Jonah?"

"Go ahead," said Jonah, completely unfazed by Trace's doubt. "Make fun. But if you think we're here for a little kids' camp, then you're about as smart as the donut I ate for breakfast. Listen," said Jonah, lowering his voice to a whisper and glancing up at the driver again as he leaned in closer to me. "You probably haven't been paying attention to the special science magazines or the recent rumors about NASA's lunar project. Mysterious launches? Unexplained missions? Well, if you've been reading those articles like me, then you'll know that NASA is having some serious problems. Something's going totally wrong."

"Fine," I said, "maybe that's true. But what makes you think that has anything to do with us?"

"Well," admitted Jonah, "that part I can't figure out. It just seems like the space program should be awfully busy with other things rather than worrying about a space camp right now. It seems like a funny time to send a couple of top astronauts out to round up kids from across America, doesn't it? And that's another thing: Isn't this an odd time for a camp? Don't they normally do camps in the summer?"

I hadn't really thought about that. It was the end of October, right in the middle of school.

"And another thing," said Jonah. He was on a roll. "This whole invitation came out of the blue. Like Trace, I just heard about this last week. They told me they were inviting me late because some kid from Nebraska dropped out, and there was an open spot. How about you? When did they invite you?"

"Um. Like, yesterday," I admitted. "But wait, they told me I got the Nebraska kid's spot!"

Even Trace looked surprised now. "That's weird. They told me I got the last spot. But it was a kid from Kansas who dropped out."

Jonah let out a low whistle.

I didn't have an answer. But to be honest, it didn't bother me in the slightest. I was just excited to be off on an adventure. "Nebraska, Kansas, whatever," I cut in. "I just think this sounds awesome, whatever it's called and whyever they're doing it."

Jonah sank back into his seat with a sigh, and our conversation turned to our homes, our schools, and Trace's recent go-kart victory. She was telling us about her thrilling pass on the final lap when she realized we were no longer listening. As her voice faded away, she noticed that Jonah and I were craning our necks to stare out the front window.

The van was heading due east and had passed across a long causeway over water. The expanse of land in front of us was hard baked and treeless, with clumps of shrubs and clusters of buildings. Visible now in the distance were several hulking towers rising up into the hazy sky. I knew right away what they were. They weren't radio or TV towers. We were looking at the launchpad towers at Cape Canaveral.

We were looking at the home base of the American space program.

We passed under a huge sign that read WELCOME TO THE KENNEDY SPACE CENTER AT CAPE CANAVERAL. A guard waved us through. We were traveling slowly now. A line of cars and RVs clogged the road leading to a large parking lot and a big white visitors' center.

Our van turned out of the traffic, however, taking a small, unmarked road to the right, heading for a low, one-story building at the edge of a tall fence. I realized it was actually two fences about ten feet apart. Both had barbed wire on the top. As the van slowed to approach the gate, the driver said over his shoulder, "Welcome to Kennedy. That's the public area over on the left. We're heading into the restricted area. Not many people get to go through this fence."

"I think I've died and gone to heaven. This is awesome!" said Jonah.

"I think I've died and gone to Weirdissippi. This is bizarre," said Trace.

They both looked at me for the deciding vote.

"Give me a little more time," I said. "I'm on the fence."

As the van rolled forward, Jonah said, "Too late now, Mickey from Orlando. We're through the fence. And Trace? I have a feeling this is going to get even weirder before it's all over."

CHAPTER 7

The Secrets of the Space Program

Once inside the gate, we pulled into a small parking lot on the other side of the guard building. A tall woman in a crisp, white shirt and pants was waiting for us. She emerged from the shade of a palm tree when she saw us and took a few quick steps forward. She pulled open the door while the van was still rolling and hopped skillfully into the passenger seat as the driver hit the gas again and pulled back out onto the road without stopping. Black letters on a shiny, white road sign spelled out Apollo Drive.

"Trace, Mickey, Jonah," she said as she nodded at each of us, "welcome to Kennedy. I'm Amanda Collins, and you can call me Amanda. I'm assigned to the Moon Project Task Force, and I'll be spending a lot of time with you three, and the others, for the next few weeks."

"The others?" Jonah interrupted. I was beginning to understand that Jonah was never afraid to speak up.

"Yes, the other kids in the program. Seventeen others, twenty total." Amanda saw that Jonah was about to interrupt again, so she held up a palm, making a quick stop sign. "Now wait, I know you all have a ton of questions. Or at least *you* do, Jonah. You'll get a chance to ask them very soon. Just—" Amanda pushed her hand forward again as Jonah opened his mouth. Jonah sank back in his seat, almost as though she had used some magical force to propel him backwards, "Relax. And let me tell you about where you are."

I turned my attention back to the windows of the van as we rolled along Apollo Drive. Bushes and short trees a bit taller than the van were growing on either side of the road, but they soon gave way to shorter, stubby bushes, giving us a better view of the buildings scattered around the area. "This is the John F. Kennedy Space Center at Cape Canaveral. There are almost fifteen thousand employees here, all working together on the space program.

"There are engineers who help design and maintain the rockets, the landing vehicles, and other spacecraft. There are specialists who run our computer and communications systems and thousands of others who keep everything else going. We're like a small city. And of course, there are the astronauts who live here and train in the weeks leading up to their missions."

"We're heading toward the—." Her words were suddenly drowned out by a thunderous rumble of sound. My head quickly spun left, right, and then up to see what was making the noise. I saw a flash of gray out the left window that quickly disappeared over the roof and then reappeared on the right side of the van. It was a plane—a jet plane—flying extremely low. It must have been some kind of Air Force fighter jet.

"And how could I forget," said Amanda after the rumble died down. "We also have an airport: the Cape Canaveral Air Force Station."

"Whoa. Now *that* plane was fast. And I know fast!" said Trace, awestruck and clearly impressed.

"Well, you'll get used to those. Most of the astronauts come from the Air Force, and they like to show off by flying their toys. Anyway," Amanda continued, "NASA's other major facility is the Johnson Space Center in Texas. A lot of our design and training takes place there. But this," she waved out the window, "is where the action happens. Kennedy is where the rockets are launched. All our missions start from here, but they don't end here. As you know, a command module carrying the astronauts reenters the Earth's atmosphere and then is slowed down with huge parachutes before splashing down in the ocean.

"Someday we'll have a rocket that can return to dry land, just like an airplane. Our scientists are working on an exciting new program called the Space Shuttle. It looks more like an airplane than a rocket, and it will land on a regular runway instead of splashing down in the ocean."

"I'll believe *that* when I see it," Jonah snorted sarcastically.

"Someday soon, you'll see," replied Amanda, smiling. We pulled up to a group of one-story buildings. Painted white rocks lined the circular driveway in front of the first building, with a flagpole bearing a large American flag. They obviously watered the grass here, because the lawn between the buildings was as smooth and green as a golf course. There were even flowers lining some of the pathways.

"Welcome to the Astronaut Center. Camp Alpha, we call it. It has classrooms, a cafeteria, sleeping quarters, a gym, and a swimming pool. You'll be calling it home for the next few weeks. You three are the last ones to arrive, but don't worry, you haven't missed much. Follow me. It's time to meet the other kids here—your fellow campers."

Amanda sprang out of the van, again before it stopped. She told us to leave our bags, which would be taken where they needed to go, and motioned for us to follow her.

She led us down a hall and then stopped at an open door and pointed inside, smiling. Jonah walked in first and stopped short, making me crash into his back. It looked like a classroom, with several rows of chairs and tables facing a chalkboard. The front rows were filled with kids, each of them wearing a dark blue jumpsuit that looked a little like the one my friend Mack wore at the Sunoco gas station near the Dairy Queen, except without the stains from grease and last week's burrito. Each jumpsuit had a small American flag on each arm, a glittering "USA" patch sewn onto the left side in the front, and a NASA patch with an eagle on the right side.

I glanced down at my green, striped shorts and cartoon T-shirt that read Dirt Bike Racer. Nice choice, Mickey, I thought to myself, crossing my arms and shuffling into the room.

The other kids stared at us, and there were a few whispers as we came in. Then they quickly swiveled to face forward as Amanda walked briskly to the front of the room. Jonah, Trace, and I scooted quickly into three empty seats in the third row.

I noticed there were five men standing at the front, behind a large table. All five had short, military-style buzzcut hair. Each was wearing a blue jumpsuit just like the campers. And they were all wearing those incredibly cool gold sunglasses. One of them had a toothpick hanging out of his mouth and gave me a scowl and then sighed and checked his watch. He obviously wanted to be somewhere else.

"Welcome to Young Astronaut Academy," announced Amanda in an official tone.

Jonah leaned toward me and whispered, "Young Astronaut Academy? Young Explorers Academy? Astronaut Adventure Camp? See, they can't even keep the name of this camp straight! Very fishy. Am I right? Am I right?"

Boy, that kid was suspicious about everything.

More men and women in uniforms were filtering into the back of the room and now filled every seat behind the kids in the first three rows.

"First of all, congratulations. There are about three million fifth graders in America. NASA could have invited any one of them. But they picked twenty. They picked you. You're lucky to be here, and we're lucky to have you.

"This week will be full of surprises, just like the space program," Amanda continued. "We will be treating you like real astronauts. You will sleep where they sleep and eat where they eat. You will receive some of the training they receive and take the tests they take. There are three main parts of training for our astronauts: physical, technical and mental. And you will receive all three."

"We want you to feel like real astronauts. Yes, we want you to follow our rules, but we also want you to be curious. We want you to ask questions."

As Amanda kept talking, I noticed that Jonah's hand was up in the air. Trace noticed, too, and turned to look at him. The table on our left noticed as well and started staring at him. Finally, Amanda noticed what we had noticed and stopped talking.

"Okay, Jonah, shoot," she said.

"You meant what you said about being curious and asking questions?"

"Absolutely, Jonah, go ahead."

"Can you discuss the problems faced by the recent lunar missions?" asked Jonah. "It was the third mission in one year, and it seemed like there was a big hurry to get it up there. The newspapers had almost no information about the purpose of the mission. NASA said the mission was just collecting rock samples. But I think there's something else going on. Can you explain?" Jonah looked intently at Amanda. I shot a look sideways at Trace, who rolled her eyes at Jonah for the fifth time today. We were afraid our new friend might be a little crazy.

"Well," Amanda looked at her feet, "that's a very good question, and I think we'll be discussing the recent missions at some point during your camp experience. You see, it's true, there was a ... well ... a small, you know … a problem that—" Amanda Collins looked very relieved when she was interrupted by a voice from the back of the room. The voice wasn't loud, but it was strong and deep and Southern and filled the room. Everyone swiveled around to face the speaker.

"Some people might call it a problem. But for the space program, it's a *challenge*. Do you understand what I'm saying?" This came from a tall man with piercing blue eyes, wearing a dark blue uniform and standing in the open doorway.

His question was hanging over the room as he scanned the kids in the front three rows. None of us answered. The man turned to the five adults in the front of the room. "Do *you* understand what I'm saying?"

"Yes, sir!" came the response from the adults, speaking as one.

"Good," said the man as he strolled forward. "Our newcomers may not understand it now. But you will all appreciate and comprehend, before too long, that we don't see things as *problems* here. We see them as *challenges* that have to be overcome." He spoke slowly, giving certain words extra punch for emphasis.

"I'm Director Marshall. I'm in charge here. This is my base. I run the United States Space Program. I'm responsible for the success of our missions and the safety of our astronauts. I'm responsible for everything that goes on here," he pointed around the room, "and up there," he gestured to the ceiling and beyond. "I'm responsible for every brilliant idea and success. And I'm responsible for every bad mistake and failure.

"And I hope you'll all fall into the first category and not the second," he said, mumbling the last few words. Then he continued firmly, "The men standing behind me are astronauts who will be leading the next expedition to the moon. This is Team Varsity, led by Commander Riker."

The man with the toothpick took a half step forward and nodded. He still looked sour.

"And now, young . . ." Director Marshall glanced down at a piece of paper in his left hand, "Jonah Jones, I will address your question."

Director Marshall told us about the history of missions to the moon: the first missions that simply got close and took pictures of the moon, the ones that orbited the moon, the first mission to actually land astronauts on the moon in 1969, and other trips to the moon in the early 1970s to do experiments and gather moon rocks. Then he told us about how on one trip, the crew had discovered a very special, highly magnetic metal called pleurinium. It was far more powerful than the strongest magnet found on Earth. He told us about the mining center that had been built last year to dig for the special rock.

And he told us that nothing about the pleurinium and the special mining center was in the newspapers.

The public had been told that the recent missions to the moon were just routine, boring trips to make maps and collect samples of moon dust. The real purpose— the mystery metal, the special mining center—this had all been kept secret. The U.S. government didn't want the Russians to learn about pleurinium.

I looked over at Jonah. His mouth was hanging open and his eyes, already wide open, looked like they were getting bigger and bigger with every word coming from Director Marshall.

"But now, here's where it gets interesting," said Director Marshall. At that point, there was a crash to my right side as Jonah fell straight out of his chair. I think Jonah had been listening so hard that he forgot . . . well, as crazy as it sounds, I think he forgot how to sit. He scrambled back up into his seat, having somehow managed to close his mouth. The Director raised one eyebrow and seemed about to smile before he continued.

"As I said, the interesting part. After the first large load of pleurinium was pulled to the surface, something happened. Our astronauts got sick, and fast. We had to evacuate the first group within one day. We sent another group a month later and the same thing happened. We sent a third group three months later and the same thing happened again. Each time, they started getting sick only a few hours after arriving. After about twelve hours, some of them couldn't stand up any more. After eighteen, we had to evacuate them, every one of them, every time. Nobody has been able to stay there for even one day."

"I bet I know what causes the illness," Jonah interrupted. "It must be that highly magnetic rock. The pleurinium. It's the pleurinium, isn't it?"

All eyes were on Jonah, who was leaning dangerously forward in his chair again.

Director Marshall raised his eyebrows. "Good guess, Jonah. That's what our scientists guessed, as well. And it's more than a guess. They have proved it by bringing some of that special rock back to the laboratory and watching how people react to it. We now know that it's the pleurinium that causes the strange illness. Something about its remarkably strong magnetic force. And the moon base was built right on top of a huge deposit of pleurinium, the largest one on the moon.

"Our top scientists and doctors . . ." At this point, Director Marshall paused and gestured toward a row of women and men in white coats standing in the back of the room. Then he frowned and continued, sounding frustrated. "At least, people tell me they are the best scientists and doctors we could find. They have been trying to figure out why the pleurinium affects our astronauts this way and how to prevent it, as well as how to send astronauts back to the moon base without having them get sick. Any luck?"

We all turned to look back at the row of doctors and scientists who were now shuffling nervously from one foot to the other. One of them mumbled something that sounded like "Not yet."

"Well," barked the director, "*keep working!* We're kind of in a hurry!" He waved his hands like you do when you shoo a cat, and the adults in white coats scurried out of the room.

"So anyway," the director continued, "last month we sent a final mission to shut down the facility and turn off the nuclear reactor that powers the mining station. We sent five of our best: Commander Riker led the team, along with Jackson, Austen, Strider and Dr. Yang. But they ran into some unexpected challenges. With nobody there to keep things running right, some of the machinery started to fail."

He paused. "Commander Riker's team was unable to turn off the nuclear reactor that generates power for the moon base. Nuclear reactors can create a lot of energy if they're working right. But if they're not working right, you'd better watch out. Our moon base reactor is broken and is now in danger of exploding, which would shower the moon with dangerous, radioactive material. If you know anything about dangerous, radioactive material, you know that's not a good thing."

There was a stunned silence in the room.

None of us could believe what we were hearing. Especially me.

Just one day ago at this time, I had been sneaking out of the Home to get ice cream with Taco and Big Linus. The biggest secret I knew was the location of my special stash of comic books, stored under a squeaky floorboard in the northeast corner of our attic. And now, less than a day later, I was learning the secrets of the U.S. space program.

"And you probably don't want to admit to the Russians and the world that you're having these problems, now do you?" asked Jonah.

Director Marshall glared at him. "You're darn right about that. At least, you're almost right. Because this is a challenge, not a problem. We're working hard on the next mission. The next mission will get it right. The next mission will save the moon."

"ROGER THAT!" barked Commander Riker, causing Director Marshall to jump, despite his otherwise cool, confident demeanor. "Team Varsity is working

24/7 on the preparations. Twenty-four hours a day, seven days a week. We don't take a break. We don't sleep. We're ready to go as soon as you say the word, sir!"

"Good man." Faced by Commander Riker's intensity, Director Marshall looked a little uneasy. "You, um, you have my permission to sleep once in a while, though."

Riker didn't crack a smile. He just stared straight forward. The only thing moving was the toothpick, which he jiggled between his front teeth.

CHAPTER 8
Some Kind of Supercamper

Amanda led us out of the main building into a grassy courtyard with a white cement pathway cutting diagonally across the grass in an X pattern. In the middle of the X was a paved circle surrounded by stone benches. And in the middle of the paved circle stood a huge flagpole with an enormous American flag flapping at the top. We walked across the X toward another two-story building that looked a lot like the first one. Amanda explained that this was the training dormitory where astronaut candidates lived during their training. We would have the east wing all to ourselves.

She showed us to a large, common room area with tables and chairs, a ping-pong table, and a big TV. "Girls down the left hallway, boys down the right," said Amanda as she swept quickly into the room. "The bags you brought with you are already in your rooms. You won't be needing them, though. In your rooms you'll find your camp supplies: uniforms, books, everything you'll need for the next two weeks."

Jonah and I were assigned to share a room at the end of the hall. It was a little smaller than my room at home, but everything was spotless and shiny. I saw that both neatly made beds had an equally neat stack of clothes.

We raced over to our beds. It was like a birthday or Christmas, except all the presents were already opened. Just like my birthday, there were new socks and underpants. But next to those were two dark-blue astronaut jumpsuits. And gray shorts and gray T-shirts with the NASA badge on the front. And baseball hats. One read KENNEDY SPACE CENTER, and another had NASA underneath a rocket that was arching up, up and away.

I glanced over and saw that Jonah had moved right past the items on the bed and was flipping through the items on his desk. There were stacks of notebooks and pens and a tower of thick, heavy books.

I picked up one of the heavy books. It looked promising. There was an awesome, full-color photo on the front, showing a gleaming black-and-white rocket blasting off, shooting yellow flames and white clouds from the bottom. The inside of the book did not live up to its promise. There was page after page of tiny text with confusing diagrams of machinery—probably details about the inside of the rocket engines. It looked absolutely, completely, impossibly complicated.

I put down the book and turned back to the bed. Shoes. A small bag of bathroom supplies. And then, on the brown blanket next to the hats, was a pair of sunglasses. Just like the ones worn by the two recruiters. Gold.

"Jonah," I said, "put down that book. Look what we *got*!" I slipped on the sunglasses and squared to face the mirror. Totally cool.

"Mmmm-hmmm." Jonah glanced up from his book. His eyes were on me, but his mind was obviously still deep within the book's pages. "Nice."

"Nice? Is that all you can say?" I looked at the mirror and saw myself, wearing gold sunglasses, reflected in the lenses of the sunglasses. Totally cool.

"Okay, Mr. Italian Fashion Model," laughed Jonah. "Your sunglasses go well with your Dirt Bike Racer T-shirt."

Gah! I grabbed my astronaut jumpsuit and started to climb in, covering up my former middle-school self.

"You know why those sunglasses are gold, don't you? And why the helmet visors used by astronauts in space are gold?" asked Jonah, watching me fumble with the snaps on my jumpsuit.

"Because gold is totally cool and better than silver, and way better than bronze," I said quickly, stating the obvious. "Don't you watch the Olympics?"

"Um, not exactly, Mick. It's all about protection. They use real gold on the astronauts' visors to block the most harmful of the infrared rays coming from the sun. It turns out that gold does that better than just about anything else. These sunglasses look like they have a micro-thin layer of real gold on them, too."

"Man, how do you get so smart?" I asked. "You're a walking library. You must have one heck of a science teacher!"

"Science class? Well, that helps. But I read the really cool stuff outside of school. I found out about how the space program uses gold in my *International Journal of Advanced Science Research* magazine. You should really check it out. It's not as complicated as it sounds. It's even got a comic strip section."

"Now you're talking."

"Yeah," continued Jonah, chuckling, "the comic strip stars this subatomic particle named Zippy. He has adventures with other subatomic particles and different types of energy and electromagnetic forces. His best friend is a charm quark named Ray. In one episode, they surf this cosmic wave through the outer galaxy, and then suddenly they get bombarded by electrons—"

"Dude," I interrupted, "you're frightening me. I feel like you're actually sucking intelligence out of my head to feed your giant brain." I shook my head. "You're reading comics about complicated science. Last Sunday morning, I had to ask Sister Rinaldi to explain the Charlie Brown comic strip to me."

✪ ✪ ✪ ✪ ✪

Jonah and I were still putting away all of our new stuff when I heard a voice in the doorway behind us. "Come on, y'all, it's lunch time. Ya hungry? And hot dang! Will you take your sunglasses off indoors? You're fixin' to walk into a wall with those on. Save 'em for the sun, friend."

A tall boy with red hair and freckles had leaned into our room from the hallway. He had the thickest, heaviest Southern accent I had ever heard.

"Yeah, sure," I said as I quickly took off my glasses and set them carefully on my dresser. "By the way, where's lunch?"

But he had already turned and was sauntering down the hallway. "Just hurry up," his voice floated back to us, "and follow your ears to the noise."

Jonah threw on his jumpsuit, and we tore out of our room into the hallway. We heard the chatter of boys' and girls' voices coming from the direction of the common room, and when we got there we followed the stragglers down the main hallway to the stairs and then into the cafeteria.

We caught up with the red-haired boy with freckles who introduced himself as Dale from Texas. And then he introduced us to his friend from Texas, a kid with black hair whose name was also Dale.

"Dale and Dale? Two Dales?" I asked.

They both laughed. "Nah," said the black-haired boy. "I'm Dale. He's Dale."

I looked over at Jonah, who just shrugged back at me.

"Come on," drawled the red-haired Texan, "you boys from the North got the same ears they give out in Texas. I'm Dale, D-A-L-E. This here's Dell, D-E-L-L. Big difference, you hear?"

The two boys from Texas grinned broadly at us. I got the feeling they enjoyed introducing themselves to people.

I figured out pretty soon that everybody just called them "The Texans," so their exact names didn't matter anyway.

The Texans led us over to the lunch line where

we grabbed a tray and silverware. The cafeteria was filled with a mix of kids and adults. Some adults were wearing astronaut jumpsuits, others were dressed in dark pants and white shirts, and a few were wearing military uniforms. As we walked through the line, the servers behind the counter slid plates of cheeseburgers, chicken sandwiches, and grilled cheeses into rows, along with paper containers of fries, bowls of canned fruit, and Jell-O. There was also a salad bar and machines where you could fill up on milk and soda. I grabbed two cheeseburgers, a plate of fries, and a shiny red apple.

After I had poured out two glasses of milk, I scanned the room and saw Trace waving from a table by the windows. She was sitting with three other girls, but there was still room for me along with Jonah and the Texans. Trace introduced us to her roommate, Cat Obando from Cupertino, California.

"Boys, you'll like Cat," said Trace in her excited, 80 mile-per-hour way of talking. "Her real name is Catalina," she slowed down for the name, drawing out the sounds to get the pronunciation right as if she had been practicing. "Her parents are from Costa Rica and she's named after an island there, but she says just call her Cat. And here's the good part, you won't believe this. She actually has her own computer. And she brought it with her."

I gasped. "No. Way. An entire computer? Did you drive it here in a truck or something?"

"No, silly," said Cat, a girl with small features and a huge bloom of tangled, frizzy, brown hair. "Come on, it's 1977. Computers are small as can be now. My whole computer fits into a suitcase."

"Yeah, can you believe it? It's cute," Trace explained. "Cat tried to turn it on and show me something on it, but it wouldn't work. It kept crushing."

Cat sighed. "It's called 'crashing,' but I'll fix it, I just need some time. That's the challenge with computers. These things are complicated, and it's not as easy as switching on a lightbulb."

Jonah winced, but nobody noticed.

Trace continued happily. "Whatever. It didn't bother me that it crashed. I still thought it was cool. And Cat even has a pet name for it. She calls it her Apple."

"It's not just a pet name, that's its official name, the Apple One," explained Cat. "My neighbors in California are trying to start a company to sell them, and the Apple One is their first computer. My dad says they'll never make a dime, but he doesn't know anything. I think they'll be famous all over California one day."

"I don't see that thang catchin' on," said one of the Texans, shaking his head. "Why would ordinary folk want one?"

"You'd be surprised," said Cat quietly. "Do you like baseball?"

"Well, heck yeah. My daddy and I drive to Dallas every summer to watch the Rangers play. They're going to win the World Series next year, you mark my words."

Cat shook her head and frowned. "Sounds like you could use a computer. See, it's like this. My mom loves baseball, so I wrote a computer program for her that'll predict the winners in baseball games. I enter all of the information I can get about the players: their batting averages, how they hit against left-handed pitchers and right-handed pitchers, how they play in the daytime and at night, how they play at home and away, how they play at the beginning of the season or the end of the season. If it's a number, I put it into the computer program. Then you tell the computer who is playing and—"

"And it tells you who's going to win the game!?" I gasped.

"Well, kind of," continued Cat. "It doesn't know for sure. But it's usually right. And I hate to break it to you Dale or Dell or whichever Texan you are, but I don't think the Rangers have much of a chance next year unless they replace their entire team."

"Awww, come awwn!" yelled the Texan. "That's a bunch of cow patties if I ever heard it. You're tellin' me your computer can predict the future?"

Cat blinked and seemed to shrink a little against the force of the larger boy's yelling.

"Hey, Tex, calm down," Jonah jumped in. "She didn't say anything about predicting the future. She said it helps make sense of the numbers, and it can venture a pretty good guess."

The Texan saw Cat hang her head and quickly apologized. "Pardon me for raisin' my voice, miss. Mighty unkind of me. I didn't mean any disrespect to you or your Pineapple computer."

"All I'm sayin'," he continued, "is I'll do just fine without a computer in my life." He proceeded to entertain us with stories of his ranch back home. He and the other Texan told stories that were more and more incredible—how they would rope cattle and drive off wolves and ride their horses with the buffalo herds under moonlit skies. The tales sounded so cowboy hokey, I started to suspect both of them lived in a regular neighborhood in the suburbs and went to a regular school. But I didn't want to say anything, because their stories were so entertaining.

I was just finishing my dry, stiff cheeseburger when I saw Trace and Jonah sit up straighter, looking at someone approaching the table behind me. As I turned, I saw a tall boy with short, buzz-cut brown hair. He pulled up a chair, spun it around, and sat down on it front-to-back at the end of the table. He smiled broadly as he grabbed a french fry off my plate and popped it into his mouth.

"So, it's the new kids," he said, chewing with his mouth open. "Hi, new kids. Welcome to Kennedy. You must be overwhelmed. Totally confused." He dipped his head so he could see Jonah's eyes. "Right, new kid with the crazy dreadlocks hair?"

Although his words were friendly enough, they were as fake as a cardboard penny.

He was wearing the collar of his jumpsuit turned up like Mr. Cool. I noticed he had "Lance M." stitched onto his uniform under his space program patch. This guy thought he was some kind of supercamper.

"I'm going to give you the lay of the land here," said Lance M. "You know, explain who's who. What's what. Which end is up. You're playing catch up, you know?

"You see that kid with the blond hair sitting against the wall?" He gestured toward a big kid across the room who was leaning back casually with his feet on the table, laughing loudly at something. "That's Brad Stimple. Sitting next to him is Mandy Rockwell. Maybe you've heard of her father, Senator Rockwell from Tennessee? The three of us have been here training for three weeks already. Pretty intense stuff."

He paused for a moment to let that part sink in before continuing in a lazy tone of voice. "I think it's great they invited you other kids to come along. You know, to watch and learn. But let me give you a little advice, okay new kids? Stay out of our way. There's some important business happening here, and we can't let you—the space campers, that is—mess things up. I know you get it," he said, nodding once at me. "You're a smart kid, right?" As he said the last part, he casually reached for another one of my fries.

But I was too quick. I slid my tray quickly to the left so that his hand missed my fries, landing instead in a puddle of ketchup.

"Easy, old timer," I said. If I had learned one thing at the Home, it was how to protect my food. "I guess you're still figuring things out, too. These are *my* fries. But you can get your own up there. For free. Pretty good deal." I tipped my head toward the food counter and gave him my best ear-to-ear grin.

His eyes narrowed for just a second before he returned my grin with one of his own. "Nah, keep your fries, Mickey Price from the mean streets of Orlando." I must have looked surprised that he knew my name, because he gave a satisfied smile. "And Trace Daniels, the bumper car champ. And Jonah Jones, the mad scientist. And frizzy haired computer girl and two guys from Texas whose names I can't be bothered to learn—no offense, y'all. Nice to meet you. I'm Lance, in case you didn't know that already."

With that, he spun around and strolled back toward the table where Stimple and Rockwell were telling jokes.

One of the Texans was the first to speak. "That boy's got a bad attitude as big as the Texas sky. When I see a horse, ornery like that, I just keep out of its way. Same for him. Best just to let him run wild." The other Texan nodded his head in agreement.

Trace was fuming. "Bumper car champ? Who does he think he is? Called me a *bumper car* champ!? Gah!"

"Easy, Trace," I said. "He might be a jerk, but don't turn him into an enemy. It's only our first day. Keep your cool."

But I wasn't convinced by my own words. I didn't like Lance M. the supercamper, either.

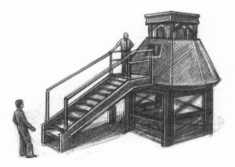

CHAPTER 9
An Unplanned Encounter with Chihuahuas

It sounded like a doorbell. *Bling, blong.* Pause. *Bling, blong.* Pause. *Bling, blong.* I blinked and noticed that the overhead lights in the dormitory room had clicked on automatically. I guess this was their way of waking us up.

There was only the faintest glimmer of dawn in the sky outside our bedroom window. They were starting us early on the first morning of space camp.

Back at home, I usually woke up to the sound of Taco's voice. Taco was the first one to fall asleep at night, sometimes right in the middle of things while we were all watching TV, or curled up on a couch in our common room while the rest of us were playing a game. And he was *always* the first one to wake up. He usually woke me up next just by talking at me nonstop until I finally gave in and talked back.

Sometimes I'd pretend I was asleep as he kept talking. And he'd say things that were more and more ridiculous just to get me to admit I was awake.

One time, it couldn't have been much past six in the morning, I counted how many times he said my name. Seventy-two. I managed to lie perfectly still and not move a muscle as he said "Mickey, Mickey, Mickey" seventy-two times. He must have known I was awake, because Mickey fifty through Mickey seventy-two were pretty loud.

But instead of saying Mickey a seventy-third time, he started to tell a tall tale about how the cypress tree outside our window had become haunted during the night and had tried to reach in through the window, attack me, and drag me out to my doom.

"It was stealthy at first," Taco had said, almost in a whisper. "Sliiiiiidin' the window open and streeeeeetchin' across the room in the pale moonlight. That's when I heard it, with its leaves going *flick, flick, flick* as they slid over the windowsill. Then I realized the eeeeeevil tree was goin' after you, Mickey. Slowly, steadily across the floor toward your bed. So I grabbed my trusty axe and started attacking that creeping branch."

I lay still, trying to suppress a giggle and keep my breathing normal.

Taco continued. "I cut the sucker right down the middle, but it kept coming. The more I cut, the faster it moved. And then came a second branch. And then a third, like an unstoppable army of snakes sliiiiiidin' in through the window.

"So there I was, screamin' my head off, whackin' at the branches with this huge axe as it tried to grab you and pull you out the window. It had you around the ankle, Mickey, but I finally distracted it, and it turned to attack me. I was backed up into the corner. My axe was useless against its mighty force. So I grabbed my trusty chainsaw!

This wasn't easy. I refused to give in, but it was almost impossible to keep from cracking up.

"*Brrr-AWWW, gug-guh-guh-guh. Brrr-AWWW, guh-guh-guh-guh!*" Taco had screamed at the top of his lungs. "I was loppin' off branches left and right. But the tree kept comin'. *Brrr-AWWW.* You kept sleeping, but I was hard at work. Wood chips and sawdust were flyin' everywhere. Branches and leaves all over the place. I was covered with sap. Oh, the sap, the horrible sap! The tree was . . . it was . . . and . . . oh geez, come on, Mickey. Will you wake up already?"

Right then, I had jumped out of bed. "YES! I win! You gave up, you stopped your story! Victory!" I danced around the room. "Victory is mine!"

Taco was grinning from ear to ear. "No, Mick. I won. Look who's out of bed."

I realized I had a smile on my face, thinking back about my goofy sidekick. I sighed when I realized I was lying in a strange bed a hundred miles away from Orlando, listening to a chime that sounded like a doorbell ringing over and over and over.

My mind quickly returned to reality and I was jolted by curiosity. What on earth was going to happen at space camp today?

Jonah and I jumped up from our beds at the same time, just as the chiming stopped. I heard voices in the hallway. Then a piece of paper came sliding under our door.

GOOD MORNING CAMPERS

Monday, October 23, 1977

Kennedy Young Astronauts' Adventure Academy

DAY ONE SCHEDULE

6:30 A.M.   Wake up

Shower – Breakfast

8:00 A.M.   Morning Classroom Time – Meeting Room B

10:00 A.M. Flight Simulator

12:00 P.M. Lunch

1:00 P.M.   Games and Free Time

3:00 P.M.   Swimming Pool

5:00 P.M.   Dinner

6:00 P.M.   Evening Classroom Time – Meeting Room B

9:00 P.M.   Lights Out

"There you go, Jonah," I said with a grin. "Are you satisfied now? This looks like an official camp schedule to me. All perfectly innocent. Nothing sneaky, no mystery. Just a plain, old-fashioned camp. Right?"

Jonah scowled at me. Maybe he wasn't a morning person.

✪ ✪ ✪ ✪ ✪

After a breakfast of waffles, eggs, and grapefruit, we all reported to Meeting Room B to start our training.

We had assigned seats. On my left was Mandy Rockwell, one of the supercampers. She turned her back on me as soon as I sat down and continued talking to the boy on the other side of her, bragging about how she and Lance had gone on a special tour of the local Air Force base the day before. The empty seat to my right was soon filled by Cat Obando. I asked her a few more questions about her prized computer. We didn't have much time to talk, however, because the class started as soon as everyone found their seats.

The training started with a movie about the history of the space program. It described how scientists had developed rockets with longer and longer ranges. It explained how the scientists eventually figured out how to send rockets up out of the Earth's atmosphere and back down again. There were lots of fiery crashes back then, so luckily the rockets didn't have people in them.

The first animal successfully launched into space was a monkey named Ziggy 2.

They didn't explain what happened to Ziggy 1, but I could guess.

They launched mice. Dogs. More monkeys. Guinea pigs. Frogs. A cat named Felix. And then, finally, a human.

After the movie, the lights came back on, and we blinked at each other under the bright overhead lights.

Team Varsity was lined up along the side wall. They must have entered while the movie was playing. Commander Riker and the other four members were standing at attention as they were reintroduced by Amanda.

"We're lucky to have our best astronauts here for a few minutes this morning, campers," said Amanda. "You're among the first to hear this. It hasn't been announced yet to the newspapers. Commander Riker is leading Team Varsity through their final week of preparation before they leave on their important mission. The launch is scheduled for next week. Next Monday morning."

Riker puffed out his chest as a ripple of excitement spread through the classroom.

"Each member of Team Varsity has a special job in the mission," continued Amanda. "There are five seats in the launch vehicle and five very special jobs." She explained how Riker was the flight commander and pilot. He was the leader, the quarterback, the astronaut in charge. Number two on the team was the copilot and sat next to the flight commander in the front row. The other three sat in the back row of the command module. The third crew member was the navigator, who kept close track of the rocket's location and direction and maps, basically making sure the space craft stayed on course and didn't end up flying into the sun. The fourth astronaut was the computer engineer, keeping track of the complicated computer programs and onboard electronics.

"And number five, that's me," said a short, smiley man who seemed a little on the plump side for an astronaut. "I'm pretty much just a passenger during the flight. But if we encounter anything strange or unexplained, that's where I come in. I'm Jack Binkman, but people around here just call me the Professor. I'm a nuclear physicist. I'm going to make sure we solve this problem and turn off that nuclear reactor if it's the last thing I do!"

The astronaut to the Professor's left gave him a high five.

Riker cleared his throat with a sharp *ahem* and both men jumped to attention. They quickly replaced their grins with stern scowls to match Riker's.

Amanda asked us to stand and give them all a big round of applause. Team Varsity left the room as we clapped, off to their next important training destination. The Professor paused in the doorway, allowing his fellow astronauts to move down the hall. The smile returned to his face, and he raised his hands in the air triumphantly. Our applause grew, and several kids added whoops above the clapping.

The Professor leaned back inside and said uncertainly, "Hey, anyone want to do a cheer? Let's go NASA? Gimme an N?"

"ENNNN!" came the response.

"Gimme an A," he yelled, louder now, slapping his hands together above his head and making the shape of an A.

"AYYYYYY!" we roared back.

"GI . . . MMEE . . . AN . . . S!" He was really getting into it now, for some reason flapping his arms like a chicken.

"ESSSSSS!" we screamed, so loud that the lightbulbs rattled.

"GI . . . MMEE . . . AN—" Suddenly his cheer was cut short. A hand clamped down on Professor Binkman's shoulder and yanked him backward into the hall.

Commander Riker was not amused.

✪ ✪ ✪ ✪ ✪

After two more speakers, we had a snack break of Fig Newtons and orange Tang. Amanda then led us to a building across the courtyard, into a large room filled with computer equipment and monitors. There was a wide bank of TV screens along the front wall. Facing those screens were two rows of attendants at desks, about eight of them, each one sitting in front of computer monitors and dials and blinking lights. They all wore crisp, white shirts and had turned to watch us enter.

That's when a dark-haired man wearing head-phones with a mini-microphone emerged from be-hind a computer the size of a refrigerator and began to speak.

"Good morning, campers. I'm Dr. Grover Yang— the rocket science kind of doctor, not the medical kind. I'm the guidance officer here at Mission Control. This means I'm the main person talking to the astronauts during the mission—the voice they hear on the radio every step of their trip. Their link to home. I've handled every mission since Apollo 13, and that one was a doozie. I pass along important instructions, but most of all, I just try to keep everyone cool and calm. Cooool and calm. Got it?"

We all nodded.

He went on to explain about the room we were in—the flight simulator center—and how this was a key part of astronaut training.

"That strange contraption over in the corner might not look like much, but on the inside it's an exact replica of the Artemis command module cockpit. Same seats. Same controls. Same radio. The experience is just like flying the real Artemis rocket, just not as fast."

We all stared at the peculiar mass of metal in the corner. It was about the size of a small bus, with hundreds of wires running out of the top and sides.

"Everything you do in the flight simulator shows up on the monitors out here, and it's all powered by a giant computer," Dr. Yang went on. "Think of it as the world's most complicated video game. The astronaut trainee moves the controls in the flight simulator, and the capsule responds. We can practice every part of the trip—blastoff, flying through space, landing on the moon, lifting off from the moon, and reentering the Earth's atmosphere. We can go to the moon and back without ever leaving this room.

"And today, it's your turn. We're going to take each of you through the reentry procedure: the part at the end of the mission when the capsule approaches the Earth's atmosphere—reenters the atmosphere—and deploys three huge parachutes to slow it down. If you follow the instructions right, you'll splash down in the target zone somewhere in the Pacific Ocean near Hawaii where a Navy ship would be waiting."

One of the Texans had raised his hand in the front row. Dr. Yang pointed at him. "You there, go ahead."

"Sir, I got one question," he drawled. "I can ride a horse, but my daddy don't even let me drive his pickup truck. If I can't do that, how do you expect me to drive a spaceship?"

"Don't you worry, son," Dr. Yang said calmly. "There's a computer program that guides the real command modules back into the Earth's atmosphere. It's called Program 64, and we use the same computer program in this flight simulator. It does all the work. You just need to trust Program 64 and the folks at Mission Control. We know where you are, how fast you're going, and where you're going to end up. We'll tell you what to do and when to do it. The test this morning is all about listening and following directions. It's that simple."

We noticed that Dr. Yang was looking off to his left at a boy who had wandered over to the capsule and was peering in through its tiny window.

The scientist cleared his throat. "Young man?" he said. "Young *man*! Did you hear me? What's the test all about this morning?"

"Um, we gotta figure out how to fly this thing?" he said uncertainly.

"Not exactly. Anyone else?"

"I know, I know!" said a girl named Madison, waving her hand eagerly. "It's about listening and following directions." She looked very pleased with herself. She pursed her lips and nodded slowly at the boy standing next to the space capsule.

"Right you are, young lady," said Dr. Yang. "And that means you, my fine young volunteer," pointing at the boy, "will go first."

✪ ✪ ✪ ✪ ✪

After all the buildup, the test itself didn't seem too hard. The campers went one at a time into the test capsule, were buckled into the pilot's chair, and were given radio headsets. We watched on the TV monitors as they went through a series of instructions. Read numbers from this dial or that dial. Push this button or that button. Fire thruster rockets. Make an adjustment here or there.

A couple of the kids didn't do so well. To the delight of many, Madison failed to turn off her thruster rocket, even after Dr. Yang reminded her five times to hit the big red OFF button. This ended up sending her out toward Saturn. So her test ended early.

One of the Texans flicked the wrong switch and shut off the oxygen, which ended his test early, too.

Lance was one of the only people to do it absolutely perfectly. So were Rockwell and Stimple. As much as I hated to admit it, those three were living up to the Supercamper label.

The morning wore on, and my attention started to fade. Plus, it was kind of warm in the room. And the electric lights overhead were making a nice, soothing, buzzing sound. Kind of like bees.

Yeah, bees, I thought to myself. Big, fuzzy bees buzzing around lazily on a sunny summer afternoon. My head started to nod, and ...

"Price!" shouted the loudspeaker.

I scrambled to my feet, aware that everyone in the room was staring at me. I guess it was my turn. I scrambled over to the corner of the room, passing Jonah, who had just finished his turn and was giving me a thumbs up of encouragement.

At the test module, an engineer handed me a helmet, which she helped me adjust and put on my head. It was heavy and uncomfortable. I said, "Hi, can you hear me?" My voice must have carried through the room's loudspeakers loud and clear because I could see Lance look up and whisper something to Stimple, who gave a mile-wide smirk.

As I strapped myself into the flight commander's seat, Dr. Yang's voice filled the radio headset. "Okay, Mickey, we'll get started as soon as you're ready. Just remember: Follow the instructions, trust the computer, and you'll do just fine."

Piece of cake, I thought, staring at the dizzying array of buttons and knobs and computer displays and switches and gauges and dials and readouts and flashing lights surrounding the flight commander's chair.

I started following the commands, one at a time. They had sounded easy when the others were taking their turn. But it was harder now that I was the one actually in the pilot's chair, doing things like "find the fifth row of switches to the left of the round glowing dial at the center and flick the first three." Or "Check your speed, fourth dial from the top in Row J."

Surely all these instruments and switches weren't really necessary?

"Mickey," said Dr. Yang, "you are now four minutes from reentry. The center panel should say 'Program 64.' Can you confirm?"

"Let's see. Center panel . . .uh . . ." My eyes raced over the dizzying array of numbers and lights and dials. Bingo. "Oh yeah! Roger!"

I had noticed that all of the astronauts, as well as Lance and his buddies, used the word *Roger* to mean yes. I guess it was all part of being an astronaut.

"It says 'Program 64 Active,'" I continued. "What does that mean again?"

"Mickey, Program 64 is the final reentry program. The computer makes the final calculations and fires your booster rockets to get you at the perfect angle for reentry. It then tells you exactly when to deploy your parachutes."

"Roger that," I said, feeling confident now. "Program 64, take me home."

"Good job, Mickey, three minutes to reentry. Remember, reentry is when you hit the Earth's atmosphere. You will lose radio contact for a few minutes. The radios we use to talk to you in space won't work because you won't be in space anymore. The radios we use to talk to you in the Earth's atmosphere won't work because you're not quite home yet. And the command module will shake. In a real reentry, it would shake so hard and be so loud, you wouldn't be able to talk anyway."

A gentle beeping rang out through my headset, and the main screen flashed the words "Course Adjustment."

"Um, Mission Control, Mickey Price here. Can I say something?"

"Go ahead, Mickey. And you don't need to say who you are. We kind of know that."

"Oh, sorry, Mission Control. Um, the main screen says "Course Adjustment: right booster 75 percent, 17 seconds.""

"Roger that, Mickey. Good job. So let's make the course adjustment."

Dr. Yang walked me through the process to adjust course, finding the right control to set the direction of the booster rocket and fire it for exactly the right amount of time.

I thought I had done it right, but a few seconds later the "Course Adjustment" warning came on again. I fired the booster rocket again. And then again a third time.

Suddenly a shrill warning buzzer, louder and more insistent, filled the cabin.

It went downhill from there. According to Yang, I had done something wrong, even though I swear I had followed all the instructions perfectly. I was off course—and it was apparently too late to do anything about it.

After I finished going through the outer atmosphere, I got the verdict: "Mickey, you were lucky. A little more off course and you would have burned up like a flaming marshmallow coming through the atmosphere. The bad news is that you'll miss your landing spot in the Pacific and will impact on land in central Mexico. Prepare for ELCI."

"ELCI?" I asked.

"Emergency Land Crash Impact," came the reply. "If this was a real ELCI, NASA would scramble helicopters and ambulances and get the rescue team to the crash site as soon as possible."

"Can't I steer? Change course? Zoom a little to the left or something?"

"Negative, Mickey. The Command Module has no booster rockets and no steering. I'm afraid you're falling like a brick."

"What's the big deal about coming down on land?" I asked. "I've got parachutes, right?"

"We always aim for the water, Mickey. It's possible to survive an ELCI, but there's a lot that can go wrong. Even with a parachute, you're going 30-40 miles per hour. It's like jumping from a high dive onto a sidewalk. Or driving your car into a brick wall. The impact is hard. There could be a fire. The door could jam shut. All sorts of things could go wrong."

My mind raced. I never gave up on anything, and I didn't want to quit, but they weren't giving me any options. "What can I do, Mission Control? Give me instructions!"

"Mickey, Program 64 will take it from here. You might still survive the impact, so it's not a complete failure. Parachutes deploy in five . . . four . . . three . . . two . . . one . . . main parachutes have deployed and you're now a floater. Computer is calculating the exact crash site . . . it . . . is . . . okay, it's the desert, 52 miles east of the city of Chihuahua in Mexico."

At that moment, the hatch door opened on my right and the engineer eased herself into the cabin to help me with the buckles. She told me we could end the test early because there was nothing more I could do now that the parachutes had deployed. "Don't worry, Mickey," she said. "At least you made it through the atmosphere."

My face burned as I walked back toward my fellow campers on the other side of the test room, knowing they had all just heard every detail of my crash broadcast over the loudspeakers in the room. Jonah gave me a slap on the shoulder and said, "Hey, not all that bad, Mick. A lot of kids did worse."

As I headed over to the drinking fountain, I heard some high-pitched barking and panting coming from Lance and a group of kids standing around him.

It took me a minute to get the joke.

They were being Chihuahuas. Very funny.

CHAPTER 10
Checkers

An hour later, I was leaning back in my chair in the cafeteria after devouring three cheeseburgers and a large piece of chocolate cake. Jonah and one of the Texans were having an animated argument about Jonah's great idea for ranch management. Jonah proposed putting special collars onto the cows and using robots with powerful magnets to round them up, instead of having cowboys do it with ropes and lassos.

"That ain't right. Ain't no robot alive that can rope a calf like I can," bragged one of the Texans.

Jonah sighed. "First of all, robots aren't alive. And second of all, you just wait. It won't be long before you have robot ranchers. They'll be much more efficient than humans. Think about it. They could work all day and all night. And they'd be fast as anything if you gave them backpacks with jet engines."

I grinned, thinking about renaming the local NFL football team. No more Dallas Cowboys. A huge crowd in ten-gallon hats would cheer for the Dallas Robot Ranchers.

Over in the corner, Supercamper Lance was sitting with a few adult astronauts from Team Varsity, along with Rockwell and Stimple. They were all leaning forward, with their heads over the table, having what looked like a very important, private conversation. Commander Riker was holding a saltshaker in one hand, swooping it around like a rocket as he explained something. He didn't seem to realize that every time his rocket tilted, salt poured onto the table.

To be honest, at that moment, it didn't bother me that Lance was over there discussing the trip the real astronauts were about to take. I was stuffed full of cheeseburgers, and Space Camp was going pretty well so far. Despite my fiery simulated death in the test rocket.

Over behind the Team Varsity table, I noticed that Cat and Trace had just come through the food line and were standing at the edge of the cafeteria, scanning the room for a familiar face. I stood up and waved both hands like a sailor on a ship, signaling to shore.

Trace burst into a smile and started weaving her way through the crowded tables toward us, Cat right behind her.

"Hey, where have you guys been?" I asked. "We waited for you in line, and now we're almost done."

"You. Would. Not. Believe. What this girl did!" Trace presented her friend with a mix of excitement and awe, while Cat sheepishly slid into a chair at the end of our table. "She's some sort of genius, I swear. Tell them, Cat. Come on, tell."

"It was nothing. I just, it was nothing," Cat mumbled into her tray. She was looking down slightly, so her bushy hair covered most of her face.

"Come *on*, girl!" said Trace, her face bright and beaming. "Okay, okay. If you won't tell, I will. Listen up, boys. Remember how Cat was the last one to go on the flight simulator, right after Mickey? And she crash-landed at the North Pole, right?"

"You give my order to Santa?" asked Jonah with a grin. "A red bicycle and an electron microscope?"

Trace ignored him. "She crash-landed, and then you all left to come to lunch. And I was about to leave, too, when I saw Cat tapping away at a computer in the corner. Soon the other Mission Control engineers were gathered around her. One of them was trying to make her stop, saying she was going to ruin everything. But Director Marshall said, 'No, let her keep going. Let's see what she can do.'"

"Wait, she was trying the flight simulator again?" I asked.

"Not doing it. Fixing it. You see, she had a hunch that it was somehow broken since Mickey and she had both crashed after doing everything right. Well, the way she explains it, the whole thing is just like a video game. Cat said something in the game program must have gone wrong, and she had some idea about how to fix it. Right, Cat?"

"Fix the game? Where would you even start?" I asked.

Cat looked up. "It's just a computer program. A computer program is a set of instructions. Do this, do that. If this happens, do this. If that happens, do that. It's not magic. A computer does exactly what you tell it to do. So if it misbehaves, it could be because the program contains an error. A mistake in the programming code."

"Yeah, go figure," said Trace with a shrug. "You think these NASA people would have this stuff figured out, but they say these computer errors happen all the time. Anyway, this girl is sitting there at the computer in the corner, with all these NASA engineers huddled around her, whispering to each other. I'm hearing things like 'Oh my gosh, she's tapped into the mainframe,' and 'Holy cow, she's fixing the root formula,' and 'Golly, she's fixing the whats-a-magibbit.'

"And then all of a sudden, Cat pushes her chair back and says, 'Okay, that should do it. Try it again.' Just like that. La-dee-da, I'm done. The NASA guys swarm around the computer, and one of them runs into the capsule to check something. You should have seen the looks on their faces when they realized that she'd fixed it."

"The looks on their faces?" I asked. "Were they mad?"

"Mad? Heck no!" said Trace. "They carried Cat around the room on their shoulders like she'd just won the 500-mile race at the Rockingham Motor Speedway. Somebody even asked for her autograph. There was whooping and hollering and cheering. Sure, the room got pretty quiet when Director Marshall said maybe he should fire everybody and replace them with a bunch of kids like Cat. But then he laughed and said he was probably kidding. Tell you what, the party pretty much ended right there. The NASA engineers didn't start dancing around again. So we left and came to lunch."

Cat's head was still tipped toward her tray, but I could see through her bushy hair that she had cracked a small grin.

"Come on, girl!" Trace concluded. "You've got to celebrate your victories. Whoop it up when you win, 'cause you're not going to win every time."

"Whoopie, hooray," Cat said quietly.

Trace shook her head in dramatic disappointment. "We'll have to work on your celebration skills, Catalina Obando, Computer Genius. I'll teach you my signature Victory Dance before this camp is over."

After congratulating Cat for a while, Jonah shifted the conversation back to his robot cowboys, and how Cat could write a computer program that would control the entire ranch so the head rancher could take long vacations in Hawaii while the robots took care of things back in Texas. Of course, the Texans were all over that idea.

After a while, Amanda Collins started making her way from table to table, and the other campers got up to put away their empty trays. "Kids," she said when she got to our table, "you've had a full morning, and we still have a lot to do today. We'll start off with some relaxation. We have a special game room set up on the other side of the compound. So take care of your trays, grab your backpacks, and meet in the lobby."

Without another word, Amanda turned and disappeared through the open door. We scrambled to follow. We met her in the lobby, where she had been joined by three scientists in white coats, carrying thick notebooks. When everyone was there, they led us back through the building to a rear exit.

I blinked and squinted in the bright sunlight for a few steps before noticing that Lance had slipped on his gold astronaut sunglasses. I dug deep into my bag and pulled out mine.

We had turned onto a cement path that ran along a narrow drainage creek. Frogs hiding in the long grass beside the path jumped into the creek with a chirp as we walked past.

We crossed a service road and continued along the creek for a few more minutes before I saw the small, white building. It was actually a trailer without a cab but with the rear wheels still on it. A shiny new air conditioner stuck out the back, whirring loudly and dripping moisture into a puddle.

Amanda paused at the bottom of a small metal ladder leading up to the door. "Okay, you guys can hang out here for a while. You've been working hard, and we wanted to give you a break. There are games inside and a movie to watch."

"Go on in, follow the instructions, and we'll see you in a couple hours."

"You're not coming along?" asked Jonah, eyeing the trailer suspiciously.

"Nope, I've got some . . . paperwork to do. As I said, this is just hang-out time. In you go!"

The first kids in line piled into the trailer. It was larger inside than I had thought from the outside. There were comfy cushions on the ground and a few beanbag chairs, all scattered around five or six low tables. The air inside the trailer was cool and dry and smelled like fresh paint.

I plunked down next to Jonah, who started reading aloud from a card sitting on the nearest table:

CHECKERS

Time to test your skill against your friends.
Have a checkers tournament for an hour.
Play a game, then the winner moves
on and plays another winner.
Keep going until there is a champion.
If you lose, find a friend and keep playing!
Your movie will start in one hour.

"Jonah," I said, "you are *so* going down in flames. Prepare to face the checkers master." I opened up the red-and-black checked board and placed it between us as Jonah opened the metal box containing the game pieces. The sound of clinking mixed with chatter as we all started plinking the heavy metal pieces onto the game boards.

The bossy girl named Madison decided it was a good time to give us all a lecture about checkers. "Okay, people. Place all your pieces on the dark squares. No moving sideways or backward unless you're a king. And always jump diagonally," she trilled like an annoying substitute teacher.

Jonah and I were the first to get the game board set up, and he moved his first piece with a thunk.

"And if you capture a piece," Madison continued, "pick it up and place it neatly at the right side of the game board."

"We know how to play checkers," came the singsong reply from Lance in a perfect imitation of Madison. There was scattered laughter for a few seconds, then a hush fell on the room again as we concentrated on our games.

I quickly realized that Jonah was going to destroy me. My stack of defeated checkers pieces started to pile up quickly, and I had only captured one of his. I plinked the defeated pieces together. They were heavy, with a rubbery red coating. I found that if you stacked two together in the right direction, they grabbed each other with a pull, and if you flipped one upside down, it would push the other one away. I put my six captured pieces together into a mini skyscraper.

Jonah finished me off in an amazing triple jump.

After a few more games, we all clustered together to watch Jonah beat a boy named Elvis from Mississippi in the championship round. Most of us were pretty much through with checkers at that point. Trace and I joined a few others in the center of the room, piling our checkers together into a giant tower that reached almost to the ceiling.

It wasn't much longer before the movie projector in the corner jumped to life and started whirring, seemingly by magic. The lights dimmed, and the movie flickered onto the wall at the far end. All of us quickly scooted the checker boards aside and jockeyed for prime position in front of the movie screen. It wasn't really necessary because the movie filled almost the whole wall and nearly every position had a great view.

To my delight, the movie was *Godzilla*.

★ ★ ★ ★ ★

Just as the movie ended, there was a light rap at the door. The door opened a crack, letting bright sunshine spill into the room, along with Amanda's voice. "All right, hope you liked the show. Leave everything in the room—absolutely everything—don't bring anything with you but your backpacks. Who wants to head to the swimming pool?"

The room was suddenly thrown into chaos. After a morning in the classroom and flight simulator and then another three hours inside, a swimming pool was exactly what we needed. There was a flurry of arms and legs as everybody scrambled for their backpacks and burst through the door to the outside. This time I remembered to put on my sunglasses before heading out into the afternoon sun. Amanda led the first of us away from the trailer and over to a shady cluster of palm trees.

The three scientists in white coats walked around among us, taking attendance. Or maybe they were doctors. One of them asked me how I was feeling. He had me stick out my arms straight sideways and then bend my elbows and touch my nose. He seemed strangely impressed when I succeeded.

Madison was standing next to me trying to stuff one of the checkers boxes into her backpack when it slipped out and dropped onto the ground with a flop. The checkers scattered onto the hard-packed earth.

Amanda instinctively reached down to help Madison pick up what she had dropped, but then suddenly pulled her hand back in surprise and took several startled steps away.

"Why did you bring those out? You were supposed to leave them inside," said Amanda. The scientist standing beside me jumped and moved back, too.

"It's just the checkers. Sorry," said Madison as she plunked the pieces back into the box.

"You can't choose to ignore some of the rules here. The rules are important—all of them," said Amanda sharply. "Pick those up and put them back into the trailer. Right now."

As Madison fumbled with the box, all of us moved away from her instinctively and clustered around Amanda, who looked down at us. "Wait, nobody else brought anything out with them, did they?"

Jonah broke the silence with an "umm..." as he unzipped his backpack and pulled out a checkers box. One of the Texans did the same, saying, "I kind of need the practice."

Amanda's head spun left and right as she took several more quick steps back. Amanda raised her right hand and pointed back at the door of the trailer. "Put those back! Put them back now!"

Jonah turned and took a few steps toward the trailer, but then stopped and gave Amanda a strange look. One of his classic looking-right-through-you looks.

I didn't know Jonah very well, way back then. I'd only met him one day earlier. But I knew him well enough to know that his brain was working overtime. He stopped moving toward the trailer and turned to Amanda, holding the checkers box right out to her.

"Here you go," said Jonah, taking a step forward.

She took a step back.

"No really, you can have them," said Jonah, advancing again. Amanda retreated again. I almost had to laugh as Jonah chased Amanda in a slow circle around the group. She took a step back for every one of his steps forward.

"Ms. Collins," said Jonah, "if you don't tell them about these checkers, I will." Amanda pursed her lips disapprovingly, so Jonah continued. "Pleurinium," he said. "The dangerous moon magnet. Tell me I'm wrong."

He and Amanda locked eyes and stared at each other angrily.

Amanda was the first to look away.

"They're made of pleurinium," Jonah repeated. "And you were trying to see how it affected us, how it affects kids. Weren't you?"

I heard a squeaky scream and then a crash as Madison's box hit the ground. The Texan with the checkers did the same thing. They both dropped their boxes like hot potatoes and scurried away from them.

"Ms. Collins? Why would you do that to us? Pleurinium is poisonous!" said Trace angrily.

"Okay, okay," Amanda replied, clearly frustrated. "Yes, they're made of pleurinium. The checkers are made of pleurinium. You're right. But dangerous?

Poisonous? Really? Trace, tell me how you feel. Are you tired? Dizzy? Sick? One little bit?"

Trace shook her head.

"Anyone?" Amanda pressed. "Feel bad? Strange? Anything?"

We all shook our heads.

"All right then, Jonah Jones," Amanda sighed, "would you tell your friends all about it, since you evidently have it all figured out?"

"Sure thing," said Jonah, brandishing the box of pleurinium checkers. "We've all heard how the pleurinium has a negative effect on adults, causing exhaustion, dizziness, and nausea almost immediately. And then, after minutes and hours, causing worse symptoms like fainting or unconsciousness. That's for adults. But for kids, it doesn't have that effect. It doesn't have any effect. None. Zero."

"Correct, Mr. Jones, correct," one of the white-coated scientists interrupted. "All of our tests show that pleurinium does not affect kids under about thirteen years old. Anyone over thirteen, well, that's a different story. And this test proved it again. The funny thing is, we still have no idea why. But we're doing everything we can to figure it out. And we've got to figure it out before Team Varsity goes back to the moon. Or else their mission will fail just like the others, and we'll be looking at a lunar nuclear meltdown."

★ ★ ★ ★ ★

That evening, after dinner and ice cream sundaes, we watched a movie about how the moon base was built and listened to a long speech by one of the astronauts who had helped build it the year before. It was almost ten o'clock by the time we got back to the dormitory, but they still gave us thirty minutes until lights out.

The comfy couches and bean bag chairs were a welcome change from the hard-backed metal chairs in the classroom. As we scattered ourselves around the room, Jonah introduced a new, crazy theory about how we were being trained to go to the moon.

"Don't you see? Pleurinium doesn't affect kids? Are you finally buying it? That's why we're here. They're sending us to the moon!"

That statement was met by a chorus of whoops and laughter from the other kids. One of the Texans jumped up onto the back of the couch and cupped his hands together to make a tinny radio sound.

"This is Mission Control. We're about to witness the first kids walkin' in space. Hold on to your hats. Ladeez and gentlemen, here he comes. Jumpin' Jonah Jones is away from the air lock and is . . . actually . . . walkin' . . . on the moon!"

The other Texan rose in fake slow motion and pretended to space-walk around the room. The rest of the group laughed as he churned his arms in slow circles and bounce-hopped over the back of the couch and onto a table.

The rest of the group laughed, but I didn't feel like joining them. I had a funny sensation in my stomach. Strangely enough, I noticed that Lance wasn't laughing, either.

Jonah scowled. He turned toward me, giving me another one of his pleading looks. Then his gaze changed suddenly and he stood up, staring straight at me. He must have seen something in my eyes.

"Wait! Wait a minute!" Jonah said slowly. "Mickey, you . . . you . . . agree with me, don't you?"

The funny feeling in my stomach grew more intense. I ran through Jonah's arguments again in my head. Why had everybody been invited to space camp at the last minute? How had I been invited without even applying? Why couldn't our leaders seem to agree on the name of our camp? Was it really a coincidence that all this was happening while there was an emergency on the moon? Why were they studying our reaction to pleurinium? And why was Commander Riker always so negative, so nasty toward all of us in the space camp? It was almost like he felt . . . threatened by us.

I realized that most of the kids in the room had stopped watching the Texans and were now watching Jonah and me as we stood facing each other. Even the Texans had stopped clowning around and were staring at us.

Then the last piece hit me.

"Team Varsity," I said.

"Team Varsity?" asked Jonah. "What about it?"

"Varsity," I said again. "You know what *varsity* means?" I didn't wait for an answer. "High schools have varsity sports teams. Colleges, too. It means the best team at a school, the top team. But you don't call it a varsity team if it's the only one. If there was only one team, you'd just call it 'team.' Right?"

"Um . . . dude . . . I thought you were on my side," said Jonah, disappointment spelled across his face.

"Now you're sounding like a crazy person. What's all this about sports teams?"

I scanned the crowd and locked eyes with Trace, who cracked a smile. "Oh, he's making sense," she said. "What he's trying to say is, the top team is called the varsity. The second team is called the junior varsity. You don't have one without the other."

"So," continued Trace, "what does that make us?"

"Exactly," said Jonah. "That makes us the junior varsity. They brought us here—they're putting us through tests—because they need a team of kids. A backup team to send to the moon, in case they can't send the adults. And if the genius NASA scientists can't solve the pleurinium problem soon, that's exactly what they're going to do."

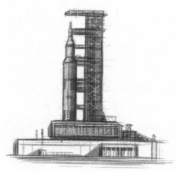

CHAPTER 11
Greatest. Field Trip. Ever.

The next morning was sunny. Low, puffy white clouds raced overhead, pushed in from the Atlantic Ocean by a steady breeze. After a breakfast of pancakes and sausage, all twenty of us loaded into a white school bus that pulled up in front of the main entrance. When asked what we were doing, Amanda replied simply, "We're going to see the rocket."

A buzz of excitement spread through the group as we settled into our seats and immediately pulled out onto Apollo Drive heading north. After a while we turned right toward the ocean and then left again onto a broad, straight road with no traffic. The land was flat and barren here, with patches of gnarly brown grass and scrub bushes, nothing taller than knee high. Except for the row of metal towers stretching out in front of us, reaching into the sky.

As we headed north, we passed a dusty, pot-holed cement road cutting away at an angle to the right, leading to the first tower. We passed another road leading to another lonely tower. Then a third.

I watched as a row of white sea birds lifted off from the top rim of one tower, their wings flapping quickly for seven, eight, nine beats until they caught the breeze and eased steadily back down the beach toward the next abandoned tower.

"These towers were used to launch the early test rockets out over the Atlantic," said Amanda, pointing back at the launchpads we had just passed. She had turned in her seat to sit backward, facing us. "The next ones were used by the Mercury program to send the first American astronauts into orbit. Then came the Gemini program, with longer space flights and the first space walk. All the Gemini missions blasted off from that launchpad right over there: number 19."

My eyes returned to the towers we were approaching straight ahead. They were enormous, much larger than the first ones.

"The next two launchpads were used for the Apollo program. These towers were bigger to support the much larger rockets—larger and more powerful, because they needed enough fuel to take the spacecraft all the way to the moon and back. The first to get to the moon was *Apollo 11*, carrying Neil Armstrong, Buzz Aldrin, and Michael Collins. It blasted off from launch complex 39, right over there."

All of our heads turned to follow her finger, as though we might still catch a glimpse of the actual rockets if we looked quickly enough.

"I didn't work for NASA back then. I was still in

college," said Amanda. "But I watched the Apollo 11 launch from right over there, standing with my mom and dad at the public viewing area at Piney Point. It's something I'll never forget, and it changed my life forever. At that point I realized I had to be a part of the space program.

"You see," Amanda continued, turning from the window to face us, "even from a mile away, I could feel the power and rumble of the rocket right in my stomach. It shook the ground under my feet. I can only imagine what it would be like to be actually inside the launch vehicle, experiencing it myself. Few people ever do."

She had us all in a bit of a trance, imagining the liftoff. I looked at Trace, Jonah, and the other kids in the bus and saw that their eyes were all turned up to the sky, tracing the imagined path of a rocket.

Amanda seemed to shake out of her dream. "Well anyway," she said abruptly, "that's your history lesson for the day. We just drove through thirty years of the early space program's history. Mercury, Gemini, Apollo. These programs were important building blocks and got us where we are today: the Artemis program."

And that's when I noticed that the final red tower in the line was not empty. It was even taller than the last two, sitting on top of what looked like a cement hill at the end of an enormous ramp. As we pulled closer to it, I saw a huge shape appearing from behind the tower. It was smooth—black and white at the bottom, with a large American flag on its side. About two-thirds of the way up, it narrowed and was capped by a shining golden section with a thin point at the very top.

"And here's Launch Complex 40 with the *Artemis 7*, ready for launch."

We got out of the bus, which had pulled up alongside some other cars next to the launchpad. A steep cement wall angled up to the base of the rocket. I guessed that's what the "pad" was: an enormous cement slab that the rocket and tower sat on. Right now, we were climbing up a thin, metal staircase to the top of that slab. A couple times I glanced up—almost straight up—at the rocket pointing into space.

When I got to the top of the stairs, I saw that the launchpad was a beehive of activity. There were small trucks shuttling supplies to the base of the rocket, plus dozens of workers with clipboards or tools or electronic instruments, all busy at some task.

Amanda introduced the person in charge of the launch complex and told us to "huddle up" so we could hear him. That was a good idea. Even by squeezing in close, and even with him barking out his words in something close to a yell, it was hard to hear him above the commotion.

I nudged Trace on the arm and pointed to an elevator creeping slowly up the heavy red metal tower to the top of the rocket.

Jonah saw what we were looking at. "Yeah, I'd give my right arm for a ride on that. That's how you get to the command module, the area for the crew. The astronauts ride that elevator on the day of the launch. Can you imagine?"

"Man," I said, looking down the coastline, "just think of the view from up there. I wonder if I could see Orlando." I thought of home for the first time in almost twenty-four hours. But it didn't last long, because I heard the word *elevator.*

"I see you all looking at the elevator," yelled the launch complex director. "It runs thirty-six stories up the tower to the command module, the crew compartment."

"So, anybody want to go up?" Amanda asked brightly.

Right. That was officially the dumbest question in the history of questions.

Twenty hands shot straight up. Actually, it was twenty-one hands. Our van driver had followed us up the steps and had been standing next to me, listening to the speech.

He shrugged his shoulders when I looked at him curiously. "Hey, come on," he said, "I've worked at Kennedy for ten years and never got to ride up to the top. It was worth a try."

I shrugged right back and then realized I'd fallen behind. I jogged forward to catch up to the rest of the kids who had followed Amanda under the frame of the tower and toward the base of the elevator.

"No pushing, settle down," Amanda chided the group. "We'll do this in groups of five. The elevator isn't large, and there's not much room at the top. Five at a time up to the top, where you'll have a chance to look around the real command module of the *Artemis 7* spacecraft. Then you'll walk down thirty-six stories." There were immediate groans from some of the kids. "Yes, *walk* down the stairs, which should be totally awesome, right? I mean, how many kids in America get this kind of close-up look at the Artemis?"

She had a point.

"So this will take a while. While you wait your turn at the bottom here, Mr.—" She paused to glance down at the launch complex director's name tag. "Mr. Dulmore here will keep you entertained with fascinating stories about . . . well . . . about whatever it is that he does around here. Right, Mr. Dulmore?"

"Oh, of course, right!" said Dulmore, who looked rather surprised to hear his name in the same sentence as the words *entertained* and *fascinating*.

Amanda started counting heads and swept five kids to her left toward the elevator door. Her path was blocked by Lance, who was pushing Rockwell, Stimple and two other girls to the front of the pack.

"Now, Lance," said Amanda lightly, "I've got my first five already. You'll get your turn, don't worry."

Lance kept walking forward, a smug grin on his face. "Look, Amanda," his voice was quiet and mocking, and he used a tone and enunciation that might be used when speaking to a preschooler. "You don't want me to tell my father that you're interfering with my training, do you?"

Trace shot me a quizzical look, her eyes saying "what?" I gave a tiny shrug.

"Young man," said Amanda, turning to face him. Her face still wore a smile, but her voice was sharper than usual. "You can tell the director anything you like. I have a job to do, and I'm going to keep doing it. And you're going to wait—your—turn."

Trace shot me another look, but this time her eyes said "aha!" Wait a minute, his father? Director

Marshall. Lance had the name "Lance M." on his jumpsuit. Lance Marshall.

Lance stood still, facing Amanda. He was almost her height, and his chest was puffed out like a soldier at attention. But then I saw his shoulders slump a bit. He had made up his mind. He backed down. Lance gave a little laugh and made an exaggerated bow to Amanda and the five campers as he waved them toward the elevator.

Trace leaned in toward Jonah and me. "Of course. Now it makes sense," she groaned in a whisper. "I was beginning to wonder why Supercamper acts like he runs this place. It's because he practically does."

✪ ✪ ✪ ✪ ✪

The elevator came back five minutes later with only Amanda inside. Dulmore had been telling us about the special kind of cement used to make the base of the launchpad, how thick the cement was, how many cement trucks it had taken to deliver the cement, and how long it takes cement to dry. Boy, that guy loved cement.

I was thrilled when Amanda stepped out of the elevator and called my name, along with Trace's, Cat's, Jonah's and Elvis-from-Mississippi's. Lance looked like hot smoke was going to shoot out of his ears.

"We'll send a postcard," Trace whispered to Lance as we stepped past him. Then she stuck her hand out behind her back to give me a mini high five.

The elevator was different from any elevator I had ever been in. It was a metal mesh cage with holes in the floor so you could look down. And the walls only went up to my shoulder level, leaving the rest open to the air.

As we started the ascent, Amanda pointed out what the workers were doing. "We're in final preparation mode," she said. "With launch just a couple days away, we're working twenty-four hours a day, every day, on all the final details. The engineers are checking and rechecking all the machinery and the electronics. The food is being loaded into the command module. The oxygen tanks are being filled.

"This bottom section we're passing now is called the stage-one rocket. It contains a huge amount of rocket fuel. It burns for the first six minutes of flight and gets the spacecraft about thirty miles into the air. And when that fuel is gone—"

"Forty-two miles," said Jonah.

"Excuse me?" said Amanda, surprised.

"I'm sorry, Ms. Collins, I didn't mean to interrupt," said Jonah politely, but of course he had meant to interrupt. "It's just that stage one burns for forty-two miles, not thirty. At that point the spacecraft is traveling about six thousand miles per hour. The empty stage-one rocket detaches and falls into the ocean, you know, so the spacecraft doesn't need to carry the weight of the huge, empty fuel tank."

"Um, that's right, Jonah. You mind telling me how you know all that?"

"Aren't we *all* supposed to know this already?" asked Jonah, looking honestly confused. "I mean, that was covered in the materials you gave us when we arrived.

You know, the green binder, volume seventeen, section six? The part about rocket propulsion?"

"Dude," said Elvis in amazement. "You didn't actually read all that stuff and understand everything, did you?"

Jonah shrugged. Amanda politely asked Jonah to please pick up where she had left off and muttered something about how she might learn something.

Jonah cleared his throat and proceeded. As our elevator slowly continued its climb, Jonah explained to us that we were now passing the stage-two section of the rocket, which carried the spacecraft to the outer part of the Earth's atmosphere at a speed of over twenty thousand miles per hour. "Exit velocity" he called it, the speed at which the spacecraft would exit the Earth's atmosphere.

After a while, the sides of the rocket started to taper inward, and its body got narrower. We were nearing the top.

"Here, above the stage-three rocket, are the last two sections of the spacecraft. The sections we have passed so far do the work and carry the fuel to get it up and out of the atmosphere, and then they fall away during the flight. These top two sections are the ones that land on the moon. The big lower section is called the service module. It has rocket engines that are small compared to the ones needed to blast off from Earth, and it also carries fuel, a bunch of equipment, oxygen tanks, and an air lock used to enter and exit the spacecraft on the moon. The service module doesn't return to Earth, though. At the end of the return trip, right before reentering the atmosphere, the service module detaches and floats away. That leaves only the command module—the small golden section at the very top—to come back to Earth."

"Perfect timing, Jonah," said Amanda. The elevator slowed as it moved up and into a little building at the top of the tower. "We're now in the ready center: the room where the astronauts gather before boarding the spacecraft."

We squeezed our way through a handful of workers. One of them was loading packages of Fig Newtons and small bags of dried apricots into a plastic container.

"These are the final preparations. The food, the special equipment—everything is being loaded for the launch," explained Amanda as we stepped outside onto a thin metal walkway heading toward the top of the enormous spaceship.

I had to admit, it was dizzying to look down at the ocean and launchpad thirty-six floors below. I noticed that Cat had grabbed Jonah's hand as she moved out onto the walkway. Her eyes were terrified, and she stared straight ahead. Jonah looked completely embarrassed. I grinned and flashed him a thumbs-up sign, causing him to blush so hard that his face matched the color of the red safety railing.

We took turns peering inside the command module through the small opening, about half the size of a regular door. "Is this all there is?" exclaimed Elvis, the first one to look. "Isn't there another room where the astronauts can, you know, move around and stretch their legs?"

"No, Elvis," Amanda smiled as Trace pushed Elvis aside and leaned her head in through the entrance. "What you see is what you get. It's cramped, but it has everything the astronauts need for the trip to the moon and back."

"But come on," said Trace with her head still inside, "why not give them a little more space? A little room with beanbag chairs? A foosball table?"

"Jonah?" asked Amanda, realizing he was itching to give the answer.

"No unnecessary weight, that's why," said Jonah. "It's hard enough to get this stripped-down command module up out of the atmosphere. We just came up a skyscraper worth of rocket and rocket fuel, remember? It's cramped and small, but after all, it's all they need for a three-day trip to the moon."

Trace pulled her head out, and I leaned forward, blinking to get my eyes adjusted to the darkness inside the command module. I saw what Elvis and Trace were talking about. Even empty, it looked cramped, no bigger than the inside of a car. A compact car. I tried to imagine what it would be like with five full-size adult astronauts inside.

There were two seats in the front row, facing a narrow slit window on top of an enormous display of switches and computer screens and dials, just like in the test module we had seen the day before. There were even switches and buttons on the ceiling directly above the two captains' seats. Then, squeezed in right behind them in a second row were three more seats.

"What's the little door in the back?" I asked, wonder-

ing about the hatch that was about the size of a large
pizza box. I pulled out my head to allow Cat a turn.

"That door leads down into the service module,"
said Amanda. "When the astronauts arrive at their
destination, they head through that door, into the air
lock, and then out onto the moon."

After Jonah had looked around the cabin, Amanda
led us back across the narrow walkway to the tower and
showed us the head of the staircase. While we were at
the top, peering into the shining, golden capsule that
would take five brave astronauts into space, I was able
to imagine we were the ones who would be making
the trip.

As we walked down the stairs, however, it was like
we were returning to the real world where we were kids
at a space camp. The golden capsule was, once again,
far above us and out of reach.

CHAPTER 12
The Second Test

"On your marks!" After we returned from the field trip, we all had lunch in the cafeteria and were hustled straight to the gymnasium for our afternoon activities. We were divided into four teams of five. I was on team three, along with Trace, Cat, Jonah and Madison. We stood with our toes behind the end line of the basketball court in the gym, leaning forward, ready to spring into action.

"Get set!"

The other three teams of five were clumped together farther down the end line. The Texans, Elvis, and two others were on our left. They had confidently predicted victory, but Trace had told us quietly to "let them talk, let them talk." As usual, Lance was on what seemed to be the "A" team, along with Stimple, Rockwell and two athletic-looking girls from Massachusetts. They were on the far left, staring forward resolutely.

I clutched my sheet of paper with the instructions

and noticed that my shoe was untied. I wondered if I had time to tie it. It would only take a few seconds....

"GO!"

Instantly forgetting about my shoelace, I rocketed forward with my team toward the open doors at the far end of the gym. The Great Space Race was on!

✪ ✪ ✪ ✪ ✪

"Dad. Dad. DAD!"

Dad looked up, pulled from deep inside his story that had taken him far away and far back in time.

"Yes, Tom. What is it?"

"Dad, the Great Space Race?" asked Tom. "What was the goal? Why were there teams? What were the rules?"

"Oh, right," said Dad. "I need to explain that part, don't I."

"Don't worry about it, Dad. This story is way more complicated than your usual ones, and I get it, it's hard to make all this stuff up. It's only natural to mess up sometimes. Just go ahead, keep making it up."

Dad couldn't see the sly expression on Tom's face in the dark, but he could hear that Tom was baiting him.

"Make it up? Come on, Tom. This is a true story. I just jumped ahead, that's all."

"Okay, whatever, Dad. Make it up, tell it, whatever. I was just pointing out that you left something out. It's late. You're tired. No problem."

"Thanks for your incredible understanding, Tom," said Dad. "And it is late. You still with us, Tess?"

"Of course," came a voice from out of the darkness.

"All right, the Great Space Race. It was a big team competition. You know, like the decathlon in the Olympics, when the athletes have to do all the track-and-field sport: the long jump, the high jump, the shot put, sprinting, distance running? This was like a decathlon of space camp activities. We started with a foot race. Then took a space trivia test. Then we had an obstacle course in the gym. Then our team was tied together with ropes, kind of like a leash connecting each one of us to the other, and we had to make it through a maze blindfolded. One thing after another. Each team of five competing against the other."

"And the prize?" asked Tess.

"Oh yeah, the prize. What was the prize? I can't even remember. I think it was a special gift bag for everyone on the team. It had a NASA jacket and a little piece of moon rock and a book about space in it, something like that. But we knew there was something more at stake. They were watching us. Watching how we performed."

"So Dad, is this the main part of the story?" asked Tess. "The Great Space Race?"

Dad paused and glanced over at the camping clock. 12:45 A.M.

"You getting tired? You want me to make this the end? The grand finale?"

"*Make it* the grand finale?" asked Tom. "Wait, it either is or it isn't the grand finale. If you *make it* the grand finale, that means you're making up the whole story, right?"

Dad paused. "No, I just meant, you know, make

it the grand finale for tonight. This story has already happened. I'm just recalling it from memory."

"Fine, Mr. Space Camper," said Tom, "you go ahead with the story."

"Thanks for your kind permission," said Dad. "I'll go ahead with the story. Back to the Great Space Race. Our team was in second place. Maybe third. We had a problem in the maze. Madison kept wanting to lead, and it took us a while to realize she had a terrible sense of direction. We kept walking in circles and ending up back at the beginning of the maze. So after we finally finished the maze, we were in third place with only one part to go. Our instruction sheet just called it Final Test—Conference Room B.

✪ ✪ ✪ ✪ ✪

Cat and I went racing into the conference room with Jonah, Trace, and Madison right behind. At first, my heart sank when I saw Lance sitting at a desk in the far corner of the room. Stimple, Rockwell and the rest of their team was in the room too, sitting at desks, already concentrating hard on the final stage of the test. But at least they were still working. They hadn't finished yet. There was still time.

I saw a red envelope with my name on it on a table in the first row. I sprinted over and tore open the cover. Cat found her envelope in the back row and ripped it open as well. I sat down at my desk pulled out two pieces of paper. The first asked simply: "*What is the most important part of any mission?*" The second was this:

— — — — — — —
O

I shook the envelope, hoping something else would fall out, then desperately peered inside. Empty. I flipped the pages over, back and front. Nothing more than I had already seen. *"What is the most important part of any mission?"* And then the second paper with that strange collection of dashes and a circle beneath.

"You've got to be kidding me," I muttered to the ceiling.

Lance's head spun around to look at me, but he wasn't gloating. I saw a look of desperate confusion on his face before he turned back to study his own pieces of paper.

Well, I thought, at least he was just as clueless as I was.

I looked at the dashes and circle again. I spun it sideways. It looked kind of like a basketball pole and hoop.

Nah, couldn't be.

I spun it upside down. It looked like . . . of course . . . it was a word. A series of blanks and an O. Like hangman.

Except how was I supposed to guess it with only one letter? The most important part of any mission. Helmet. Food. Air. Toilet. No, those words were too short.

Space suit. Oxygen tank. Parachute. No, too long.

Rocket. Liftoff. Blastoff.

A jolt went through my brain. Wait a minute. That fit! B-L-A-S-T-O-F-F. That was it! Sweet!

But as I started to fill in the letter B, I was hit by a second jolt. This time, it was a jolt of uncertainty. Was blastoff really the most important part of a mission? Sure, it was a big part. But so was the flight. And landing on the moon. And then successfully doing the work. And then lifting off from the moon. And coming back into the atmosphere. And, of course, landing safely. After what happened in the flight simulator test, how could I forget about the crash landing? How could any one of these parts be more important than the others?

I started to panic and checked the others in the classroom to see if they were having any more luck than I was. By this time, Jonah had arrived and had the same befuddled look as everybody else, isolated at separate desks. Trace, sitting in the back row, had a look of determination on her face but wasn't writing anything down.

I was officially stuck. I decided there was only one thing to do. I walked down the center aisle to Trace's desk. "Hey Trace, you got it?" I whispered.

"Yeah, of course. I got it about ten minutes ago." She spat at me with a frustrated whisper. "I just thought I'd sit here and draw a picture of a purple unicorn to waste some time. *Of course I don't have it!*" Boy, was she frustrated.

Rockwell glared over at us and said "SHHHHH!" before returning to her work.

"Gee, sorry," I mumbled.

"Yeah, whatever," said Trace. "I feel like I've come up with every eight-letter word ending in K in the dictionary. It's a pretty impressive list: backpack, sunblock, doorlock. I'm not sure that's a word, though—"

"Wait!" I interrupted. "What did you say?"

"I said door lock. You know, a lock on a door? But I'm not sure if that's one word or two. Doorlock. Door lock. You know what I mean?"

I grabbed her sheet of paper and stared at her clue. It had this printed on it:

"Trace, you rock!"

"Wait. Y-O-U-R-O-C-K. That's not enough letters, Mick. It's only seven," whispered Trace. I ignored her and sneaked over to Cat's desk. I grabbed Cat's page, then quickly reached for Jonah's, and walked over to pick up Madison's. With the rest of the team following me, I returned to Trace's desk and lined up the pieces of paper, one above the other.

Each one had eight blanks. But each one had a different letter filled in. Cat's clue started with a T. The next two spaces were blank on all of our clues. Madison's clue had an M in the fourth spot. Jonah's had a W in the fifth. Mine had an O in the sixth. And Trace's ended in a K.

T __ __ M W O __ K.

"The most important part of a mission," I said simply.

"You got it, Mick," said Cat excitedly, looking over my shoulder. She mouthed the answer at the rest

of us. A feeling like electricity swept through me—
through all of us—as we quickly filled in the blanks.
Cat gathered our answer sheets, and we bolted for
the door, suddenly in first place, with our entire team
heading back to the finish line in the gymnasium.

We sprinted the short distance between buildings
in record time and skidded as a group into the
gymnasium, where we found Amanda Collins and
Major Jackson (wearing his gold sunglasses, of course)
waiting with a group of scientists and engineers.

"So, it's you five. I can't say I'm surprised," said
Amanda, smiling.

As Cat handed in our answer sheets, we heard the
sound of heavy footsteps in the hall behind us. Lance
burst into the room, red in the face.

"I got it. I got the answer on my own. But it's my
duty to report that these five totally cheated."

"Cheated?" asked Amanda, raising her eyebrows.

"Yes ma'am, cheated," said Lance, standing up
straight like some kind of soldier with a smirk on his
face. "They were talking and working together, and
everybody else saw it. You can ask anyone. They officially
broke the rules."

There was another commotion in the hallway, and
the remaining fourteen kids came bursting into the
room and jostled their way to the front, pushing each
other aside as they tried to hand their answer sheets to
Major Jackson.

"Ma'am," continued Lance as Amanda put the
papers in order and the crowd backed away a few steps,
"those five will be disqualified, right?"

"Not at all," said Amanda. "You each got an envelope with your name on it, but the rules don't say anything about having to work alone. Besides," she continued, flipping through the answer sheets to find his, "you didn't get it right. Blastoff is not the answer we were looking for."

I couldn't help bursting into a smile.

"Trace, Mickey, Cat, Jonah, Madison, you got it right," said Major Jackson with a grin. "Teamwork is the answer. There are many important parts of a mission. The blastoff is certainly one of the important parts. But each part, each individual task, is impossible without the help of your teammates. It's all about teamwork."

Amanda jumped in. "You see, answering this question alone was almost impossible. But working together, you could figure it out. Congratulations to team three, you win. And also, congratulations to the rest of the teams. It looks like you all got it right, too. I guess you followed the example set by team three and figured out you needed to cooperate. Good work, everybody, and sorry, nice try, Lance." Lance took a step back. His mouth opened and closed as though he was talking, but no sound came out.

Jonah had his arm around Cat's shoulders, and they were both smiling broadly. Trace had her lips pursed firmly together and pumped her fist several times in silent celebration.

I was ecstatic. It felt great to win and even better to win with my friends.

"Okay," said Amanda, checking her watch. "It's 5:30 P.M. We'll break for dinner in a little while. But first, find a seat. We need to talk about what we learned."

As we shuffled back toward the chairs, two men in white shirts carrying walkie-talkies came bursting into the room. They spoke in low voices to Major Jackson, and Amanda leaned in to listen. I watched her face and saw a look of complete shock fill her wide eyes. Her hand flew to her mouth as she glanced quickly at the kids retreating to the chairs, then she turned again to listen to the two visitors.

Everyone in the room realized something was up. The lively chatter had stopped, and I was frozen, halfway between standing and sitting.

The two men took a step backward to let Amanda speak.

Something was different. Her usual confidence and polish was gone. She looked nervous. "There's been a change of p-plan," she stammered. "I'll be walking you back to the dormitory right now. You'll still have some time before dinner. It's been a long day, so this is ... um ... this is good. Some time for you all to relax."

"If you ask me," said Jonah, leaning in toward me, "it looks like *she's* the one who could use some time to relax."

CHAPTER 13
Ready or Not

When we got back to the dormitory, we all headed to the common room to hang out. Trace, Cat, Jonah, and I—and even Madison—received a few high fives for winning the race. Lance had stopped calling us cheaters, at least, but instead he started loudly making fun of the whole competition.

"Yeah, they figured out that word problem but big deal. Being good at a crossword puzzle doesn't have anything to do with being an astronaut," he sneered, shooting a sideways glance at our group. That seemed to make him feel better, and a few other kids nodded in agreement and went over to sit near Lance as he started to tell a story about visiting the White House with his father.

Trace was ready to burst. "That no good, arrogant, lousy attitude, boneheaded, meatheaded, bigheaded . . . aagh!" She rose from the couch with her hands balled into fists, looking like she was ready to march over to Lance and kick him in the shins. Or worse.

I grabbed her shirt and tugged her back onto the couch, which she hit with a thud. I think she was happy to be back on the couch instead of marching her way across the room to confront Lance and his fan club.

"Trace, you know he's just doing that to get a reaction, right?" I asked. "Yank your chain? Get your goat?"

"Well, he got my goat all right. Let's see if he's still smiling after a nice knuckle sandwich." She slapped her right fist against her left palm with a loud *thwack*. Then she burst out laughing. "Or we could just beat him again in the next contest. What do you say?"

The response was unanimous. Jonah, Cat, and I showed our agreement by piling on top of her on the couch. Then I felt the weight of Madison and a couple of Texans pile on top of us, too.

When I finally pulled myself free from the dog pile of kids, I saw a pair of women's shoes with two pairs of men's shoes in the doorway. Not just the shoes, of course. They were attached to people. But it was the shoes I saw first.

The shoes belonged to Amanda Collins, Major Jackson, and Major Austen.

They weren't smiling.

As I stood up and patted down my messed-up hair, they stepped aside. In walked Director Marshall.

A sudden hush fell over the room, so the only sounds were the snorting and giggling coming from the two Texans who were still piled on top of each other on the couch, wrestling. Cat gave one of them a sharp kick with her sneaker. He howled. "Hey, no fair! Why'd you—?" But he scrambled quickly to his feet when he saw our visitors.

"Oh . . . howdy there, I mean, good evening Mr. Director Marshall, sir." He couldn't stop babbling. "I didn't see you standing there. Mighty nice of you to come by for a visit. I'll . . . well, um . . . sorry . . . I think I'll just be quiet now."

Marshall regarded the Texan with raised eyebrows. Then he spoke.

"Young astronauts, our engineers have received some disturbing news from our monitoring equipment on the moon. The nuclear reactor is in worse shape than we had feared. We have to move quickly. Very quickly. We cannot wait until the planned launch date next week. We have to move up the launch . . . to tomorrow morning."

There was complete silence now in the room.

I could even hear the mechanical buzz-hum of the long, skinny lightbulbs overhead.

"You will all have a good view of the launch, which will mark the start of one of the most exciting, important, and unusual missions in the history of the space program. A few of you will be . . . separated . . . from the main group. You will be watching from a different location."

I glanced sideways at Jonah, but he didn't take his eyes off Director Marshall. Jonah's lips were moving, but noiselessly, and I couldn't figure out what he was saying.

"Don't ask why," the director continued. "That's not important. What's important is the mission. And the launch is just a few hours away."

There were a couple hands in the air, but the director brushed them aside. "No time for questions. Amanda will stay with you and can tell you about the evening's activities. I have to go to Mission Control. Five of you will come with Major Jackson, Major Austen, and me."

He paused.

He nodded at the tallest boy in the room, who had already started to walk toward the door. "Lance," he said, "step out with us."

Rockwell and Stimple also got to their feet, and kids started to scoot out of the way, making room for them as they followed Lance to the door. But the director closed his eyes for just a second before raising his right palm at them and shaking his head slightly. "Trace Daniels. Catalina Obando. Jonah Jones. Step out with us."

Lance gasped and stared at his father in shock. "But Dad, that's crazy. What about . . .? You gotta be kidding me!"

The director turned swiftly. With a loud crack, he snapped his fingers and pointed sharply at Lance's nose. "Not one more word, son. That's an order, and it's crystal clear. And you *know* how to follow orders."

Lance sagged and hung his head. Rockwell and Stimple stood frozen in the middle of the room, their mouths hanging open in disbelief.

Marshall turned back to face the group. "And . . ." he continued, then paused to scan the room, looking for one more person. Amanda stepped forward and whispered in his ear. "Oh right," said the director.

"Price. Mickey Price. Step out with us. The rest of you, carry on."

Marshall spun on his heels and was out the door almost before his words traveled across the room to my ears—or at least before his words had sunk in.

Cat and Jonah were headed toward the door, but my butt was still firmly glued to the couch. I felt Trace take my hand and give it a strong tug, pulling me to my feet.

As I walked past Amanda, she said, "Good luck, kids."

Out in the hall, Lance, Cat, and Jonah were standing next to Major Jackson when Trace and I approached.

The major took a deep breath. "Kids, you are the five. You're Team Junior Varsity. Let's get you ready."

"Do you mean—," I asked, unable to finish the sentence.

"Yes, Price," said the major, looking intensely at me. "We can't solve the pleurinium problem, and we need to send up the rescue team immediately. So you're the five. You're going up."

✪ ✪ ✪ ✪ ✪

We were whisked into a van for the short ride to the Mission Control complex and herded into a conference room where the director was waiting with Team Varsity. Commander Riker did not look happy. His mouth was drawn in a thin, straight line, toothpick sticking out at an angle.

The director paired each one of us with a member of Team Varsity, who would tell us about our special jobs and give us instructions. Lance would be our flight commander and was paired with Riker. I was assigned to Lieutenant Strider, the gruff-looking copilot. Trace was paired with Major Jackson and would be our navigator, in charge of our maps and direction. Cat was paired with Major Austen and would be our computer engineer, keeping track of our electronics and computer systems. And Jonah, of course, was our mission scientist, paired with Dr. Yang, the scientist on Team Varsity.

For the next two hours, Strider flooded me with information about the copilot's duties during all stages of the flight, from prelaunch and liftoff at the beginning to splashdown in the ocean at the end of the mission, and everything in between. All the time, he flipped through a binder the size of the New York City phone book, showing me photos and diagrams of the copilot's seat in the command module and the instruments that surrounded it. I paid as much attention as I could, I really did. I nodded my head and said "got it" or "roger that" at all the right times.

But after a while, I began to wonder whether I would actually remember any of this. Did I remember what he had said two minutes ago? What was the first thing he had told me? Had I forgotten some absolutely critical piece of information?

"Price? Price! PRICE! Are you okay?" I looked up. Strider was giving me a very concerned look.

"Oh, sure. No problem. I was just wondering . . . I mean . . . do you honestly expect me to remember all of this? Seriously?"

Strider looked startled at first and paused, then sighed and broke into a big grin. "Look, Price, you'll have it easy. You're not leaving us behind, we're going with you in a way. We'll be watching you. We'll be reading your instrument panel readouts. We'll be connected by radio. We'll be there every step of the way. I'm going through all this so it will be familiar when it happens. And a lot of this is preprogrammed into the computer. So, you don't need to memorize everything right this second."

I must not have looked convinced.

"Look," Strider continued. "Imagine this: You need to draw the Mona Lisa on a piece of paper. It's hard if you're drawing on a blank page, right? But it's easy if you're doing a connect-the-dots. Every dot is numbered. You just follow the numbers. That's what you're doing on this mission. We'll worry about the dots, you just connect them. Okay?

"It's just like what you did in the flight simulator," Strider continued, "where you practiced following instructions. If you leave it to us, everything will turn out just right."

"Um, you might not remember," I cut in, "but in the flight simulator test, I followed the instructions, and my command module missed the landing zone by a thousand miles and crashed in Chihuahua, Mexico."

Strider's smile vanished, and he shifted nervously in his seat. "Well, then I guess you thank your lucky stars that was just a test. We'll get it right this time. Trust us." Strider finished with an unconvincing smile.

"Now look," he plowed ahead, happy to change the subject, "let me give you a few pointers about the moon base. We call it Oblivion Base. First, don't expect anything fancy or comfortable at Oblivion. It's like living in a factory, with metal walls and pipes and wires everywhere. Second, the food stinks. The chewy peanut butter sticks are pretty good, but don't get your hopes up about the freeze-dried burgers. And finally, watch the sun rise around the corner of the Earth sometime and make sure you're wearing your special sunglasses, because the glare can really hurt your eyes. It's a sight you'll never forget."

It seemed like Strider had run out of advice, and he looked relieved when the director chose that exact moment to sweep back into the room. He clapped his hands twice, quickly. "Eyes up here!" he barked. The room was immediately silent. The clock over his shoulder said 12:10 A.M. It was past midnight.

"Junior Varsity, I have just two things to tell you before we'll let you get some sleep."

"Number one: No matter what you think, the primary goal of the *Artemis 7* mission is to keep you safe. Remember that. Our mission is to bring you back, every one of you. Shutting down the nuclear reactor, that's just icing on the cake. Got it?"

He pointed his finger at each of us. Lance, Trace, Jonah, Cat, and then me. We nodded.

"Got that?" He pointed his finger at Team Varsity and the other adults crowding into the room. "Yes, sir!" came the reply.

"Good. Now, number two: I'm not going to say good luck. Luck is what rescues you when you make a mistake. Luck is what saves you when you fail. Well, let me tell you something, kids. You can't rely on luck. Sometimes it's there. Sometimes it's not. I can tell each one of you, NASA will not need luck on this mission. We have the best equipment, the best plan, and the best people in the world. We will not need luck."

He looked around the room. The astronauts on Team Varsity were nodding their heads in agreement. The astronauts on Team Junior Varsity just looked sleepy.

"So instead of good luck, I will just say follow the plan."

To tell the truth, I expected something a little more encouraging, coming from a guy who was about to strap us to the tip of a skyscraper filled with explosive fuel and light a match. But at least his instructions were simple. And at that moment, sitting there in the bright conference room at the Kennedy Space Center, I had complete confidence in the man with the perfect, simple plan.

✪ ✪ ✪ ✪ ✪

Dad looked over at Tess, who was now sitting up in her sleeping bag, eyes wide, mouth wide open. Speechless, but not for long. Out spilled a jumbled assortment of words. "That's . . . but the . . . secret . . . with the . . . but how did . . . a rocket? And then . . . really?"

"Yes, Tess, really. I was gonna be strapped tight in a command module atop the biggest rocket ever made. I had four companions. And I was only twelve."

"Woah. Wo-wo-woah!" said Tess, shaking her head.

Dad looked over at Tom, who wasn't saying anything but whose mind was obviously moving one hundred miles an hour behind his eyes, which narrowed slightly.

Finally Tom spoke. "No way. Not gonna buy it. Good story. Great story even. But I'm not gonna buy it being real."

Dad simply cracked a halfway grin and shrugged his shoulders.

Tom continued. "Just like last April Fools' Day, when you woke us up in the morning and told us we had missed the helicopter landing in our backyard the night before. Or the time when we were four and you told us Congress had voted to cancel Christmas because of the bad economy—"

"Hold on, Tom," Dad interrupted. "I apologized for that one. A lot. And I think Santa didn't appreciate my joke because you got a little extra that year, right?"

"True. But that's not the point," said Tom. "I'm just saying, you don't have the world's best record on truthfulness, right? How do we know this one's not another big, fat, tall tale?"

"For starters, Tess believes me. Right, Tess?"

Tess looked from her brother to her father, then back again, clearly torn. "I dunno. I want to believe it. But it does seem, I don't know, kind of crazy. I think you would've said something about this before, right? You know what I mean?"

"Yeah, Dad," pressed Tom. "How come we've never heard about this before? Why aren't you in the space travel hall of fame? Or the *Guinness Book of World Records*? Why don't you have old photos up on the walls? Or your space suit in the attic? Come on. This is a good story. But it's made up, right?"

"Who says I don't have proof? If you make me show you, I'll do it," said Dad. "But there's a good reason why this wasn't made public. Things were different back in the 1970s. The United States wasn't the only country with a space program. The Soviet Union—the big country that later broke apart and became Russia and a few others—they had a space program, too. A great one. The Soviets were actually the first ones to send an astronaut into space. The Americans and Soviets didn't get along, so the American government was obsessed with beating the Soviets to the moon— and beating them in finding out what the moon had to offer. That's what the Artemis missions were all about.

"So, think about it," continued Dad. "With so much pressure to beat the Soviets, with the whole world watching, the American government felt like it couldn't admit failure. And NASA didn't want to admit that it had to turn to a bunch of kids to save the day. On that morning back in 1977, there were fewer than one hundred people in the world who knew NASA was sending kids up to the moon instead of the Team Varsity astronauts.

"Just a few dozen engineers and scientists in Mission Control. And our parents—or for me, Sister Rinaldi. And the President. NASA told the rest of the world it was Team Varsity inside the rocket that morning. All the newspapers and TV stations reported it that way. Imagine if they had known the truth. . . ."

⭐ ⭐ ⭐ ⭐ ⭐

"Ten." That morning, the five of us had ridden together to the launchpad in a van with dark, tinted windows. As we passed the Mission Control complex, we had slowed to weave through some TV trucks with satellite dishes on top. The news channels were probably showing the rocket on the launchpad, talking about Commander Riker and the other four adult astronauts inside. Little did they know that Riker and the rest of Team Varsity were sitting in a small room without windows next to Mission Control, watching everything on special cameras and listening to the radio transmission.

"Nine." All across America, kids were getting ready for school. Maybe putting on their sneakers before heading out to the sidewalk or to the bus. At the Orlando Home for Boys, the older boys were just leaving to walk the seven blocks to the middle school, while the younger ones waited on the corner for the Pinecrest Elementary school bus.

"Eight." Boy, I was strapped in tight. I could move my hands freely and jiggle my legs up and down, but my shoulders were strapped into my seat and my head was firmly wedged into my helmet. A seagull landed on the front window. Boy, was *he* in for a surprise.

"Seven." I rolled my eyes left and saw Lance sitting beside me in the flight commander's seat. His eyes were alive with excitement, and there was a faint smile on his lips.

"Six." I wondered what Jonah, Trace, and Cat were doing in the row behind me. Probably just like me: trying to imagine what would happen next.

"Five." The engines must have started to ignite. I could feel the rocket shudder, and there was a dull rumble from behind me.

"Four." I was actually a little hungry. I wondered when we'd get time for a snack.

"Three." Each second seemed to last forever, but the countdown was relentless.

"Two." No stopping now.

"One." Gulp.

"Main engine ignition. We have LIFTOFF! Liftoff of *Artemis 7*!"

The rumble grew to a roar, and my seat began to vibrate harder. But nothing else. The blue sky above me was still blue, and it wasn't getting any closer. I angled my eyes down to the altitude meter, however, and it confirmed that we weren't just sitting still. The numbers were slowly climbing as we cleared the tower and started to pull away from the ground.

The noise built slowly and so did the pressure, thrusting us back into our seats. In a car, you can step on the gas, and it only takes a few seconds to get up to full speed. In this spacecraft, full speed was like nothing I could have possibly imagined. The enormous, explosive rockets kept pushing us faster and faster. Just when it felt like we would break apart with any more thrust, they would kick it up to another level.

After a while, I just closed my eyes. After all, there wasn't anything to see, and I didn't exactly have a steering wheel. Over the roar of the engines, I heard the radio squawk: "*Artemis 7*, this is Control. Power up thrusters to one hundred percent. Over."

"Roger that, Control. Powering up to one hundred percent. Over." Lance sounded cool as a cucumber. I watched as he moved his right hand cleanly over to the control lever and nudged it up to full power. I immediately felt my body pushed back even harder into my seat. I tried lifting my hand but it felt like it was glued to the chair arm. These were the g-forces Lieutenant Strider had told me about last night.

Our maximum speed—escape velocity, Jonah had called it—was 24,000 miles per hour.

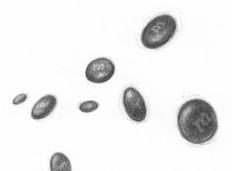

CHAPTER 14
Playing with M&Ms

"He shoots!" I said with great expectation, tossing a green M&M gently through the air. It floated, end over end, weightlessly, in a straight line across the cabin. Jonah eased himself into position and opened his mouth. He focused on the M&M as it slowly and relentlessly sailed toward him. And then he went cross-eyed watching it come closer, closer, closer, and finally into his mouth.

"And. He. Scores!" I yelled. "The crowd goes crazy. *Haaahhh. Haaahhh.* The young man from Orlando wins the national championship from the three-point range!"

Lance was not amused.

"If anyone hits me with an M&M, I'll pull over and make you walk," he snarled.

Trace flicked an M&M right at the back of Lance's head, but I snatched it out of the air and mouthed "dummy" to her. She stuck out her tongue.

It had been about three hours since blastoff, and we were most certainly in outer space. Jonah kept saying, "You are now free to unbuckle your seatbelts and move freely about the cabin," which I guess means something if you've been on an airplane. But I hadn't.

We realized, though, that we had to keep our seatbelts buckled just to keep ourselves in our chairs. It was the weirdest thing. If I unbuckled my seatbelt, I would immediately start to drift up out of my seat. If I shifted my weight and gave just one little bump off the chair, that was enough: That part of my body would rise slightly, slowly, steadily. With the slightest push of my pinkie against any fixed surface, I could start moving and spinning in the other direction.

I looked back at Trace. She was completely mesmerized by a pen. She flicked it with her index finger and started it spinning like a propeller right in front of her nose. It kept spinning. And spinning. And spinning. I wondered if it would ever stop.

Jonah had been in some kind of trance too, shaking his head slowly from side to side. His shoulder-length braids, mostly tame on earth, were spiking out in every direction like some kind of crazy sea anemone. The NASA staff had pressured him to cut it all off for the trip but he refused. As a compromise, they gave him a thick red rubber band, which he looped around his hair and brought things under control.

He glanced over at Cat with a look of concern. "Come on, Cat, what's wrong?" he asked, giving her a gentle shake on the shoulder. Cat had been strangely quiet recently, showing no interest in our M&M game.

"Cat? Are you feeling all right?" asked Trace, sounding concerned.

I swiveled the other way to look at Cat. She did look a little green and had her eyes closed.

"Ugh. Not good," came the quiet reply. "Not good at all."

"Not good, like your head kind of hurts? Because mine does, too. Or not good, like you might . . ." Jonah's voice trailed off. But I could almost hear his brain working overtime. "Gee," he continued. "I wonder what would happen in space if you—"

Jonah didn't get to finish his sentence.

Right then, Cat made a lunge for an airsickness bag in the small pouch on the side of her chair. I saw her pull the bag up to her mouth as she lurched forward and . . . let's just say the next part was not pretty.

She threw up. Loudly. Big time. She did get some of it into the opening of the airsickness bag. When I say "some," I really mean "not much." A lot of orange-colored barf missed the opening, instead hitting the side of the bag.

What happened next is hard to explain. I had never seen anything quite like it—and I hope I never see it again. The flying pool of barf hit the side of the bag and then started floating. There was a main glob of it that hovered, spinning slightly, about one foot in front of Cat's face.

But then there was a large breakaway cloud of barf that slowly moved, spinning through the air, away from Cat and toward Trace. It was the strangest thing, watching this rotating galaxy of vomit slowly but unstoppably inch its way through the air. There were medium-sized and small-sized drops of orangey liquid spinning around the central glob like little moons orbiting a planet. Each drop seemed to change shape from round, to oval, to flat coin-like shapes, and then kind of round again. A couple of the orbiting moon-things were connected to the blob by shiny, thin, gooey tendrils.

I told you it wasn't pretty.

Suspended in the main glob were chunks—bits of granola bar and, yes, I could see clearly a couple lumps of banana, no doubt about it. I remembered then: Cat had definitely grabbed a banana before our van ride to the rocket this morning. I was suddenly thankful I had not grabbed one, too.

The idea of a banana was very unappealing at that precise moment because the smell was something horrible.

While weightlessness did strange things to the shape of barf, it had no effect at all on its smell. I can assure you, blowing chunks smells just as bad in space as it does on Earth, maybe worse. Imagine going into a closet with four friends, and one of you throws up. That's how crowded it was, and that's how great it smelled.

All five of us were watching this incredible slow-motion spectacle. The main blob was still hovering in front of Cat, but the breakaway cloud was inching ever closer to Trace, who was strapped into her seat and wedged into the corner of the tiny command module with nowhere to escape. And it was Trace who broke the silence.

"Aaaaggghhhh! It's coming straight at me! Stop, stop, stop, stop, stop!" Trace yelled at the blob. "Go back! Reverse! Do a U-turn! Get away!"

The blob did not respond. It just kept moving, straight toward her face. I guess a barf blob has a mind of its own, if you know what I mean.

At this point, strapped in and unable to move left or right, Trace did the only thing she could do. She put her hands up in front of her face, cupping them slightly, allowing the blob to nestle into the bowl she had made with them. Then slowly and carefully and completely on purpose, she redirected it away from her—straight toward Jonah. Incredibly, the blob responded very well. It was slightly more compact, since Trace had packed it together like a snowball. And moving with a little more speed toward its new target.

With the crisis averted, Trace looked at her hands. The blob had left its signature on them. They were covered in stinky orange and yellow chunks.

"Nice one, Trace," I said, very impressed. "But do not wipe those hands on your pants."

"Tell me you didn't just do that, Trace!" exclaimed Jonah. "It's totally coming my way now. You're gonna pay!"

Jonah frantically started to grab at his safety belt buckles but quickly realized there was nowhere for him to hide. He raised his hands to defend his face.

Our fearless leader finally chimed in. "Nice work, Cat," said Lance. "Brilliant. If that gets into the controls, we're toast. How hard is it to throw up into a bag?"

"Ease off, Lance." I shot him an angry look. "Why don't you try asking Cat how she feels? How do you feel, by the way, Cat?"

"Amazingly better, thanks! Maybe not ready to eat another banana at this point, but much better. I'm

kind of wondering what to do about this, though."
Cat pointed to the main blob of barf, which was now
beginning to drift forward toward the main control
panel.

"A little help here?" came a panicked squeak from
Jonah. "It's closing in on me! I've got about five seconds
until a really gross impact."

Spurred to action, I snapped open one of the
overhead compartments, flicked aside a box of
bandages and a small flashlight, and pulled out a tight
roll of plastic bags. I quickly peeled off one and thrust
it at Cat, while opening a second and, like capturing a
mouse or bug, scooped the unsuspecting barf blob out
of the air.

Jonah breathed a sigh of relief.

Cat captured the other floating mass, and the five
of us spent the next couple of minutes catching stray
mini-blobs with pieces of Kleenex and stuffing all of the
disgusting bags and tissues into a single garbage bag.

All that was left was the smell.

Lance decided to call home. "Mission Control,
this is Flight Commander Lance Marshall here. We're
wondering if you packed any air freshener for us. Cat
threw up, and thanks to her, our cabin smells like baby
puke."

"Oh, go stick your head out the window!" snapped
Trace.

"*Artemis 7*, this is Mission Control," came the
familiar, smooth voice of Dr. Grover Yang, the mission
guidance officer. "How's Cat? Is she all right?"

"She's fi—"

"I'm fine." Cat hit the talk switch and cut off Lance. "I've been feeling a little sick since the launch, and it finally caught up to me. But I feel better now that I . . . well . . . you know."

"Good. Let us know if it continues, Cat," Dr. Yang replied. "Now, did you get any fluids into the controls? That could cause a problem."

"Mission Control, we handled the situation," said Lance, regaining command. "The crew decided to play a little barf tennis at first, but then I made sure they performed a thorough clean-up. We're good. Over and out."

Trace let out a grunt of frustration. "Cat, next time that happens, make sure you aim for our esteemed flight commander."

✪ ✪ ✪ ✪ ✪

If anyone tells you that space travel is exciting, give them my phone number. I'll set them straight.

Sure, the liftoff was insane. There were times when the rocket thrusters were so strong, I felt like my eyeballs were seriously going to be pulled back into my brain or that my teeth might pop out, backward. When it was all over and we were drifting in space, I checked my seat to see if my body had made a permanent dent.

Sure, we were excited about what we would find on the moon. We had gotten only the briefest description of the moon base the night before blastoff. Strider had tried to describe the feeling of walking on the moon, but then stopped and stared off at the wall, saying only, "You'll just have to experience it yourselves. It's amazing."

But between blastoff and the destination, there were three days and three nights crammed inside our little command module. There was nothing to look at out the window. And it still smelled like barf.

"At least on road trips you get to look forward to stopping at McDonald's," said Jonah, breaking a long silence.

"And you get to look at things out the window," I sighed.

"And when you're driving at night, you can play the padiddle game," Jonah sighed right back.

"You do *what* in the car?" asked Cat, joining in.

"Play the padiddle game. . . .Wait a minute. Don't tell me you've never played padiddle?" Jonah stared at Cat with a look of astonishment. He turned to me. "Can you believe that, Mickey? Cat doesn't know what a padiddle is!"

I gulped. "Oh, yeah," I said, pretending to know what he was talking about. "Amazing. I mean, all we talk about in Orlando is padiddles. I love them. I must have fifty padiddles in my room. I collect them."

I thought Jonah's mouth might get permanently stuck, it was hanging open so wide.

"YOU DON'T KNOW ABOUT PADIDDLES, EITHER? First of all, you *no way* have fifty of them in your room. Second of all, are you kidding me? Third of all, are you two sure you're from America?"

Cat and I both shrugged.

"A padiddle is a car with only one headlight. If you

see one you've gotta yell 'padiddle.' Have you guys seriously never played?"

Cat and I both shrugged again.

"Well, you can look it up. But anyway," he paused as he stared out the window at the black, star-studded sky, "I'm not counting on seeing any UFOs missing a headlight up here."

I joined him in staring out the window.

Cat was the one to break the silence again. "Um, Mickey? Jonah? I've got to ask you guys something." She glanced over at Lance, who was reclining in his seat with his eyes closed and his radio headphones on. I could just make out the sound of the Rolling Stones. Trace was asleep, curled up like a cat in her chair.

"When you were meeting with your astronaut tutors the night before liftoff . . . you know, when they were telling us about what to expect? Did they tell you about something out there, on the surface of the moon? You know, something strange?"

I just looked at her and shrugged. She continued. "Something on the far side of the canyon, a mile or so from Oblivion Base? Something they called The Glint?"

Jonah leaned forward, suddenly alert. "Nooooooooo," he said, his voice falling and then rising again as he drew out the word. "But you got my attention. Keep going."

"Well, okay." Cat tapped her fingers on her chin. "Let's see. I was paired with Major Austen—the tall, bony, bald guy who looks like some kind of zombie? Anyway, he didn't seem very interested in telling me about the space flight or the moon base. He hit the basic stuff: how to drink something when you're in zero gravity without spilling on yourself, how you need to hop up a little bit when walking on the moon so you don't stub your toe and fall on your face, how you should never take off your helmet on the moon or else you'll totally die. You know, the basics.

"But then he lowered his voice and kind of looked over his shoulder toward Commander Riker. You know, to make sure the commander couldn't hear. Then, he told me that on the last trip, he and Riker had seen something fly overhead and actually crash-land on the surface of the moon. I'm serious, I wouldn't make this up."

Jonah's eyes got big. He leaned even closer.

Cat was practically whispering by now. "They actually saw it flying and hit the ground."

"What did it look like?" I asked.

"Yeah, what was it?" asked Jonah eagerly. "Did it have wheels? An engine? LEGS?"

"Well," continued Cat, cracking a grin and enjoying Jonah's captivation. "They didn't get a good look. And apparently, half of Mission Control thinks they made it up, or imagined it, or their minds were just playing tricks on them. But Major Austen swears they both saw it. Something big. Something fast. Something metal. Like the size of a refrigerator or a small car flying through the air and then crashing into the ground.

"And get this: Austen said that NASA did some investigating. They confirmed it wasn't something NASA sent up there. They checked with the Soviets and the Chinese. Neither of them has a moon mission going on right now. So at this point, that shining speck, that reflection across the canyon is just a glint of light. An unidentified glint. And that's what they call it. The Glint."

Cat sat back, apparently quite pleased with her little story, and watched us speechless boys as we stared at her. "So anyway, Austen said this has been driving Riker half crazy. He didn't want any of us to know about it. You know, so we wouldn't get there before him."

Jonah, who hadn't buckled himself back into his seat, had been slowly spinning as Cat told the story and was now floating completely upside down, his head resting in the chair where his behind should have been. He let out a slow, cool whistle. "Ho-leeeeeeee cow!" he said. "The Glint. A genuine UFO."

Jonah grabbed the side of his seat and spun himself around. "We've got to go check it out. I mean, no question, we've got to find it. Don't you think, Mick? But wait. How'll we find it? How'll we even know where to look with our binoculars? Boy, it's going to take a long time, and we probably won't have much free time. But we'll go out there every day with our binoculars and look for it. Unless . . . unless . . ."

Jonah stopped talking. His eyes were focused on a folded piece of paper Cat had pulled from a little zipper pocket on the sleeve of her coveralls. Jonah and I craned our necks to see the page as she unfolded it. It was a map.

"You asked how we would find it? Easy. If it exists, that is. Austen drew a map."

And there it was.

A piece of lined paper ripped from a spiral notebook, the frilled edges still attached. The drawing was simple but good. I could identify the cluster of buildings representing Oblivion Base in the lower left-hand corner. In the bottom center of the page was a large circle labeled LANDING PAD. The middle of the page was a belt of black, thick near Oblivion Base at the center of the page but narrowing slightly as it moved off to the right. The BOTTOMLESS CANYON.

And then, on the far side of the canyon, right in the top center of the page, was a small X.

As the three of us stared intently at the map, studying the strange details, it was suddenly whisked out of Cat's hands and pulled up toward the front of the cabin.

Lance.

I realized I couldn't hear the faint music coming out of his headphones anymore. He had been listening to us.

"So, you know about the Glint business, do you?" his arrogant voice rang out in the cabin, just a little louder than necessary. "Riker warned me that some of you might pick up little pieces of Major Austen's crazy story. He told me to keep all of you focused on your mission and to make sure you just followed orders and not go chasing Austen's wild imagination."

Lance carefully folded the map back into a small square and slipped it into his pocket. "You see," Lance continued, as though lecturing a class of preschoolers, "Riker told me that when you're up on the moon, your eyes sometimes play tricks on you. And your mind. As you know, the grown-ups on the last couple missions didn't do too well once the pleurinium mining started. So that's all The Glint is. They imagined it, and the reflection is probably just a shiny rock." Lance yawned with perfect timing. "Case closed."

I could sense the outrage boiling up inside Jonah. "And you believed Riker?" Jonah blurted out. "You've got to be kidding me! Did you hear what Cat said? According to Austen, Riker is obsessed with this thing, The Glint. He just doesn't want anybody to get there before he does. He's curious, too. Or maybe he even knows what it is! Either way, he knows it's important."

Lance raised his eyebrows, his eyelids drooping slightly, looking completely bored. "Oh Jonah, you're a dreamer, too. Just like Major Austen."

The two of them stared at each other. "Well, guess what?" Lance tapped the pocket holding the folded map. "There's nothing you can do about it. Last time I checked, I'm flight commander, and I don't give you permission to go wasting time on a wild goose chase. But when you get back home, you can start a UFO club with Major Austen, okay?"

Lance ended the conversation by popping his music headphones back on. He cranked up the volume, and I could hear the rhythms of the Rolling Stones once again.

"C'mon guys! Do you really believe that?" Jonah turned back to us, appealing for support.

Cat spoke first. "You know, Lance might be right. Austen said nobody got a good look at it. Maybe their eyes were playing tricks on them. Maybe it was just a reflection. It could be anything."

"Cat, listen to yourself." Jonah was exasperated. "This is real evidence of aliens, and Riker is trying to keep us away from it. We have a duty to the human race! We've got to check this out!"

"Aliens?" said Trace, waking up from her nap. "Aliens? What did I miss, Mickey?"

"Hard to say, Trace," I replied, suddenly distracted by what was coming into view out the front window. "Right now, I've got something much more interesting for you. Check this out." I pointed out the front window. Just coming into view at the edge of the window as our spacecraft streaked forward was the moon—bigger and closer and more detailed than I could have dreamed. Mountains gleamed white, casting enormous shadows over dark valleys. And huge craters created by ages-old meteors striking the surface.

So close I felt I could reach out and touch it.

CHAPTER 15
Touchdown

The descent was so smooth and silent, I expected our craft to alight softly on the powdery surface. Turns out, I should have imagined an anvil rather than a feather.

Lance had made a final adjustment to the booster rockets about twenty seconds earlier, but he apparently completely botched Mission Control's careful instructions.

The impact was a sickening jolt that I felt right up my spine, accompanied by a deep, echoing wham. I felt certain our spacecraft would split in two. We bounced. There were a few seconds of silence until a second, somewhat softer impact. Then a third. Then a fourth.

Well, it wasn't pretty, but we had officially landed.

"Mission Control, this is *Artemis 7*," Lance's voice filled the command module and crackled in our headphones. "Landing successful."

I heard a loud "HAH!" coming from Trace's direction.

"*Artemis 7*, Mission Control here. Seemed like you set down a little hard. Any problems?"

"Negative. Slight bounce. We're good."

I turned and caught Lance's eye. He gave his head a slight shake. I raised my eyebrows in disbelief.

His response? He tapped the flight commander patch on his shoulder, shook his head again, and continued his discussion with Mission Control back on Earth.

Great, I thought. I sure hope he knows what he's doing.

There was no time to argue, however, about whether to describe the landing as a bounce, a thud, or a wham. All five of us started getting questions and instructions. We all had different dials to read and measurements to report. We had to put the rockets into "sleep" mode, find our helmets and gloves and other moonwalk gear, and get ready to step outside.

We also had to get our radios ready. Dr. Yang had explained about the radios we would use on the moon, and we tested them to make sure they worked properly. We each had a little radio sewn into our uniforms at the front of the left shoulder. It had a little volume dial, with a red talk button and a blue talk button. The red button was for channel one or long distance—for talking to Mission Control. The blue button was for local radio, meaning just between us kids on the moon.

Our space helmets had microphones and speakers in them, too, and our space suits had the talk buttons sewn into our gloves. A big button for channel one to Mission Control. And a little button for local chitchat.

They told us to keep off channel one as much as possible so they could send important messages to us.

So we tested the radios, checked each others' helmets, gloves, and about a thousand other things. And then, finally, they told us we were ready.

Though we had landed hard, we were right on target, inside a large landing circle marked by white rocks. Parked just outside the circle was a moon buggy about the size of a go-kart, with two seats and a cargo space in back. And off in the distance, about two hundred yards away, was a small cluster of low-lying buildings. Oblivion Base. Our home for the next . . . who knew? For the next week or so.

Trace, Jonah, and I would go first. Trace would drive us over to the base in the moon buggy and then come back to get Lance and Cat.

In my full space suit and helmet, I squeezed through a small door located between Cat's and Jonah's seats in the back row of the crew cabin and slid into a small air lock, the gateway between the friendly oxygen-filled crew cabin and the harsh outside world. One at a time, we were supposed to slide into the air lock and tightly close the small door behind us to protect the crew cabin when we opened the door to the outside.

So there I was, wedged into the small airlock with my hand on the heavy metal lever that opened the door to the outside. It had probably taken us three hours to prepare to leave the command module, but when it was finally time, my brain kept yelling, "Stop! This is crazy!"

"Mickey, you are clear to open the hatch," the radio crackled. "Go ahead."

I took a deep breath but stayed frozen in place.

"Mickey? Are you with us? Our sensors show the door is still closed. Is it stuck?"

"Negative," I responded. "More like, I'm stuck. I mean, I'm not really stuck. It's just that, you know . . . aw, heck." I wrenched the lever downward and pushed hard. A brilliant sliver of light appeared at the edge of the hatch and grew larger as the door swung open.

I pushed my legs down through the opening. After two hops down the rungs of the little ladder, I was outside, standing on the white, powdery, dusty surface. I stomped my boots against the surface just to feel the impact and to make sure it was real. The surface of the moon stretched out in front of me, beside me, behind me. The surface was whiter and finer than sand. Except for us, everything was completely lifeless, stretching out to a black sky filled with a million stars. It was so much to take in, it took my breath away.

"Mickey, report back please," came Yang's voice through the radio. "Are you outside?"

"Guuuh, dummm, yeah! I am *so* outside. I'm . . . wow . . . totally outside, Mission Control."

"Okay, then. Shut the hatch! And wait for Jonah and Trace."

I grabbed the outside handle on the hatch and locked it back into place with a sharp twist.

And then I realized that I'd totally blown it. Aw nuts! For three days, for the whole trip up, I had thought about what brilliant and memorable words I would say when stepping out onto the moon.

Neil Armstrong had gone down in history with the

first moonwalk: "One small step for a man. One giant leap for mankind." Perfect!

And here I was. The very first kid to put his size-seven boots on the moon. I had decided to say something like: "Mickey Price—a humble step for kids everywhere—I'm number one!" But it had totally slipped my mind.

What had I come up with instead? "Guuuh, dummm, yeah . . . I am so outside"?

Ugh. So I blew my grand arrival onto the moon. I decided I had to go to Mars sometime just to get a chance at a better opening line.

Suddenly, I saw a movement behind me, and Jonah's feet appeared on the ladder.

When his feet hit the surface, the radio crackled with his voice: "Jonah Jones. Claiming the moon for Chicago football fans everywhere. Go Bears!" He hopped over toward me. "Nice one, Mickey. You're the first kid on the moon and the best you can come up with is 'Guh dum yeah'?"

I sighed, which instantly made the inside of my mask steam up. "Okay, you're right, Jonah. If only I had your gift of intelligence. Giving a shout out to the Bears is much more historic. What, didn't they win two and lose twelve last year? Come on."

"The Bears will be back," said Jonah confidently. "Mark my words."

"Oh yeah?" My mind raced for a good comeback. "By the time they're back, we'll have cities with skyscrapers on the moon. There's no getting past my Dolphins as long as Bob Griese is playing quarterback."

Trace appeared next to us. "Seriously, boys. I honestly can't understand why NASA didn't send five girls on this mission. We land on the moon, and the first thing you do is argue about your favorite football team? Are you kidding?"

There was silence. I think Jonah was yelling something back at her, but he had forgotten to press his radio talk switch.

"For the record," Trace continued, "Cleveland Browns rule. Their quarterback is a total hubba-hubba. Now stop talking football and follow me."

She started moving in slow, two-footed bunny hops away from the command module, toward the four-wheeled buggy about thirty yards away, across the dusty surface.

I wanted to remind Trace that my Dolphins had beaten her Browns 42-10 the last time they played. But I decided not to say anything because, seriously, I was on the moon. And for the first time in my life, I realized there was something just as important as the Miami Dolphins. Or maybe . . . just possibly . . . even more important.

My thoughts shifted quickly back to the moon. We weren't completely weightless like we had been in the command module on the way up, with no downward tug of gravity. At least on the moon, you could tell what was up and what was down.

I started out doing bunny-hops like Trace, afraid to take a real step. But by the time I was halfway to the moon buggy, I was taking full, slow steps, pushing off hard with my back foot. Each time, I would glide several feet across the surface before being tugged gently back down by the moon's weak gravity.

I pressed the local talk button. "Hey, Jonah, check this out." Standing still, I bent my knees as far as I could in my stiff space suit and pushed up hard. The ground dropped away from me, and I felt a lurch in my stomach like I was on a roller coaster. Two, three, four seconds and then the small jolt of landing again on the ground.

"Sign that boy up for the Olympics!" shouted Jonah. "You were, like, four feet off the ground!"

"Trace, come on, measure how high our jumps are," I said excitedly. "Me versus Jonah. Come on, measure our jumps. See who wins."

"For the second time in two minutes," said Trace, "your boy-ness has amazed me. First an NFL argument. Now you're competing in the Leap Frog Olympics. Do I need to remind you that you have been sent here by the United States of America to save the moon from permanent destruction?"

Jonah and I hung our heads and looked at our feet through our gold-plated astronaut masks.

"Yes, ma'am," we said in unison.

"Now, get in the car," said Trace. "Let's go for a drive."

★ ★ ★ ★ ★

Trace slowly, cautiously inched the zip buggy forward, following tire tracks that curved around the edge of the landing area and cut across a dusty field.

"Uh, Trace. I admire your caution," I said into my radio, "but I don't want to die of old age on this trip. Can you step on it?"

"Yeah, Trace," said Jonah, "did you leave your racing skill back on Earth?"

"Knock it off, passengers," said Trace, a frustrated edge in her voice. "Believe it or not, this appears to be the top speed."

"Top speed?" I exclaimed. "Are you kidding! I could walk faster than this."

"An ant could walk faster than this," laughed Jonah. "In fact, I think I just saw one. A moon ant passed us and left us in the moon dust."

Trace decided to check in with home. She pressed the channel one talk button in her glove. "Mission Control, this is Trace. Is there any way to give this zip buggy a little more . . . zip?"

"Negative, Trace," came the reply from Earth. "The zip buggy has a 30-horsepower engine, but that's way too much power for usual driving on the moon. So there's a little electronic box in the engine called a governor that restricts the engine's power and limits the top speed. Get used to it—your maximum is six miles per hour."

"Six! Oh, come on, I'm not a baby!" complained Trace as the zip buggy inched along the pathway toward the base.

"Six is plenty, trust me. We've had a couple accidents on past trips. Having only a little gravity makes it a lot harder to drive. Just think about walking on the moon. Any bump or jump would send you flying up in the air. Anyway, you're in no hurry."

Trace continued to grumble, but I was already done with that argument. I looked around. Six miles an hour was just fine with me. We had covered about half the distance between the command module and Oblivion Base, about the length of a football field. I could now make out rows of small, round windows, running down the side of the building nearest to us. There were lights on inside, almost as if someone was there waiting for us.

As we started to come around the corner of one of the buildings, I could see a small courtyard that looked like a parking lot. From a distance, I had seen the top of what looked like a huge orange truck peeking over the top of one of the moon base buildings. Now that we were coming around that building, I could see it was indeed a truck. A ladder ran up the front side to the driver's cabin. The enormous back door was open, and I could make out large bins—kind of like plastic trashcans—filled with something.

Even though he couldn't see my eyes through the reflecting gold visor, Jonah could tell what I was looking at. "Pleurinium," he said. "They call that truck the MTV, the Mineral Transport Vehicle. It's loaded full of pleurinium from the mine, ready to be hauled back to Earth. Except they were never able to unload it because of the sickness."

Trace slowly maneuvered through the parking area toward a doorway in the far corner, where two larger buildings were connected by a low hallway. Jonah and I clumsily pulled ourselves out of the zip buggy. I felt awkward and bulky, stiff-legged and stiff-armed, but light and bouncy at the same time. I was moving slowly and carefully, remembering what Lieutenant Strider had told me. It was easy to fall over, and you definitely did not want to do that. It could tear your space suit and expose you to the harsh lunar atmosphere. Let's just say that would ruin your day.

Moving slowly, Jonah and I had no problem bouncing down the short pathway to the door, where we turned to wave goodbye to Trace. She expertly backed the zip buggy around and started the slow trip back to the command module to pick up Lance and Cat.

Leaving Jonah and me to head inside together.

Jonah paused a couple of steps short of the door and raised his palm politely. "After you, sir," he said through the radio.

"Oh, don't be silly. After *you*," I replied, giving him a slight bow.

"But you're the fancy-pants copilot!" I could imagine Jonah's big, goofy grin behind the gold visor. If he hadn't been wearing his helmet, I definitely would have grabbed his head and given him a noogie. The first human noogie in the history of the moon. Wow.

"Mickey." The radio in my helmet crackled. "This is Mission Control. You will see a keypad on the right side of the door with three buttons. Press three, one, three."

Luckily the numbers were huge, because my space-suit fingers were enormous. When I pressed the buttons, the door popped outward a few inches and then slid sideways, revealing a small room about the size of the downstairs bathroom at the Home. Except with no toilet.

A fluorescent light blinked on, and Jonah and I stepped inside the air lock.

"Mickey, you should see a large button that says CLOSE. It should be flashing. Make sure you're standing away from the door and press it."

The door eased shut and snapped into place with a heavy clunk. Following instructions, Jonah and I pressed more buttons and headed through another door into a larger room with benches and hooks running along two of the walls. Just like in the first room, at first it was only lit by a small emergency bulb. But as soon as we entered, the bright, overhead lights flickered on automatically.

"Smart room!" I said to Jonah.

"Only the best. This is a taste of the future, Mickey. The future is a place without light switches. A place where the toilets flush by themselves. A place where—"

"Mickey," my radio interrupted, "look at the oxygen gauge on Jonah's chest. Is it green?"

"It's green. Roger that, Control."

"And Mickey, look at the pressure gauge next to the oxygen gauge. What does it say?"

"It reads 14.0. And it's flashing green, too."

"That means you're clear to take off your space suit. Mickey, you first."

After a full minute struggling with the complicated snaps and buckles on the side of my helmet, I was finally able to take it off. I felt a wave of cool, sweet air surround my head, and I realized how cramped and hot my helmet had been after just half an hour out on the moon. I helped Jonah take off his helmet, and then we peeled off our suits and hung them on the hooks. "Man, I feel a thousand pounds lighter," said Jonah with relief.

Free from the helmets, we looked around the room again. And I think we both noticed them at the same time. There were several large, full-sized space suits with helmets hanging on the hooks at the far end, waiting for owners who were thousands of miles away, back on Earth.

A reminder that we were kids, alone, in a place too dangerous for adults.

CHAPTER 16
Welcome to Oblivion

At the end of a long hallway was a doorway to a large room. Through the dim glow of the emergency lighting, I could see shapes of unidentifiable furniture lining the wall on the right. I stepped into the room, and the overhead lights automatically flickered on.

"The recreation room," I said, remembering the description from the maps Strider had shown me that evening before blastoff. On the right side of the room was a set of strange-looking furniture—exercise equipment. There was a treadmill for walking and running, a stationary bicycle, and three different weight lifting machines. On the other side of the room were clusters of chairs around a small table with games and playing cards piled in the middle.

"I don't think we'll have much time for hanging out here," I said.

"Yeah, and this won't do me any good," said Jonah as he strained to lift the heavy weight lifting bar. "Hey, move this outside onto the moon surface, and I could probably lift it!"

"C'mon, Jonah, let's explore some more." I was eager to see the rest of the moon base before the others arrived. "We have two doors to choose from. You pick."

Jonah made his way over to the door just beyond the stationary bicycle. Like all the others, it was gray metal, shiny and smooth. To the right of the door was a square pad about the size of a deck of playing cards, surrounded by glowing green light. The open button. Below it was a keypad, like you would find on a telephone.

Jonah punched the open button, and the door opened with a *shwoosh*. We stood in the doorway, and I waved my hand inside the entrance to turn on the automatic lights. The smell hit me a split second before the overhead light flashed on.

"Holy stinkin' cheese!" Jonah exclaimed when he saw the mess. "What the heck happened here?"

"Um, I'd say the guys up here before us had a ginormous food fight. What a mess! I haven't seen food fight wreckage this bad since Sister Rinaldi went to get a haircut and left Taco in charge. Ugh gross. Is that an old sandwich? Or some kind of fruit?"

Jonah looked closer. "No, I think it's . . . green Jell-O?" He poked at it with his shoe as if expecting it to move. Fortunately, it didn't.

There were boxes and plastic bags of food piled on the ground in front of two cabinets, with more still on the shelves. Many of the bags were ripped open, their contents spilling out onto the floor. The door of a refrigerator stood open. That's where most of the smell seemed to be coming from.

I pressed the talk button on the small radio clipped to the front of my jumpsuit. "Uh, Mission Control. This is Mickey here. We hope you don't need us to clean up the kitchen. Over."

"Mickey, Mission Control here. We don't understand. Please explain."

"I mean the mess in the kitchen," I continued. "There's food everywhere. At least, what used to be food. The people before us were total pigs." I suddenly remembered Commander Riker was probably listening on the other end of the radio. "I mean, no offense. They just didn't clean up. At all." Jonah was walking around the room, picking his way through the mess.

Riker's unmistakable, sharp voice crackled through the radio. "Riker here. Explain yourself, Mickey. That doesn't make any sense. What are you seeing?"

"Well, let's say this place gets the Bad Housekeeping Award for the year. I've seen some food fights before, but this takes it to a whole new level. Back where I come from, this would be three weeks of detention."

I felt a crunch under my feet and realized I was walking through a small pile of Froot Loops cereal.

"Mickey, I don't know what you're talking about," said Riker. "The kitchen was perfectly clean when I left it."

I looked at Jonah. He just shrugged his shoulders. "These guys are treating us like we're toddlers, or insane," I complained to Jonah. "I know a mess when I see one, and this—"

Crash!

A chill ran up my spine.

For a second, I didn't believe I had heard it. But I knew it was real because Jonah jumped at the same time I did.

A crash . . . a one-hundred-percent, definite crash . . . had come from the next room, right ahead of us. There was no way the others had arrived yet. So that meant . . .

"Come on, Jonah, let's go take a look. Time to earn our pay."

"Earn our pay?" asked Jonah. "Last time I checked, we weren't getting paid. Let somebody else check."

"Somebody else? Like who? Come on, it's up to us. Let's check it out."

I headed across the room to the door on the far side, toward where the noise had come from, and punched the Open pad. The door slid aside with a *schwoop,* revealing a short, dimly lit hallway. As I stepped inside, the main lights flickered on, activated by my movement just like in the kitchen.

Jonah was right behind me. "You know, I never thought of that. We're not getting paid. They sent us to the moon, and are we getting so much as a dime? Sheesh! I bet Riker and the rest of Team Varsity get huge salaries. But us? What's in it for us? I think we should just, um, sit and wait in that room with the games in it."

I reached the door at the end of the hall and paused to turn back to Jonah. "Are you listening to yourself? Just a few days ago you said you felt like you had won the lottery, you were so lucky. 'An adventure in science,' you called it. And now you're holding out for money?"

Jonah looked glum. "Yeah. But now it's different. I wasn't exactly chasing mystery noises on the moon at that time." He sighed as he listened to what he had just said. "Okay, okay. Adventure in science. Go ahead. I'm . . . um . . . right behind you."

We had reached the door at the end of the hallway. I pressed Open and the door slid aside, revealing nothing but darkness. I took one, two, three steps inside, expecting the lights to flicker on at any second. Jonah was so close behind me I could feel him breathing on my ear. Smelled like peanut butter.

Then the door schwooped shut, leaving us in complete blackness.

"Uh, Mick," Jonah whispered. "This sucks. Do you think—"

"SHHH!"

There was a mechanical hum and a steady, constant clicking coming from the right side of the room. Like some sort of machine or fan. But there was something else.

Occasional. Irregular. An unmistakable shuffling. Then silence. Then shuffling again. No doubt about it.

If something hadn't happened soon, I probably would have fainted. I was so nervous, I had forgotten to breathe.

But something did happen. At the far end of the room, about forty feet away, another door suddenly schwooped open. A dim glow of light spilled into the room. And right then, just as the door was sliding open, the faintest glimpse of a shadow . . . or maybe it was a small shape . . . no, definitely a shadow . . . briefly streaked through the dim light through the opening.

Before I could do anything, the door schwooped shut, leaving us again in total blackness.

That's when I sprang into action. Not in the direction of the mysterious shape, of course, but back where we'd come from. Jonah had obviously seen it, too, and had the same idea at the same time. We both spun and dove backward for the Open button, outlined in green light. I launched myself toward the sliver of bright light as the door opened, and so did Jonah, and we spilled back into the hallway, a tumbling mass of elbows and legs, knees and arms. Next thing I knew, I was crawling down the hallway as fast as I could, with Jonah riding on my back like he was on a horse. Backward. Again, I dove for the Open button and felt Jonah's shoe on my ear as he propelled himself back into the kitchen. I was holding onto his belt, so I went right with him, doing a backflip and landing in a sitting position on his head.

After the door *schwooped* shut, we lay there on the floor for a while, panting. I rubbed the huge egg-shaped bump on my forehead where I'd accidentally run into the edge of the door.

Jonah finally broke the silence. He said it, but I was thinking it. "An alien."

The word hung there in the still, stinky air of the kitchen.

"Definitely an alien. That's what we saw, and that's what made this mess. Mickey, do you know what this means? We're not alone in the universe. We're not alone on the moon. We're not even alone in this building. Mickey, we've made contact with an alien!"

✪ ✪ ✪ ✪ ✪

Tom was sitting up on his sleeping bag again, drenched in skepticism. "Okay," he said, pointing a finger straight at his dad's nose. "I was just starting to believe the story. But now, aliens? This is beginning to sound more like your regular stories now. Astronauts. Aliens. Next we'll probably have a couple of moon dinosaurs, right? Nice story. But it's just a story, right?"

"What, you believed it through the whole space camp and rocket-to-the-moon part? But as soon as you think there's an alien involved, it's a tall tale? What's so impossible about an alien? Are you absolutely certain we're alone in the universe?"

"No," said Tom, still glaring with accusation at his dad, finger still pointed accusingly. "There *could* be life on other planets. I just don't believe that you've ever met it."

Dad tilted his head as he thought about that one. "Emph. Fair enough. So I've lost the Tom vote," he said, turning to Tess. "How about the Tess vote? Are you still with me?"

Tess's face looked tense, clearly showing the battle going on in her brain. "I don't know!" she said with exasperation. "I want to believe you, but I just don't know!" She paused. "What did the alien look like? How many legs? What color? And did it talk? I need more information."

Dad smiled. "We'll get there, don't worry. Jonah and I were lying in a twisted heap on the floor of the completely messy kitchen on the moon base. We had just discovered that we weren't alone. There was something else already at the moon base, waiting for us. And just then, Lance came waltzing in with Trace and Cat. And for the first time ever, I was actually glad to see him. Which lasted about three seconds."

CHAPTER 17
We Are Not Alone

"Nice work, you two. You're the advance team with instructions to prepare the moon base for our arrival. And what do you do? Trash the kitchen and goof around wrestling. Top notch." Lance strode into the kitchen like he owned it.

Jonah and I were still lying in a tangled heap in the middle of the floor. I flung Jonah's leg off my chest and pulled myself upright.

"But wait," I started. "The kitchen was a total mess like this when we came in. Food everywhere. And then we heard a noise. So we decided to investigate. We went through that door and down a hall, and you'll never guess what we saw! There was a—"

Lance's radio crackled to life and we heard Dr. Yang's voice.

"This is Mission Control. Please confirm that all five of you have arrived at Oblivion Base. Over."

"Mission Control, this is Flight Commander Lance

Marshall," replied Lance. "We have all arrived, and the team is . . ." he cast an insulting sneer in my direction, "the team is making itself right at home here."

"Nice work so far, *Artemis 7*. But don't get too comfortable, we need you to get right to work. Lance, lead the team down to the east control room. Cat, we need you to tap into the main computer running the nuclear reactor, locate the maintenance history, and send that information back to our scientists here at the space center. That maintenance history should contain the clues we need to figure out why it's overheating, and how to shut down the reactor."

"Roger that, Mission Control," said Lance. "Over and out."

✪ ✪ ✪ ✪ ✪

"Aliens?" Trace stared incredulously at Jonah.

"Face it," said Jonah, crossing his arms and staring back at her, "it's the most logical explanation. The five of us are the only ones up here. And I definitely saw something alive. And you know what else? Mickey saw it, too."

Trace turned to me, her eyes urging me to put an end to this craziness.

The thing is, I couldn't. As much as I didn't want to believe we had encountered an alien in our first ten minutes at the moon base, I couldn't come up with any other possible explanation.

We were all crowded together in the east control room, watching Cat as she sat in front of a huge computer monitor. She alternated between tapping furiously at the keyboard and reading the dizzying scroll of computer code as it flashed up onto the screen. Lance hovered over her shoulder, occasionally saying "Yeah" and "Do that one" and "Yup, that's right." Of course, none of us had any idea what Cat was doing, especially Lance.

As I thought about the strange thing we had encountered, I stared at the view through the small windows above the control panel. A flat, rocky area sloped up gently toward a ridge of rough boulders. Beyond that ridge, and out of our range of vision, was the deep Bottomless Canyon. And still farther, lurking in the distance, was the dark, gray mass of a lunar mountain range.

I realized Trace was staring at me, waiting for a response. Oh yeah, aliens.

"Mickey?" prompted Trace again. "Mickey! You're not buying Jonah's crazy theory, are you?"

"Well," I didn't want to say it, but I had to. "I can't rule it out. We didn't see a ghost. It was something real. I think. Hey, why don't we ask Mission Control?"

Lance, who had been silently ignoring our conversation until now, suddenly spun to face us. "Are you jerks serious? Ask Mission Control? Ask Riker? 'Hi, Mickey Price here. I think there are aliens at the moon base. And big purple elephants dancing with unicorns.' Mickey, you might be a stupid little kid, but at least don't act like one on my mission."

My cheeks flashed red. I was mad and embarrassed at the same time. There should be a word for that. Madbarrassed. Or emb-angry. I was both. Before my brain could reattach to my mouth, however, Cat surprised us all by speaking up.

"Done!"

"Done with what?" asked Trace.

"Done with finding the nuclear reactor's maintenance records for the last three months, creating and running a program to decode them and eliminate the unnecessary information, compressing the file into something that can be transmitted, and then radioing it back home. Now the engineers at NASA should have all the information they need to figure out what's wrong with the reactor."

We were speechless, except for Lance. He pressed his radio talk switch and said, "Mission Control, Flight Commander Lance Marshall here. I have completed the computer work with help from my team and have transmitted the information back to Earth."

"Nice work, Lance. Very good job. We're impressed with you. Oh, and tell your team they did a good job, too," came the immediate reply from 250,000 miles away.

Cat spun her chair around and scowled at Lance. She hadn't missed the fact that he had just taken, and received, all the credit.

"One more thing, Flight Commander Marshall," said Cat. "Jonah is no liar. If he and Mickey say they saw something weird, then that's good enough for me. They're not making it up. And right now, Jonah has the only explanation that makes any sense."

"Fine," said Lance. "I'm looking forward to doing my I-told-you-so dance when I prove we don't have little green aliens running around here with us. Come on, grab your travel packs and follow me over to the sleeping area. First one there gets their choice of beds. See you, suckers."

Our flight commander turned on his heels and broke into a very undignified sprint out of the room and down the hallway.

$$\bigstar \ \bigstar \ \bigstar \ \bigstar \ \bigstar$$

Lance was first to arrive back in the kitchen area. He paused as he leaned over his backpack. Rather than pick it up, however, he drew back sharply. "Wait a minute—"

I noticed that the zipper of his pack was wide open and some clothes were hanging out the side. His toothbrush lay on the floor nearby. Next to a candy bar wrapper. An empty candy bar wrapper.

The other packs looked the same.

Something had rooted through our packs. And whoever it was . . . or whatever it was . . . it seemed to have a special hunger for our Butterfinger candy bars. There were five or six empty wrappers strewn about the floor.

"Somebody laid a finger on my Butterfinger!" said Trace.

"Believe me now?" said Jonah to Lance, who was poking nervously at his pack as though it might still contain a mouse-sized burglar.

Before Lance could respond, we all heard a noise directly above us that sent a chill of terror through our bones.

It was a frantic, scrambling sound. Like the sound a dog makes when it scratches at the back door trying to get in. And it was coming from right above us, up in the crawl space above the ceiling panels.

Then it began to move away, down the hall.

There was something in the ceiling.

Something alive.

"Uhhhhhh, not good," Lance said, his voice shaking. He took several steps back toward the wall, moving behind Trace and holding Cat in front of him like a shield. "What is it? What-is-it? What-is-it? WHAT-IS-IT!" Then, composing himself slightly, he managed to squeak, "As flight commander, I order Mickey and . . . um . . . Jason to go follow that thing."

"Jason? Who's Jason?" said Jonah. He stuck out his arm toward Lance as if to shake hands. "Nice to meet you, I'm Jonah. J-O-N-A-H. Are you a little scared of something, Flight Commander?"

We all laughed nervously. But to be honest, nobody was in the laughing mood. Truth be told, we were all seriously freaked out at this point.

The scraping sound was getting farther away. I knew we had to move fast. "Come on, guys! Strength in numbers. Let's all go. Follow me!"

I set out down the hall at a slow jog, looking up for, well, I had no idea what I was looking for. I tilted my head for maximum hearing.

Down hallway after hallway, through laboratory rooms and back through the living room and the kitchen, we stayed a few steps behind the scraping, shuffling sound up in the ceiling.

The thing slowed as we neared the end of a long hallway and reached a sign marking the west control room.

"Uh-oh," said Jonah. "Dead end. End of the line. Ground zero. Cornered. The big one. Showdown at the O-K Corral. No escape—"

"Jonah?" said Trace.

"Yes, Trace?"

"Shut. Up. We get the picture."

We all stood there at the doorway to the west control room, our eyes riveted to the ceiling. Unless there was some kind of escape hatch in the roof, we had it cornered. The west control room wasn't that big, maybe the size of a ping pong table. The only way out was the way it had come, back down the hallway above us. Or through us.

I decided there was only one thing left to do. I had to take a look.

I had Lance and Trace get on all fours to make a ledge with their backs, and then Jonah stood with one foot on each back. I climbed up onto Jonah's shoulders, holding onto the wall with one hand as I wobbled to a standing position.

This seemed like a good idea when I imagined it, but now that I was standing with my head wedged against the ceiling, it seemed slightly crazy. The ceiling was made up of square, plastic panels, each one about two feet by two feet. The panel above my head tipped up easily when I pushed it, and I eased my head into the crawl space.

Total darkness.

I pulled my head back down into the hallway.

"Guys, it's totally dark," I whispered. "Anyone got a flashlight?"

I heard some rustling below, and Cat handed one up to Jonah, who passed it up to me. I flicked it on and saw that it cast a bright beam even in the lighted hallway. My eyes met Trace's, and she nodded in encouragement. Well, here goes nothing, I thought.

I poked my head back up into the crawl space and pointed the flashlight into the area above the west control room.

At first, all I saw were pipes and wires. The crawl space was only about a foot tall, a little extra space between the ceiling panels and the hard cement that formed the outer wall of the moon base. I swung the beam toward the right. More pipes. More wires. And then—

Like a flash it came at me. Two glaring red eyes, at first small but then getting suddenly larger as it came straight at my face. And teeth, gleaming teeth that flashed as they charged right at me. And I heard a scream. Maybe it was the creature's. Or maybe it was mine.

Forgetting that I was perched atop a human pyramid, I launched myself backward. My arms and legs windmilled desperately but found nothing to grasp onto. As I sailed through the air, I was horrified to see that the charging creature had come through the ceiling panel and was still coming at me.

As I tumbled toward the ground, the last thing I saw before my head smacked onto the rock-hard floor of the hallway were the creature's legs and . . . yes, no doubt about it . . . a long, hairy, alien's tail.

★ ★ ★ ★ ★

A huge pair of eyes blinked above me, an inch away from mine.

Though the face was close, the voice sounded like it was coming from far away. "Wait, guys. He's not dead. I think he's actually alive!"

I closed my eyes, a searing pain filling my skull, and I emitted a good, long groan. When I opened my eyes again, I saw Trace leaning above me. She was patting my forehead with a warm washcloth.

I tilted my head and saw Jonah, who was looking at me with obvious concern. Next to him was Lance, who looked . . . unbelievably . . . I'm sure I saw a look of disappointment when he realized I was alive.

I tipped my head the other way and saw Cat. On her shoulder was something I couldn't identify. I blinked hard. OHMYGOSH! THE ALIEN!

I closed my eyes tight and blinked hard again.

When I looked back, there she was, clear as day. Cat. With, wait a minute . . .

I leaned up on one elbow. "Hey!" I croaked. "Can someone explain why Cat has a monkey on her shoulder?"

The monkey stared at me with small, intense eyes. When I met its gaze, it quickly buried its face in Cat's bushy hair. It certainly looked like an Earth monkey and not some sort of alien monkey. That's when I noticed that it was wearing a blue jumpsuit just like ours, with a little American flag sewn onto one of the arms. Under the flag was the name ZIGGY 3 in small, white letters.

The monkey pulled its head up, and I saw one eye emerge from Cat's tangle of hair. It looked at me angrily and gave a shrill scream before it buried its head again in Cat's big hair.

"Guys," I said. "Can someone explain? Did I miss something?"

"Yeah, you kind of missed something when you fainted," said Lance, using his I'm-talking-to-a-preschooler voice again. "After you freaked out and hit your head, I called down to Mission Control and confirmed that this monkey was part of an earlier mission. Riker said the *Artemis 6* team had to leave it behind when they evacuated the moon base three months ago."

"Hold on," I raised myself up onto one elbow. "You're saying *I'm* the one who freaked out back there? I seem to remember a certain flight commander who was hiding at the back of the pack, using Cat as a human shield."

"I was giving you all a leadership opportunity," Lance replied, looking like he wanted to change the subject. "It's not fair to you if I'm always in front, making the decisions."

Jonah suddenly thumped himself on the forehead. "Oh, duhhh," he said up into the air, clearly frustrated. "As we were following the mystery noise, we passed a room with a sign that said PRIMATE ROOM. Now it makes sense."

"Excuse me?" I said in disbelief. "You saw a sign that said PRIMATE ROOM, and you didn't bother telling us?"

"Well, it didn't seem important back then," said Jonah defensively. "Remember, we were busy chasing an alien at the time, remember? If it had said ALIEN ROOM, I might have commented."

Lance brightened up, realizing his chance to change the subject from him to Jonah. "Oh, right. Aliens. So, fantasy boy, what do you have to say for yourself, now that your 'alien' has turned out to be a simple zoo animal? And 'The Glint'? Do you still think it's some alien spaceship?"

"Well, it could be an alien spaceship," said Jonah stubbornly. "Just because Ziggy turned out to be a monkey doesn't mean there's not an alien spaceship out there. Ziggy has nothing to do with The Glint."

"Oh, Jonah, don't you see? Ziggy has everything to do with The Glint. They're the same thing. Something uncertain. Something unknown in search of an explanation. Now, you're the kind of person who always thinks up the craziest, wackiest explanation and then actually believes it. But no matter how hard you believe in aliens, Jonah Jones, it doesn't make them real."

Jonah sighed. As much as I hated to admit it, Lance was probably right. I wondered whether Jonah realized it, too.

CHAPTER 18
Phone Home

The next day on the moon was probably the biggest disappointment in the history of humans. I was living the dream that millions upon millions of kids didn't even dare to dream. At age twelve, I was an astronaut on a secret mission to the moon. Our mission was to save the moon from a nuclear accident that could contaminate it for a million years.

So how did we spend our first full day at Oblivion Base?

Cleaning the kitchen. One month's worth of bad monkey table manners. Ziggy watched us clean his mess for a while with great interest. After about half an hour, I walked over, handed him a dustpan and broom, and gestured toward the piles of food. Ziggy took one look at me, chattered loudly, and ran out of the room. Without the dustpan and broom, of course. "Hey, just 'cause you've got a tail doesn't mean you can't work. You're part of the team, furball," I shouted.

Trace and Jonah shook their heads at me and went back to work. Great, now all of a sudden *I'm* the jerk for fighting with the monkey? Sheesh.

Meanwhile, Cat got a pass from kitchen duty and spent the day huddled over a computer monitor. They still hadn't solved the problem of the faulty reactor. Working with the engineers back on Earth, she searched through line after line of computer code and ran dozens of tests, trying to figure out what was wrong with the nuclear reactor's shutdown mechanism.

And our flight commander? Well, he kept inventing a series of special projects for himself. Once, after he told us that Commander Riker had ordered him outside to perform some complicated fix-it project, I took a break and went from window to window, trying to catch a glimpse of our team leader. I finally found him out in the vehicle courtyard.

He was playing golf. He was actually playing golf. I could see three golf holes set up out there with flagsticks and everything.

Jonah came up alongside me and squeezed his face into the small, round window. "Whatcha looking at?"

"Just watching our flight commander get a triple bogey," I answered. "Can you believe that guy? We're slaving away, ankle deep in stinky old food, and he's outside playing golf?"

"Hmmm. Looks like he hit his ball into a sand trap," said Jonah, laughing.

"Very funny," I answered. "This drives me crazy. I feel like going outside and dragging him back by the oxygen tank. We've still got hours left before we're done."

"Mick," said Jonah, "before you go out there, think for a minute. You really want him in here with us? The only thing less pleasant than cleaning up month-old cheese is cleaning up month-old cheese with Lance Marshall. Come on, let's go back in there with Trace and keep talking about the greatest movies in the history of movies."

"You got a point," I conceded and followed him back into the kitchen.

Two hours later, the kitchen was sparkling like a photo from *Good Housekeeping* magazine. Lance had come back inside and gave our efforts a B-minus, saying he expected the kitchen to look better given how long we had spent working on it.

Trace had just threatened to re-mop the entire kitchen with Lance's head when the radio crackled with a message from Earth. Boy, Lance had some lucky timing.

We were surprised to hear Amanda Collins' voice through the loudspeaker. It was a welcome change from the no-nonsense messages we usually got from Commander Riker and the others. Dr. Yang had seemed fun the first time we had met him down on Earth, but once the mission had started, he was all business.

Amanda explained that they all understood how long we had been away from our families and how we might be homesick. She said she had arranged for each of us to have a five-minute conversation with a family member.

"All of you head down to the east control room where you can take the call in private," continued Amanda. "And Lance, honey, you're first."

We all rolled our eyes.

"The director, your dad, is waiting to talk to you."

Lance, who had looked as excited as the rest of us for a minute, suddenly deflated. I was sure he had been looking forward to hearing from his mom, his grandmother, or even the mail carrier—anybody but his dad.

"I almost feel sorry for him," I confided to Trace as the four of us waited in the hallway for our turn. "Imagine getting tucked in at night by Director Marshall."

"Dude!" said Trace, sternly pointing a finger at me. "Don't you dare feel sorry for him. Remember the B-minus."

Lance emerged from the east control room only about two minutes after going in. "You're up, Cat," he mumbled before shuffling slowly away from us down the hall.

Trace caught my eye. "Okay. You're allowed to feel sorry for our flight commander for the next sixty seconds. But that's it."

Jonah and I smiled at each other as Trace crossed her arms defiantly, her jaw firm. I could tell she was allowing herself exactly one minute of sympathy for Lance, counting backward from sixty.

Five minutes later, Cat came out into the hallway, her eyes red and puffy but with a huge smile on her face. "My mom and dad were both on the call!" The words burst out of her, followed by a giggle. "My mom kept asking me if I was getting enough food. Enough food? Sure, Mom, I'm getting protein paste from a tube and plenty of powdered bananas. My dad was speechless. Speechless! My dad! All he could say was that I made him proud. Can you believe it?" Cat walked right past us and kept on talking to the air.

Trace went next and then Jonah, both of them emerging from their phone calls noticeably different from how they went in, as though they had received a burst of powerful medicine. I guess, in a way, they had.

And then came my turn. I imagined myself in Cat's place, or Jonah's, or Trace's. I wondered whether I would feel the same way as they did after my five minutes with Sister Rinaldi. I felt a sudden pang of guilt, realizing that I wouldn't. Sister Rinaldi would probably make sure I was saying my prayers and obeying orders and other important things like that. Sure, she cared about me and would want to hear me say I was doing just fine. And sure, she'd have some stories about what had been going on in the two weeks since I had left the house, and it would even be kinda nice to hear her voice. But still, curiously, I felt guilty.

"Mission Control? Mickey here, ready for my call."

"Roger that, Mickey, we're making the connection." There was a series of clicks, and then the voice said, "Okay, Mickey, you're on. You can proceed."

"Hey, Astro-boy," a familiar voice came through the speaker. "Come in, Astro-boy. Are you there? I've been waiting on this phone for like half an hour, and they keep telling me 'three more minutes,' but it's never three more minutes. Are you there?"

I couldn't believe my ears. "TACO!?"

"Yeah, who'd you think would call you? Awww, man. Don't tell me you were hoping for Big Linus, because that would reeee-ally hurt my feelings. Of course it's me, you dingbat. How are you? How's the moon? How cool is it? Are you seriously on the moon, because if this is some sort of joke, *it's not funny at all.*"

"TACO? Is that really you?" I felt like I'd been transported thousands of miles and thousands of days away from the moon.

"Um, Mickey. Do you have some sort of moon flu? Of course it's me. I said it's me. What's with you? I know you've been gone two weeks, but it's not like my voice has changed or anything."

"Yeah, yeah. I know," I said, emerging from the fog of surprise. "It's just that I didn't expect you to be the one I got to talk to. I mean, no offense, but this is supposed to be some kind of secret mission. Super top secret. Nobody is allowed to know about it. So, like I said, no offense, but you're the worst secret keeper on the planet."

"I know," said Taco with a nervous little laugh. "Sister Rinaldi told me it was a secret and I wasn't allowed to tell anybody. And I kept it a secret for about *eight whole minutes.* I swear. And I meant to keep it a secret longer. But then it kind of slipped out in a conversation. It totally wasn't my fault. And at that point, well, once it wasn't a secret anymore, I just had to tell everybody in the whole house." He paused. "But do you know what stinks?"

"What?" I asked.

"Nobody believes me!" he wailed. "Sheesh. They think it's all some big joke. When I asked Sister Rinaldi to back me up, she got this look on her face and said, 'Why Taco, what a bunch of hogwash! Where do you come up with this stuff?' And then she actually winked at me, kind of a so-there wink."

"I think that's why the Sister told me about your secret mission, because she knew nobody would believe me. It's totally frustrating. Check this out. Hey, *Alvin!*" I heard his yell echoing through what was probably the front hall of the house.

"Yeah?" came the muffled reply from the distance.

"I'm talking to Mickey, and he's totally on the moon. He rode a rocket up there! And now he's on the moon! Isn't that awesome?"

"Yeah, whatever, Taco. Say hello to Mickey the astronaut. And when you get the Incredible Hulk and Batman on the line, let me know. Then I'll care," came the distant reply.

"See? Life's so unfair," sighed Taco. "So how was the trip? Did you get to drive the rocket? Were you totally cruising? How long did it take you?"

"Let's see," I said, trying to remember his questions and answer them in order. "Trip was great. No, I didn't get to drive. Yes, we were totally cruising faster than you can imagine. And it took three days."

"Three days?" said Taco, sounding disappointed. "That's totally slow. It only took us two days to drive all the way to Iowa that one time we went to camp. And that's like seven states away. I thought rockets were supposed to be fast!"

"Taco, I won't even bother to answer that one," I said. Sometimes I couldn't believe the things that came out of his mouth. "Oh wait," I said, "here's one cool thing. There's a monkey up here."

There was a long pause, then a tremendous shriek.

"Are you SERIOUS? MONKEYS ON THE MOON? I knew it. I knew it, I knew it! I totally knew it. Monkeys on the moon. I told you so. Or at least I should have told you because I totally thought it. I really did think it last week, I swear I did. Monkeys on the moon!? Are they like Earth monkeys, running around hairy and naked, or do they talk and wear clothes and fly spaceships?"

"Taco," I interrupted. But he kept right on going.

"Oh my gosh, do they have cities? Do they have cities of tree houses with bedrooms out on the branches? Or wait, you're on the moon. Do you even have trees up there? If you don't have trees, where do the moon monkeys live? Some sort of monkey moon hotels? How does that work?"

"Taco," I tried again. But he hadn't stopped.

"Oh my gosh, and if there aren't any trees, what do they eat? Can you grow a banana without a tree? Now that would be crazy. Anyway, it doesn't matter, because you've discovered monkeys on the moon, and now you'll be famous and—"

"TACO. STOP!" I yelled. He stopped. "Taco, get ahold of yourself. No monkeys on the moon. I said monkey. *Monkey*. One monkey. An Earth monkey. It's up here at the moon base. The astronauts before us brought it up. Sorry, but this isn't *Planet of the Apes*."

"Oh," came a small, disappointed voice.

"But he's completely cool, and we're going to bring him back. He's friendly. And, no doubt, he's way smarter than you."

"Oh, you're gonna pay for that one, Mickey. I'm totally smarter than any monkey. You can set up a test to prove it, I'm *that* confident. Seriously, set up a test, anytime, anyplace. But just don't put any math on it, because that would be totally unfair, and I'm not so sure I'd beat a monkey at math. GAH! You make me mad, Mickey. I'm *so* going to blow my nose on your bathrobe, which I just happen to be wearing right now. And you know what? You can't do anything about it."

I had to laugh as I heard a tremendous honk through the receiver, 250,000 miles away. At that point, I didn't care if he was kidding or if he had really just emptied both nostrils onto my bathrobe. I just had to laugh.

And that's when another voice broke into the line. "Moon base, this is Mission Control. We need to clear the line, Mickey. Time to say your goodbyes. We'll get you back to Earth in less than a week, and you can continue this, uh, very fascinating conversation then."

"Awww man, come on," said Taco. "Mick, that dude on the phone line sounds like a total drag. Are you going to put up with that? Does he boss you around all the time? You're totally an astronaut, and I think you should call the shots. He's just some phone operator. You should be telling him what to do. You can—"

"Taco. Slow down. Take a breath. Breathe. Now, I gotta go. There's one thing I've learned on this trip: I've gotta listen to the people on the other end of the radio. They call the shots. But like the man said, I'll see you in a few days. Can you make it?"

Taco heard my question.

But I was really asking myself.

CHAPTER 19
Hard to Resist a Gallant Monkey

"Snap to it!" Lance barked as he strode quickly into the room. Jonah looked up for just a second and then returned his attention to a thick book of moon maps he had been reviewing. He had given up asking Lance for the map showing the location of The Glint, but he hadn't given up on the idea that he would solve the mystery.

Cat, Trace, and I decided to ignore Lance and continue with our card game.

The only person or creature to move was Ziggy, who jumped to his feet and snapped a crisp salute.

"Monkey one, humans zero," pouted Lance. "How am I supposed to work with you guys if you don't give me the respect I deserve?"

"Oh, I'll give you what you deserve," said Trace, shooting Lance an angry glare.

Lance let that comment go and stood at the front of the room, puffing out his chest as he continued.

"I just got off the radio with Mission Control and have our orders for the afternoon. The engineers back home have analyzed the computer information we sent back to Earth and have figured out how to shut off the nuclear reactor. Cat and Mickey, you're making a short moonwalk over to the reactor and will turn it off, following instructions from Earth. Jonah, you'll do some basic maintenance tasks, following instructions from Major Austen on radio channel seven. And Trace," he said with a spiteful grin, "guess what? You're making our dinner."

"You're kidding," said Trace.

"Nope. Orders straight from Commander Riker, as a matter of fact. Cat and Mickey, you'd better go get suited up. And get on the radio with Mission Control, they're waiting for your call."

As much as I felt bad for Trace, I have to admit that my surge of anger at Lance didn't last long. Cat and I had been chosen for the most important part of our mission. A risky trip outside on the surface of the moon to the faulty nuclear reactor and then . . . somehow . . . who knew how? . . . We were supposed to do something that a half-dozen adult astronauts before us had failed to do.

Trace kept her emotions in check, but she couldn't control her curiosity. "So you've given the four of us our orders," she said as she stood facing Lance. "What about you?"

Oh yeah, what about Lance?

"I have my own instructions," he said, looking away quickly and then bending over to tie his shoes. "Nothing much. Just like Jonah is doing some routine fix-it things inside the moon base, I'm doing some routine fix-it things on the outside. Nothing to get excited about."

I had learned a few things from poker night at the Home. One was to be patient and not to bet all your chips on your first good hand. Another was how to tell when someone wasn't telling the truth. Lance was as easy to read as a big-print book for kindergartners. I knew he was hiding something. He always wanted to be doing the most important task. So why wasn't he upset that Cat and I had been chosen for the biggest job of all?

Trace gave me a quick sideways look and raised her eyebrows, so I knew she noticed it, too. Lance was up to something, but for now, neither of us could figure it out.

❂ ❂ ❂ ❂ ❂

Ziggy followed Cat and me to the locker room. I spent the next several minutes carefully pulling on my moon suit and helping Cat put on hers. This was pretty much a two-person job. The oxygen tanks were slotted into a bulky built-in backpack attached to the main suit. Out on the moon, with the lower gravity, they seemed lighter. But inside the moon base, this backpack was extremely heavy.

I lifted Cat's backpack as she squirmed her arms into the suit. Cat grunted as she heaved my heavy suit up onto my back.

And then came the helmets.

Each one weighed as much as a bowling ball.

And then came the checking and rechecking of the snaps and buckles and gauges to make sure the suits were completely airtight.

Finally, about ten minutes after we started, we were ready to head outside. Turning to the air lock door, I remembered Ziggy. There he was, sitting on a chair with his legs crossed, waiting patiently by the door. His moon suit and helmet were on and . . . what? Had he really done that? I think he even flashed me the thumbs-up sign.

"No way, Ziggy. You're staying here," said Cat emphatically, more sure of herself than I had ever heard her about anything. "This is way too dangerous for a monkey." She shook her head, pointed at Ziggy, and then pointed back toward the door to the kitchen.

A sharp chatter of angry monkey sounds came through the speaker in my helmet, and Ziggy thumped the door to the air lock with his little fist.

"Ummm, Cat," I said hesitantly. "I'm not sure you want to fight this battle. Let him come."

"No way," Cat said, almost pleading. "I won't allow it. This poor monkey has been through enough already. It would be cruel and dangerous for us to drag him outside onto the moon. And besides, what if he runs away or something? We don't have time to chase him around. And besides besides, Mission Control didn't tell us to take him."

I looked at Ziggy for a while, waiting expectantly by the door. He was standing at attention like a soldier. Then he gave us a salute. Okay, that did it.

"Cat, who said anybody else needs to know we're taking him? They won't have a clue if we don't mention it. And look, we're a team here, and every team member has to contribute. We don't know what Ziggy can do, but he's been here way longer than either one of us. He might just know something we don't."

Cat was clearly torn. But when Ziggy pressed the green open button and held out his paw to Cat to lead her into the air lock, the struggle was over. "Looks like *we're* going with *him*, rather than the other way around," I said. "Let's hit it."

I heard Cat sigh. She just couldn't resist a gallant monkey.

We stepped into the air lock. The door back to the locker room slid shut with a *clang*, and we heard the air whistling out of the room as the pressure changed to the harsh lunar level.

"Mission Control," I said, pressing the long-range radio button inside my right glove, "this is Mickey and Cat, reporting for duty in the south air lock. We're ready to head outside."

"Roger that, astronauts. Proceed outside when you're ready."

With that, the exterior door slid open, and the small room was instantly filled with brilliant sunlight. With an excited squeak, our pint-sized companion led us out onto the dusty surface of the moon.

✪ ✪ ✪ ✪ ✪

The entrance to the nuclear reactor looked like a port-a-potty rising up from the moon dust. As we bounce-walked across the vehicle courtyard toward it, Dr. Yang explained that astronauts on earlier trips had affectionately named it "the outhouse." But he also explained that, of course, there was more to the nuclear reactor than met the eye. Behind the door was a ladder that led deep down into the ground to a series of rooms and equipment that provided power to the moon base—enough for several moon bases someday if the reactor could be fixed.

Yang explained that the reactor was powered by uranium, a super powerful but very dangerous material that had to be handled with extreme caution. When the reactor was working, the uranium fuel rods were moved into the middle part of the reactor, creating an incredible amount of power. When the reactor was not working, these fuel rods had to be pulled out of the reactor and "parked" in a safe position so they would cool down.

That was the problem.

One of the fuel rods was stuck in the reactor. The tiny motor that pushed the fuel rod into place was jammed in the "on" position. Nothing had worked to pull it out, and the reactor was getting dangerously overheated. The solution? We would just reprogram the main computer, turn off the little motor that was causing the problem, and then the fuel rod would slide easily out of the reactor and into the "park" position.

"You make it sound easy," I said as we bounce-walked over to the outhouse.

"That's because it is easy," said Dr. Yang confidently. "Cat will log in to the reactor's main computer. And if she does just what we tell her to, this whole thing could be over in ten minutes."

With that comforting prediction ringing in our ears, we entered the outhouse. One by one, we descended the ladder rungs, down a narrow tube illuminated by a string of lights running along one side. Ziggy went first, then he and I waited at the bottom as Cat's legs slowly emerged, and then we bounce-stepped across a small room to an air lock and shut the heavy door behind us, sealing out the harsh moon environment. After only a few minutes in my suit, I was already sweaty and couldn't wait to get my helmet off.

I didn't have to wait long. After a short pause, the warning sign in the air lock turned off, replaced by a green READY sign. We unclipped our helmets and slipped off our suits.

As soon as my helmet was off, I was greeted by cool, fresh air . . . but also by an ear-splitting alarm that pulsed one second on, one second off. Like a truck horn. Only harsher and sharper.

It was so loud we couldn't talk normally. We could only communicate during the one-second gaps of silence.

"Step *honk* one *honk*," I said, filling the silence with words. "Turn *honk* off *honk* this *honk* dumb *honk* alarm!"

"Seriously *honk*," Cat yelled back. "I *honk* think *honk* we *honk* get *honk* the *honk* picture *honk* there's *honk* an *honk* emergency *honk* right? *Honk, honk.* Duh!"

As soon as Ziggy stripped off his bulky space suit, he scampered over to Cat and extended both hands upward. Of course, she was happy to give him a ride. He hugged her hard with his legs and squeezed her neck with his elbows. His paws were firmly clamped over his ears, and his eyes were shut tight. The loud noise of the alarm was clearly bothering the little guy. Heck, it was bothering me, too.

We gave up trying to speak and wended our way through a maze of tunnels.

We knew we had found the main control room when we stepped in through the low door. There was a bank of computer equipment along one wall, set in front of a long, low window overlooking the reactor in the next room.

Cat struggled to set down Ziggy, who reluctantly relented and grasped her leg. After a few quick taps on a keyboard, the brain-rattling alarm suddenly stopped mid-honk. My ears were still ringing.

Ziggy cautiously removed his paws from his ears. He looked at me angrily and let out a loud shriek.

"What?" I blurted out incredulously. "You're not blaming *me* for the alarm, are you?"

Ziggy kept staring at me angrily as he gripped Cat's leg. "Eeeeeeep."

"Oh come on, monkey. It hurt my ears, too. I would have—"

"Um, Mickey?" interrupted Cat. "Please stop arguing with the monkey. Can you do something useful, like call back home?"

"This isn't over, Ziggy," I called out as he turned his back on me and jumped up onto Cat's lap. "We'll talk more about this later."

Cat cleared her throat. "Em-hem."

"Okay, okay," I said, trying not to get irritated at a ten-pound monkey.

I contacted Mission Control and, for the next few minutes, watched and listened as Cat was led through a series of complicated procedures on the computer. It turns out, logging on to the computer system and turning off the alarm was the easy part. After that, nothing seemed to go right.

It was soon clear that the plan designed by the NASA scientists wasn't going to work. No matter what they did, the fuel rod remained stuck in the reactor. Which meant the reactor's temperature kept rising.

Just because we had turned off the honking alarm didn't mean the problem had gone away. In fact, it was getting steadily worse. If we didn't get this fixed soon, we were going to have to accept defeat and abandon the moon base altogether.

"That," said a new voice over the radio, "is not an option. Director Marshall here. Time for the Hail Mary."

Cat looked up at me. "I have a feeling that's a sports term, am I right? Please translate."

"Right." I smiled. "Here's the translation: a Hail Mary is a prayer that the priests and nuns make you say a lot in Catholic church. And on a football field, it's kind of a prayer, too: a last-second, desperation, when-all-else-has failed, long-bomb pass. Two years ago in the last game of the regular season, the most excellent Miami Dolphins were playing the Denver Broncos. Dolphins, down by four late in the fourth quarter. Things looked bleak, but Bob Griese—the Dolphins' quarterback, you know—he called a play named Eagle-Duck Left Seventeen Hook, where two receivers line up wide on the left side and run this deep crossing pattern to the end zone. Here, let me draw this out for you—"

"Mickey?"

"Yes."

"Mickey, I get the picture. Long pass. Diving catch. Touchdown. Game over. But I don't think Director Marshall is going to call an Eagle-Duck Left Seventeen Hook, okay? Let's hear his Hail Mary plan."

I sighed. "Director Marshall, please proceed. We're ready for your Hail Mary."

"Roger that, Mickey," came the NASA director's reply. "The little motor keeping the fuel rod in place is stuck in the on position. And we can't turn it off. We've tried every imaginable way to cut the power. The only thing left is a total shutdown."

"All right. Just say the word and Cat can do it."

"Well, we tried a total shutdown using the computer, but it didn't work. All that's left is doing this the old-fashioned way. We need you to cut the power wire somewhere between the master panel and the generator. Just clip it with a pair of wire cutters. With all power off, the motor that keeps the uranium fuel rod in place can't keep running. It's impossible. So the fuel rod will just slip back down the tube out of the reactor and slide into the safe park position."

Sounded easy enough.

"But I told you, this is a Hail Mary," continued the director. "It's our only hope. But we don't usually do this. It has other consequences. When we say it shuts off all power, I mean all power in your part of the base. Even the emergency power. Even the power that runs the oxygen pumps. Once you cut the power, you will have about five minutes to get back to the air lock and get your suits back on before the oxygen runs out. You think you can do that?"

"Roger that!" Cat and I said together. Not because we felt any confidence, but because, really, we didn't have any choice.

After tearing apart the control room for ten minutes, digging through every drawer and closet, we finally found the wire clippers. The three of us—two kids and an angry monkey—then followed Marshall's directions to a short hallway two levels below the control room.

We removed the floor panel and exposed a maze of pipes and strand after strand of wires. "This is it, Mickey," said Marshall. "You only get one chance. If you can't do it, we're evacuating the moon base and bringing you back home."

I looked over at Cat. "He really knows how to calm a guy down, doesn't he?" I laughed nervously.

"I don't think he was trying to calm you down, Mickey," said Cat, completely missing my sarcasm. "I think he was trying to tell you that if you don't cut the right wire, we all may die and the moon will be a toxic disaster area for a million years."

I sighed and shook my head. At that moment, Ziggy tiptoed over to me and put one furry hand on my shoulder. With his other, he made a thumbs-up sign and nodded his head.

"Cat, you see that? Take a few lessons from Ziggy here about how to calm a guy down."

I turned back to the spaghetti of wires and called back to Mission Control. "Is it okay with you if I just start clipping randomly? I'll eventually get the correct one, right?"

A chorus of voices immediately blasted through the radio. "NO!"

I got the picture.

"Mickey," Marshall explained, "if you cut the wrong wire, it could have disastrous results. Depending on which wire you cut, it could start or stop one system or another, and that could make things even worse, if that's possible to imagine. We don't have time to create new problems. You just have to clip the aqua-colored wire in bundle number seven underneath the main water tube. Not the dark blue wire. Not the baby blue wire. Not the royal blue wire. The aquamarine blue-green one. Aqua. Can you do that?"

I leaned down into the mess of pipes and wires and reached down . . . way down . . . snaking my arm downward, firmly grasping the pair of wire cutters.

And then I could see it. A twisted cluster of multi-colored wires near the bottom of the utility duct. And one of them, sticking out to one side, was definitely aqua. I reached down through the tangle of pipes.

Not even close.

"You got it yet? Mickey? You got it?"

I wedged my shoulder hard against the row of pipes at the top of the duct, shoving my arm down as far as it would go. My hand swung down, and the wire cutters snipped open air. It was just out of reach.

"Mickey, you got it?" Marshall asked again.

"I . . . can't . . . reach!" I replied, disappointed. "I just can't reach. How long do you think my arm is, anyway?"

There was a long pause. "You're right, Mickey," came Marshall's reply. "The utility duct was made with a full-grown astronaut in mind. A full-grown astronaut could reach down to those wires. By our calculations, you need to reach about thirty-two inches down into the duct. Your arm just isn't long enough."

I pulled up the clippers and rolled over onto my back. Cat crawled over and reached her hand down into the duct. Again, not even close.

We didn't say anything to each other, however, because we had a lot to listen to. Somehow, somebody had left the radio channel open, and we could hear a confused, chaotic argument coming through the radio.

Somebody suggested that Lance had the best shot at reaching the wire since he was by far the tallest member of our team. We heard Dr. Yang call for Lance over another radio channel without getting a response. Marshall started yelling, "Where the heck is Riker?" And some other voices started arguing about whether we could use a saw to cut away two of the pipes so that I could reach farther down.

Cat looked at me with a tinge of desperation in her eyes. "That does not inspire confidence," she said quite simply.

I agreed.

"Eeeep," concurred Ziggy, brandishing the wire cutters.

Cat reached to grab the tool from the monkey. "Ziggy, don't wave those around. You might poke out your little monkey eye."

I looked at Ziggy, who was angrily pulling the wire

cutters back from Cat. And I looked at the utility duct. There was no way for Ziggy to fit between the pipes. But maybe, just maybe.

"Cat, let go of the wire cutters. Ziggy's trying to tell you something. He can do this. He's our real Hail Mary."

Cat let go. Ziggy stood in front of me holding the wire cutters in both paws. They looked huge in his hands, like he was holding a pair of giant hedge clippers.

"Okay, Mickey, maybe he can get down there. And maybe he knows you need him to clip a wire. But how the heck are you going to tell him which wire? Remember, he can't just cut all of them. What's monkey for 'aqua'?"

Cat must have thought I was going crazy as I started to unzip my space suit—and even crazier when all I could say was "my underpants, my underpants, my underpants."

You see, as I explained earlier, the Miami Dolphins are my favorite football team on Earth. And the team's colors are orange and aqua. And I happened to be wearing my lucky underpants that day. My glorious orange and aqua Miami Dolphins underpants.

With the wire clippers, I snipped a hole in the fabric and tore off a strip. Ziggy looked about as confused as Cat. But when I handed him the one-inch by one-inch square of aqua material and pointed down to the utility duct and then pointed to the wire cutters, I thought, just for a split second, that I sensed a glimmer of understanding in Ziggy's little monkey eyes.

He grabbed the wire cutters from my hand and tore off down the hallway to the far end of the duct, disappearing into the tangle of pipes and wires.

"Cat. Do you think, maybe, you think he gets it?"

Cat sighed deeply and shook her head. "Mickey, I think you're a dreamer who needs a new pair of underpants. I also think it's very, very unlikely that Ziggy understood your crazy sign language."

A minute passed. Then two. Cat and I strained our ears, but we didn't hear any shuffling or movement from down in the duct.

"He should be there by now," Cat said nervously. "He should be there. And he should have cut the wire already. Something's wrong. Something's wrong, I just—"

She stopped talking abruptly because everything went suddenly black. Really, really black. I don't think I'd ever really seen black like that black before.

At night, back in Orlando, there was always a glimmer of light coming in through my bedroom window from a street lamp or the moon or some stars. Playing hide and seek in a closet, you usually have a little sliver of light coming in from under the door—or at least you know that light is just one turn of the doorknob away.

But this was something else. Complete blackness.

"I guess he found the right wire," I said into the muffled silence.

"I never doubted him for a minute," said Cat. I swiveled my head in the direction of her voice. "That was a joke, by the way."

"I know," I said, waiting for something to happen. "It was pretty funny. Remind me to laugh when we get out of this, okay? So . . . now what?"

Our long-range radios crackled and emitted a faint, choppy sound. Knocking out the power must have affected the signal, maybe turning off a booster antenna that helped the radio reach us underground. Or something like that. Where was Jonah when you needed a good explanation?

"Mission Control," I said very slowly and loudly. "The lights are out. Repeat, the lights are out. Please repeat what you said."

All I could make out was "good job" and "hurry, hurry, hurry" and then something that sounded like "flashlights."

"Mission Control, you're hard to understand. But yes, a flashlight would be useful now. Where can I get one?"

There was a pause.

Between crackles I heard "flashlight pocket" and "your right hip."

I patted my right hip, finding nothing but a flat, empty pocket.

"I don't have one, Cat, do you?" I said, feeling a jolt of panic.

"No . . . but . . . oh no! I remembered the flashlights clipped to those charging stations in the locker room back at the moon base. I remembered looking at them thinking, 'When would we ever need those?'"

The radio crackled again and I heard "hurry, hurry" and "losing oxygen."

They didn't need to tell us again.

I remembered back to the last thing I saw before the lights went out. I was pretty much facing a wall, straight ahead. That meant that I should turn left—a full, ninety-degree left turn—and then walk straight ahead, feeling for a door on the right side about ten or fifteen steps down the narrow passageway.

I turned and took a step forward, smacking immediately into Cat's forehead. Hard. We both fell backward. It was so dark that I wondered for a second whether I was standing or lying down. I reached out with my hand and patted the floor next to my head. Definitely lying down.

I heard Cat scrambling along the hallway. "Mickey, follow my voice! Hurry!"

I flipped over and started crawling toward the part of the blackness Cat's voice had come from. "Wait!" I heard her say, close up ahead. I started crawling faster and then *smack*, we clunked heads, hard, for a second time.

Great. Thirty seconds in the dark, and all we'd managed to do was ram into each other like fighting mountain goats. And we were about ten tunnels, five rooms and one hundred yards from the air lock where our suits were waiting. In the pitch black.

With a sinking feeling, I could feel the air getting colder. I heard a steady hiss: the sound of our precious oxygen leaking out of the tunnel. We were officially toast.

The second blow to the head must have been harder than the first, because I sensed a glowing over to my right side. I thought maybe I was seeing stars, because I could definitely see a glow down the hallway . . . I could see the shine of the polished floor and a couple of pipes hanging from the ceiling.

"Ziggy!" Cat yelled.

Turning the corner, scampering quickly toward us was Ziggy, carrying a little flashlight and clutching a three-inch strip of aqua wire.

"You cut the aqua one!" squealed Cat. "Good monkey!"

I made a trade with Ziggy. My last Butterfinger candy bar in exchange for his life-saving flashlight.

"Work now, party later," I said quickly. "We've got to move it, move it."

We took off down the hallway at a full sprint, Ziggy leading the way. And thank goodness for that. Several times I would have picked a right turn instead of a left. But Ziggy got us back to the air lock, and we practically leaped into our space suits, breathing heavily in the rapidly thinning air.

This time, it was a relief to get my helmet on, and I gulped down the sweet oxygen that hissed in from the tank.

As we bounced back across the parking area toward the main buildings, my heart was still pounding from the excitement of our successful Hail Mary. "Kids and monkeys: one—impossible task: ZERO!" I announced triumphantly.

Mission accomplished! It's all easy from here on in, I thought.

Guess what. I was wrong.

CHAPTER 20
Don't Forget the Parking Brake

Once Cat, Ziggy, and I got back to the main base, we found the others gathered in the kitchen area. Trace had made a huge batch of mac and cheese. The food at Oblivion Base was pretty terrible. The powdered eggs tasted just like the powdered potatoes, which tasted just like the instant oatmeal.

But this mac and cheese was going to be different, I just knew it. Even by Earth standards, it smelled awesome. Lance wasn't back yet, but we were all starving, so we took a quick vote. I'm not sure Ziggy knew what he was voting for, but he raised his hand when the rest of us did. Eat now, five; wait for Lance, big fat zero.

The food tasted even better than it smelled. Between bites, Cat and I told the full details of our adventure, including how Ziggy had saved the day and how I needed a new pair of underpants. When we finally finished our story, we had put a large dent in the huge pot of mac and cheese. Ziggy gathered up our plates and carried them over to the sink. The rest of us looked at each other, unable to ignore the empty chair at the head of the table anymore.

"Okay," I said, leaning back in my chair and patting my satisfied belly, "is anybody besides me wondering where our flight commander is?"

"Jonah and I were talking about that while you guys were gone," said Trace. "Of course, Jonah has a crazy theory about it. And this time, I think he's right. And the longer Lance is gone, the more it makes sense."

"Wow, call the newspapers!" I said, raising my eyebrows. "I can see the headline: Miracles Do Happen— Trace Agrees with Jonah."

"Very funny, Mickey," said Jonah. "But this one's obvious. I'll forgive you for not figuring it out because you were kind of busy saving the moon from total destruction."

"Mick, we think he went out looking for The Glint," Trace blurted out. "He went outside. He took a zip buggy. And remember, he has Major Austen's map. He's out there looking for The Glint. We're sure of it."

As soon as I heard it, it made so much sense I knew it had to be true. "How long has he been out there?"

"Almost two hours," replied Jonah. "And not a peep on the radio."

"Well, I don't know about you guys," I said, scrambling to my feet, "but I'm going to the west control room and try to find him with my binoculars." I scrambled out of the kitchen, with the others hot on my heels.

★ ★ ★ ★ ★

Thirty minutes later, we were ready to give up. We took turns with the binoculars, scanning the ridge and the hills beyond, looking for the mystery glint of light or the zip buggy. There was only gray dust and rocks. And rocks and more gray dust. We even tried calling him on the local radio channel but got no answer.

The silence was finally broken by the radio. But it wasn't Lance. It was his father.

"*Artemis 7*, Mission Control here. Put Lance on, please." The four of us froze and we exchanged nervous glances. Who would move to the microphone first?

"Lance, this is your . . . this is the director." His voice was more insistent this time. "Reply."

I stepped over to the microphone. Pressing the red button, I said, "Mickey here. Lance . . ." I looked over to Jonah for inspiration, but he just shrugged. "Uh, he's in the bathroom."

Jonah rolled his eyes. "Now that's creative," he whispered.

"Come on, man," I said defensively. "Could you come up with anything better?" I pointed up at the speaker where Director Marshall's voice had crackled a few seconds earlier. "Anyway, it seems like that took care of him. Right?"

Wrong.

"Mickey? Director Marshall here." His normally no-nonsense voice sounded even more serious, if that was possible. "We can't wait for Lance. This is urgent. We've discovered an issue with the oxygen tanks on the command module. Your oxygen for the ride home. I need you to confirm the readings."

Cat scooted over to my side and started tapping the keyboard. A few seconds later, a picture of four dials popped up on the computer screen. They looked kind of like the gas tank indicator on a car. "There you go," said Cat. "The oxygen tank levels. Tell Director Marshall you're looking at them now."

I pressed the talk button to open the line again with the adults back on Earth. "Okay, Mission Control, I've got it up on the screen. I'm looking at the four oxygen tank levels for the command module. What can I tell you?"

"Very good, Mickey. Tell me what they say."

"Here we go, I'll read them to you," I responded, happy to be in control. "Number one says 'empty.' Number two says 'eighty percent.' Numbers three and four both say 'empty.'" I felt the others scrunching up next to me to see for themselves. I realized now that I had said the words, the readings didn't sound good. Three tanks were empty with just one left?

"Is that a problem?" I asked.

"Mickey, remember, we don't have problems. Just challenges. We can deal with this one. Kids, we're bringing you home right now."

"Mission Control, can you repeat that? When you say 'now,' you mean, like, today?" I glanced nervously at the others.

"Negative, Mickey. 'Now' means this instant. Without delay. In fact, we've already started the launch sequence for the command module. You don't have any time to waste. You will lift off in thirty minutes."

Trace grabbed my arm and mouthed the word *Lance*, staring at me with huge, panicked eyes.

"Hey, that's cool," I said, as casually as I could. "We have a few other things to do, though. We'd rather leave in two hours. Over." I made a face and waited for the response. I had a feeling I wouldn't like it.

"Negative, Mickey. You cannot wait two hours. Tank three is empty: That was supposed to be your oxygen for the trip home. Tank four is empty: That was your emergency spare. The only oxygen left for the command module is what's in tank two, but the level is slowly dropping. Right now, it has enough for about seventy-two hours, and if you leave right now, that's just enough to get you home."

The director went on to explain that the tanks must have come loose with the hard impact of our landing, and the system had been slowly but steadily leaking oxygen for the last forty-eight hours. He explained that we needed to launch right away because of the Earth's rotation. If we waited any longer, we would have to do another entire orbit of Earth to hit our landing zone— and we didn't have enough oxygen for that.

He didn't need to explain what would happen if we ran out of oxygen in the command module while we were still in space.

As he talked, Trace nervously squeezed my arm until her fingernails dug into my skin, and I yelled, "OW! THAT HURTS!"

I didn't realize I was holding down the Talk button. Director Marshall said, "Yes, Mickey, I know that hurts.

I know there are things you still wanted to do up there. But you kids have completed the mission. You need to leave. And you need to leave now."

"Roger that. Gotta go tell the others. I'll be right back." I switched off the Talk switch and grabbed for the moon radio. But Trace already had it.

"Lance, this is Trace. Come in, Lance. Emergency. Emergency. Code red. The sky is falling. Come in, Lance."

This time, finally, there was a response. "Lance here. I leave for an hour, and you guys can't survive without me? Really, do you require adult supervision every minute of the day? What is—"

Trace cut him off. "LANCE! GET BACK HERE RIGHT NOW! The command module is low on oxygen. They've started the launch process. Blastoff is in thirty minutes. We can't delay."

Lance's voice came through the radio immediately. "Did you say thirty minutes? Is this an order from Mission Control?"

"Yes, Lance, of course it's an order from Mission Control. I'm not sitting here making stuff up. We leave in thirty minutes, so GET. BACK. HERE. NOW!"

"Roger that, Trace. I've found what I was looking for, anyway. I'm returning right now. I'll be back in twenty minutes. Walking back to my zip buggy, it's parked right on the other side of this little hill.

"And by the way, I deserve a serious award for this solo moonwalk and treasure hunt. I got an excellent . . . rock sample." Lance just couldn't help himself. For him, going an hour without bragging was like going an hour without breathing.

"Deserve?" fumed Trace. "You deserve a serious slap on the forehead, that's what you deserve, you giant meathead showoff. You're giving us a heart attack. HURRY UP!"

I rolled my eyes and waited for Lance's reply. But it didn't come. The radio remained silent.

"Are you still there, hero?" said Trace mockingly. "How long until you get back here?"

"Where the—? What the—? How the—?" Lance did not sound happy. "Who *stole my zip buggy*?"

"Very funny, hero," said Trace. "You'll be here in, what? Twenty minutes?"

"This can't be." There was no mistaking the panic that had crept into Lance's voice. "This just can't be. I parked right near this little rock pile. I stopped. I got out. I walked up this little hill for, maybe, one minute. Tops."

"Lance, did you put on the parking brake?" asked Trace.

There was a pause.

"Of course I put on the parking brake," said Lance, sounding less than sure. "Do you think I'm stupid?"

There was another pause.

"I mean, I *always* put on the brake. Everyone knows you're supposed to put on the brake when you stop. And I always do what I'm supposed to. Right?"

Nobody answered.

"Well, almost always," he continued. Now he was talking to himself. "Come on, Lance. Come on, zip buggy. Aw, come on . . . don't tell me . . . awww . . ."

Silence again. Then, "AW NUTS!" The voice was so

loud that the moon radio seemed to jump from Trace's hand, hitting the floor with a loud crack.

"NUTS, NUTS, NUTS!" Lance's voice was a little quieter since the radio had scooted under the table. Cat bent down to fish it out. "The stupid brake must have broken." We could hear Lance huffing and puffing as he apparently was bounce-running along. "My zip buggy rolled back down this little hill . . . I'm following the tracks . . . rolled down . . . and now it's . . . AW NUTS! It's nose-down in a ditch."

"Lance, now it's your turn to relax," said Trace. "Can't you back it out? You can still drive it, right?"

"OF COURSE I CAN'T! It's totally in a ditch. A real ditch. Like a twenty-foot-deep hole. It's down there so far, I can't even reach down and touch it."

Silence again. I knew what was coming next.

"Somebody's got to come get me," said Lance. "Please. Somebody's got to come. Who's coming to get me?"

"Lance, where exactly are you?" asked Trace slowly.

"I'm . . . I'm on the other side of the canyon. I'm about twenty minutes away. I'm . . . I'm at The Glint."

The words crackled like a jolt of electricity through the speaker and right through the four of us gathered in the west control room. The Glint.

I looked at my watch but didn't really need to. A first grader could have done that math. The zip buggies couldn't go more than six miles per hour. Twenty minutes to get there, twenty minutes to get back. And the command module was leaving in less than thirty.

I didn't need to explain it to Jonah or Cat, either.

Trace was obviously so freaked out that she sprinted from the control room as soon as she heard where he was.

Aw nuts was right. I couldn't see any way around this.

"Mickey," whispered Jonah, "you know what you need to do. We can't cover for Lance anymore. We've got to tell Marshall."

I knew he was right. I handed the moon radio to Jonah and said, "You deal with Lance. I'll tell his dad." I stared at the microphone. How was I going to say this?

⭐ ⭐ ⭐ ⭐ ⭐

"Mission Control, Mickey here. Director Marshall, please."

"Marshall here," came the immediate reply. "Good timing. The launch preparations are on track and confirmed that you're all set for an easy trip home. Everything looks clear and good to go. We need you to make your way to the air lock and then immediately out to the command module. Congratulations, *Artemis 7*, you're coming home."

It sounded so simple. I hated to do this.

"Um, just one slight . . . little . . . one little thing going on here. Not a problem. Just a little challenge, as you'd say." I took a deep breath and just let the words roll out. "You see, about an hour ago Lance took a zip buggy out to, uh, he told us he was going to collect rock samples. I know, I know, we told him not to go, but he really thought he was doing the right thing, and he's in charge up here, and what were we supposed to do, stop him? Well, anyway, it turns out he went looking for this thing called The Glint, and that's where he is now. But something happened with his brakes, and his zip buggy is in a ditch, and he can't get it out, so now he's stuck at The Glint. And it's going to take almost an hour to go get him." I paused to take a breath. But then I didn't dare start up again.

Director Marshall had a simple, short reply. "Roger that."

The radio was silent.

We didn't realize it at the time, but although the radio was silent, there was absolute chaos at Mission Control. My radio transmission had been broadcast over the loudspeakers in the command center room, so all of the scientists and engineers and assistants, and all of Team Varsity, had heard what I said.

Everybody had a reaction. Everybody had an opinion. And they all started talking and yelling at once. People must have been running across the room, some of them whipping out calculators and punching numbers like crazy, trying to calculate a solution to our impossible problem. Others were probably heaving huge maps of the moon onto tables and starting to measure different routes with rulers. Still others were maybe diving for bookshelves and grabbing huge books and manuals about rockets and orbiting the Earth and reentry and oxygen tanks and everything in between.

As I said, it was apparently complete, total chaos.

People in Mission Control told me later that at that moment, Director Marshall stood up on his chair, put two fingers into his mouth, and gave a whistle so loud it could have called a dog from three states over. It cut through the noise and brought everybody to a screeching halt. He told the assembled scientists, engineers, and mission specialists to calm down. He told them to please keep working, but just do it more quietly.

Apparently, while Jonah, Cat, Ziggy, and I were staring nervously at the silent radio, Marshall was explaining to the workers at Mission Control that the lunar module needed to blast off in thirty minutes—no, twenty-eight minutes to be exact—and if it didn't leave then, it wasn't coming back to Earth. And his boy was trapped two miles and forty minutes away from Oblivion Base. And for the first time, he used the word problem. He said, "This is a problem. And because I'm the father of the stranded astronaut, I can't be the one to decide what to do. I just can't."

So? Director Marshall quit. He explained that, with his own son in danger, he might make decisions based on protecting Lance rather than on what was best for the entire team. So he was stepping down as the director and turning over the job to Commander Riker.

We didn't realize it at the time, but as we sat there waiting, Marshall was actually climbing down off his chair and quietly walking out of the silent room, out into the Florida sunshine.

All we heard over the radio was silence. Two full minutes of silence.

And then, Commander Riker's voice. "*Artemis 7*, this is Mission Control. *Director* Riker here." He spoke that part slowly, clearly relishing the sound of the words. "The launch clock shows twenty-six minutes to liftoff. Proceed directly to the outer air lock, put on your suits, and head to the command module. No detours."

"Roger that," I said. "But what about Lance? Can't we...."

"Negative, *Artemis 7*. This is an order. Your safety is our primary mission. And to get back to Earth alive, the command module needs to blast off in . . . twenty-six minutes."

"But, Mission Control—" I started.

"*Artemis 7*, you need to start following orders, or else you will throw away the four lives that can still be saved. The best scientists on planet Earth are working on how to save your other crewmember. Leave that to the adults down here. That's not your job. Your job is to follow orders. So I repeat: Go directly to the outer air lock, put on your suits, and head to the command module."

"But Mission Control—" I tried one last time.

"No buts!" came Riker's voice, razor sharp and ice cold from 238,000 miles away. "And one more thing," he added, "leave the monkey behind."

✪ ✪ ✪ ✪ ✪

Cat, Jonah, and I argued half-heartedly for a minute, but we realized there was no hope. With only twenty-six minutes . . . no, twenty-five minutes left, it would be simply impossible to drive four miles round trip.

Our one act of rebellion as we left the control room was to take Ziggy. He gripped Cat's shirt hard with his little hands, holding folds of fabric tight in his furry fists. His legs were latched around her middle, squeezing her tight. And he wedged his head under her chin. I'm not sure Cat could have followed Riker's instructions even if she had tried.

I wondered for a minute whether Ziggy understood what Riker had said. Or maybe he just sensed that we were nervous and scared. Either way, he knew something bad had happened and sensed that his people were about to leave.

We jogged back through the moon base, calling Trace's name, heading toward the air lock. I felt suddenly disoriented and confused. In two short days, the moon base had come to feel like home, and now we were leaving it without any chance to say goodbye. You might not think it makes sense to say goodbye to a building, but I think it does. I certainly felt like the moon base deserved a real goodbye. It was our protector, our sanctuary on a cold, barren rock out in space. But some part of me felt, as we sped through the hallways and rooms to the exit, that I was saying "see you later" and not "goodbye." And that somehow made it feel better.

As we came through the kitchen and into the little hallway at the air lock, I realized we had something more important to worry about.

Trace.

Where the heck was she?

We had come through the entire moon base, yelling her name, without so much as a peep in response. As I entered the locker room, I saw the suits lined up on the wall. Mine. Cat's. Jonah's. And at the end, on the lowest hook, the little suit belonging to Ziggy. But the two hooks in between were empty. Lance's and Trace's. Trace's suit was gone!

Oh, no, I thought. Not Trace, too. Even if she had left immediately in a zip buggy after dropping the moon radio, that was only about five minutes ago. There was no way she could make the round trip in one of those vehicles before liftoff. Not even Trace, winner of the 1977 KF3 Go-Kart International Cup. I ran to the small window that looked out onto the courtyard.

There was Trace, wearing her space suit, bent over one of the zip buggies with its engine cover opened up. On the ground next to her was a toolbox.

At that moment, I saw her pull a small object about as big as a mini-size candy bar out of the engine compartment. Two wires dangled from either side of it. She turned to look back at our building and must have seen my face in the window. She pumped her hand with the candy-bar-wire thing above her head in a gesture of triumph. Then with her free hand, she beckoned to me frantically.

As I stood there, frozen, she threw the candy-bar-wire thingie carelessly over her shoulder and jumped into the driver's seat.

What the heck had she done to the engine of the zip buggy? As I jumped into my space suit and barked at Jonah to zip me up, it suddenly hit me.

Would the 1977 KF3 Go-Kart International Cup winner allow this mission to fail because the moon buggy was too slow? Would she seriously be satisfied with a top speed of six miles per hour?

Of course not.

She was doing what she'd wanted to do since the day we landed on the moon, since the first time she had stepped on the accelerator and felt the zip buggy creep forward at walking speed.

She was disabling the speed restrictor that Dr. Yang had told us about. The small object she had thrown over her shoulder must have been the governor, the device that limited the zip buggy's engine. She was turning the buggy into a racing machine. Through the window, I saw Trace tearing around the courtyard as she waited for me to come outside, throwing up huge clouds of dust, doing donuts like a NASCAR driver after winning a race.

"Cat, Jonah, Ziggy," I said, "take the other zip buggy to the command module and prepare for launch. Do whatever Riker tells you to do. Jonah, when you talk to Riker, you can pretend you're me if you want to. We're going after Lance. And we'll meet you there."

The others all exchanged confused looks. But I didn't have time to explain.

As I disappeared into the outer air lock and prepared to put on my helmet, I yelled back over my shoulder, "We'll see you in 24 minutes. At least, we'll see you if Trace is as good as she says she is."

CHAPTER 21
Drive Like There's No Tomorrow

Trace and I left the courtyard at top speed, the rear tires kicking up clouds of dust behind us, and started barreling up the hill away from the moon base. And toward Lance.

I quickly understood why they had put governors on the zip buggies. This was absolutely insane.

Remember, the moon has about one-sixth the gravity of Earth. A one-foot jump on Earth turns into a six-foot jump on the moon. A six-foot jump turns into a . . . well, you get the picture.

Every time a wheel hit a rock or a bump, the wheel would fly up in the air. On the trip from the landing area to the moon base at six miles per hour, the moon seemed smooth and flat. Now that we were going fast, the moon seemed like it was all rocks and bumps.

The zip buggy was soaring five, ten, sometimes twenty feet in the air. And it would bounce when it landed. We lost speed whenever we bounced, as the buggy's engine could only push us along when the wheels were touching the surface.

Sometimes if we didn't hit a bump straight on, the zip buggy would tilt dangerously to one side or the other. To stay balanced, I had to throw my weight to the left side, leaning behind Trace as far as I could go. Or to the right side, leaning as far out into the thin air as I dared. Whatever it took to tip us back and level us out.

It didn't take long for Trace to get the hang of it, though. She was always looking thirty yards ahead, picking her way between the larger boulders and flooring it on the flat parts.

In almost no time we reached the top of the first hill. What an amazing view.

In front of us, stretching from right to left as far as we could see, was a huge, dark canyon. Black like a scar across the light-gray surface of the moon. The canyon was about seventy or eighty yards wide, almost the length of a football field. And I could only guess how deep it was. The sun was at a steep angle, so the shadows were long, like you would get at sunset on Earth. Because the sun was so low on the horizon, only a few feet of the canyon wall on the other side were visible. The rest of the canyon was blackness. A deep, murky blackness far darker than the star-studded sky spreading out above the lunar surface. The thought of this deep, murky blackness caused me to lean away from the canyon as we sped along its edge.

After about a mile, just as we remembered from Major Austen's map, the canyon narrowed suddenly. I tapped Trace on the arm when I saw our target: a tiny strip where the canyon walls came so close together they touched before spreading out again on the other side. It was a thin natural bridge, stretching over the narrowest part of the canyon. A graceful, fragile arch of rock—only about ten feet wide.

When we reached the land bridge, Trace slowed sharply. The slightest bump to the left or right would have sent us plummeting into the darkness. We crept across the narrow pathway, and I peered to my right, down over the side and into the deep canyon. I glanced nervously at Trace, who fortunately was not looking down into the abyss. I couldn't see her eyes, but her helmet was pointed straight ahead, both hands clutching the steering wheel.

When we reached the far side, I instinctively grabbed the side of the zip buggy. And just in time. Trace put all of her weight on the accelerator, and the machine lurched forward, swerving to the left, back along the far side of the ravine.

"Lance, we're . . . oof . . . across the canyon bridge," I announced across the local radio channel, my voice choppy as we bounced and skipped along at top speed. "We're coming . . . baAAAAACCKKK . . . along the canyon . . . uff . . . toward you. Come to the top . . . puh . . . of the hill and wave so we see you."

"Roger that, Mickey," came Lance's reply. "Hurry."

Yeah, right, I thought. He didn't need to add that last part.

From time to time, we would see the tire tracks Lance had left, where he had driven an hour earlier. Sometimes Trace picked a different, smoother path.

And sometimes our zip buggy would leap clear over Lance's tracks as we raced against the clock clicking steadily down to liftoff.

Trace's eyes were locked on the surface ahead. I was staring beyond, scanning every hill and ridge for a sign of Lance or his zip buggy—or The Glint.

There!

Around the edge of a rocky outcropping, there was Lance, standing still and staring straight up at the distant Earth above us.

When he saw us, he started going nuts, waving his hands over his head and jumping up in the air. It was pretty impressive. I think his first jump was about five feet straight up.

Oh, to have that ability back on Earth.

I squeezed the little talk button in my left glove. "See him, Trace?"

"Got it."

Lance kept leaping straight up into the air.

My helmet was filled with Lance's whoops of excitement coming in over the radio. The only words I picked up were *awesome* and *maybe you rock*, but otherwise it was just whoops and yahoos.

Although his jumps were impressive—freakish, in fact—I was distracted by the shape in the dust next to him. At first I assumed it was his zip buggy. It was about the right size. As we got closer, however, I realized that it wasn't his buggy. The zip buggies were clunky-looking vehicles perched on top of four big rubber tires.

This thing was gray, shiny, and mysteriously elegant. Its surface was perfectly smooth, like a giant metal egg. But as we got closer, I could tell that it was broken. Its top part was smooth and intact, but the bottom was jagged and cracked, as though it had landed with a hard impact. And its surface was shiny and reflective, like metal. The Glint.

Even as we got closer, it was hard to get a good look at it because Trace was driving the zip buggy like a maniac, and my biggest concern was holding on.

When we screeched to a halt in a puff of dust at Lance's side, I stepped out and bent down to take a closer look. Whatever it was, it had definitely crashed into the ground, with the bottom part buried in the dusty surface. There were no markings on the side. No American flag. Or Soviet flag. Or Chinese flag. In fact, no words or letters at all. There were several long cracks in the side, zigzagging up from the bottom. One of them was large, almost splitting the object into two pieces.

"Nice work, team!" shouted Lance. "Trace, how'd you get that thing to go so fast? Mine drove like a golf cart. You were *flying*!"

"Lance," I took a couple steps toward the strange object lying in the lunar dust only five feet away. "What the heck? What is it?"

"No idea. Absolutely no idea. But look." He held up a jagged piece of metal with wires and pieces hanging off of it and waved it in front of us. "I've got a souvenir!"

"Guys, let's go!" urged Trace.

"I can tell you one thing," said Lance, gesturing at The Glint, "it's not one of ours. It doesn't belong to NASA. I can't tell who it belongs to. Or what it is."

I leaned forward and peered closely at the mystery object. I could see inside the crack now. What was it? Wires! And small parts. It was definitely a machine.

Some sort of machine. And on the ground next to it lay a few pieces. One of them, about eight inches long, with strange markings on it and bumps on one end.

"Mickey, NOW!" yelled Trace. I felt a tug on the back of my space suit. "We've got to go. And you know it!"

Yes, I knew it. I glanced up and saw Trace and Lance turn their backs on me and climb into her souped-up zip buggy.

I paused, taking one last look at The Glint, leaning over one more time and reaching out my hand to—

Then I followed them back into the zip buggy.

Before I had settled back in the seat, Trace already had pushed her foot down on the accelerator, and we surged away from the strange and beautiful pile of metal, turning back toward the canyon.

I was jolted back to reality as my brain reminded me what was most important right now. The time. The oxygen.

I looked down at my right wrist and couldn't believe what I saw.

My countdown timer had shown twenty-three minutes until liftoff when we left the moon base courtyard. Even though Trace had driven like a champion up the hill, along the canyon, across the land bridge, and over to The Glint, the clock had run all the way down to ten minutes.

We were toast.

"Trace, we're ten minutes from liftoff. Aw shoot, now it's nine. Only nine to go, and it took us thirteen to get here. And once we get back, we need at least a minute or two for the three of us to climb into the command module. Can you make it back in time?"

I knew the answer.

From this point on the hill, I could just make out the top of the command module in the distance, straight across on the other side of the canyon. It seemed so close. Teasing us. But we still had to turn left and travel a mile up the canyon to the land bridge, and then a mile back again to the moon base and the rocket.

"Mick, I'm sorry." Trace's reply was soft, but certain. "I can't make it. Especially with Lance's added weight. All I can do is try, but I'm sorry, I can't cut our time in half."

The truth sank in for all of us.

"We'll still be driving when Cat and Jonah lift off," Trace continued. "But at least we'll have a good view of them going home."

"What?" yelled Lance. "Are you kidding me? How can that be! What took you so long then? I thought you were some driving champ. You can't even—"

"Lance-one-more-word-and-I-swear-I'm-totally-gonna... THROW . . . YOU . . . INTO . . . THE . . . CANYON!" Trace hollered back, spitting each word angrily into the radio. All the time, we kept careening down the hill, following the tracks we had laid on the way up.

The black canyon yawned in front of us. A huge lunar canyon, separating us from our ride home.

The tire tracks turned away to the left toward the land bridge. But Trace kept pointing the zip buggy straight ahead.

"Trace, you gonna turn left and head up the canyon to the land bridge?" asked Lance.

Our zip buggy continued straight forward, picking up speed.

"Trace . . . um . . . put on your blinker?" Lance was starting to sound nervous. "Uh, left turn, please. You might have noticed the enormous *bottomless pit* straight ahead?"

"Lance," I said hoarsely, "you obviously don't know Trace very well. You might want to shut it and fasten your seat belt."

We must have been going almost seventy miles an hour at this point, flying down the hill straight to our doom.

I could hear the engine screaming under my seat. Trace had steered toward a flat, smooth stretch leading up to the lip of the canyon, which was fortunately hard-packed and dust-free, allowing the wheels to grip the ground with perfect traction.

The canyon must have been sixty yards wide at this point.

This was crazy. Absolutely crazy.

"NOOOOOO! Let me off!" screamed Lance.

It was too late for that.

The black lip hurtled at us, relentlessly, until finally the ground gave way and there was just emptiness beneath us. The screaming of the engine stopped. Trace had taken her foot off the accelerator.

We were flying.

Up, up, and steadily forward. I was pressed back into my seat, hard, the same sensation as when we had lifted off from Earth at the beginning of our mission.

We were flying.

And spinning.

When we took off, it felt like the right side of the

buggy hit a bump and kicked up harder than the left side. So as we soared, the horizon line tipped and then rotated before our eyes. Up and to my right was the bright, starry sky. Down and to the left was the deep, lifeless, total blackness of the canyon.

Then the blackness was above us. We were upside down.

As we soared and spun, I saw a flash of metal as something slipped off Lance's lap and sailed away from the zip buggy, flipping end over end, down into the canyon. His souvenir from The Glint was gone.

We kept spinning. The horizon line was now vertical again, the deep canyon on the right side. I could see a strip of bright, white moon surface straight ahead. And the starry sky was on the left.

By now, I had no idea which end was up anymore, but I could definitely feel we were no longer rising. We were beginning to fall. My body strained against the seatbelt, and I was aware that the moon buggy was pulling us down, down, down toward the beckoning blackness of the canyon.

"Come *onnnn*," Trace urged. She jammed her foot onto the accelerator and the engine roared, spinning the wheels uselessly in the air. I leaned forward, willing our buggy to just keep moving.

Then there was something white rushing at us. The white powdery surface of the far side of the canyon was rushing toward us as fast as we fell. It was a race to that far side of the canyon, with the deep darkness dragging us down, and the white moon surface pulling us forward.

And the darkness lost the fight.

The impact was unbelievable. My butt was already bruised, my neck already sore after more than twenty minutes of bumps and lumps of our mad dash. But this next impact was something else.

Wham! The front wheels cracked hard into the ground, and my heavy, helmeted head was pitched forward and slammed into my knees. Then the buggy bounced skyward, tipping back and landing on the rear bumper, pointing straight up before pitching forward again.

The impact was loud, hard, and painful—but exactly what I was hoping for. The most welcome impact of solid ground I had ever felt in my life. There were several more enormous hops, back to front, side to side. But we didn't tip over. And finally we skidded to a stop in a massive cloud of dust.

I broke the silence with a huge whoop.

"Trace, that was AWESOME! Let's do it again!"

"Not a chance, Mick." Trace's voice quavered. "That's a one-time-only ride. In fact, I might just stick to bicycles for the rest of my life."

"That was an all-eternity moon record jump, Trace. That has *Guinness Book of World Records* written all over it. Guinness Book of Universe Records! Lance, you okay?" I slapped him on the arm, surprised by his silence.

"Did anybody else, uh, pee their pants?" asked Lance.

"Wait! You serious?" I asked. "Really?"

"Yeah, didn't you guys—" Lance caught himself. "I mean, I'm kidding, of course. I didn't…." He sighed. "Aw, man."

As much as I wanted to seize this opportunity to discuss the dampness of Lance's pants, I realized I would have to wait.

I looked at my watch. "Six minutes 'til liftoff. Start 'er up, Trace. It's just over that hill."

The engine whirred to life but then whined with no result. I saw Trace press the accelerator with her right foot. Nothing.

Trace floored it and the engine screamed, just like it had during our mad dash toward the canyon less than a minute ago. But this time . . . nothing.

"Bad news, boys," said Trace, her voice firm again. "The impact broke our axel. Maybe both. We're not going anywhere. I hope you have your track boots on."

"It just keeps getting better, doesn't it?" I said, unbuckling my belt and leaping from the buggy onto the surface. My legs were like jelly after that incredible jump, and I had to catch myself with my hand to keep from falling face-first.

"Lance, move it! Last one to the command module is a rotten egg."

Or a dead duck.

★ ★ ★ ★ ★

Trace led us up the hill. At the top, we had a great view of the moon base below, down and to the right. I could see the building's rooftops, the dock area, and the huge transport vehicle filled with pleurinium. Straight ahead, just a little farther past the moon base, was the command module, a zip buggy parked nearby—the one that had carried Cat, Jonah, and Ziggy just a few minutes earlier.

A thin stream of white gas billowed from the rocket engine beneath the command module. The launch sequence had begun. We didn't have much time.

While Trace had led the way going up the hill, Lance quickly shot into the lead on our way down. His long legs carried him swiftly along with big, graceful hops.

He paused at the midpoint of the slope, turning to watch us as we picked our way along, with me second and Trace pulling up the rear. He pressed his radio Talk switch.

"Come on, guys. You can . . . you can do it." His voice was confident and encouraging. "Copy me, take long steps. Concentrate on taking long steps. Make each one count."

That was the perfect advice. Taking long, soaring steps, Trace and I moved much quicker and could almost keep up with Lance.

When we came off the hill and were on level ground again, I noticed that more cloudy white gas was billowing out of the command module. The prelaunch process was moving to the next stage.

The radio crackled, and Cat's voice filled my helmet. We were close enough for the local radio to reach us. "I see you guys," she said excitedly. "Hurry! We're at two minutes to launch. If we don't have the door closed when the timer reaches zero, I'll have to hit the Cancel button and stop the launch. HURRY!"

"Roger," was all I said. Neither Lance nor Trace responded. We were putting one hundred percent of our effort into running. I was breathing hard, and the inside of my mask was starting to steam up. I was so hot and sweaty, it felt like I was running on the sun instead of the moon.

"One minute ten," came Cat's voice. "One minute. Come on, guys," she pleaded, "the door has to be closed in one minute!"

We were now following the tire tracks from the zip buggies. The ground was packed hard in the tire tracks, so it was easier to get a good grip without slipping in the powdery moon dust. Lance was in first place, Trace right behind him run-bouncing in the left tire track, with me alongside in the right track.

"Fifty, forty-five."

Suddenly, Trace disappeared from the corner of my eye. It took me a couple steps to stop and turn my body around toward her. I saw with horror that she lay face-first on the ground, her hands flopping out beside her, her feet scrambling in the dust. She had tripped.

"*Forty!*"

Without thinking, I took four quick hops back, grabbed her hand, and pulled with all my might.

"*Thirty-five!*"

As I pulled her up, I felt myself tumbling back and stuck my foot behind me just in time to stop myself from falling.

"*Thirty!*"

There was no time to talk on the radio. No need to talk. We only had . . .

"*Twenty!*"

Ahead of us, we saw Lance's boots disappearing up through the hatch on the bottom of the command module. Trace and I continued to run, taking huge, desperate leaps.

Trace reached the ladder just before me, and as she climbed I put one hand on her belt and shoved her upward with all my might.

I paused, knowing I had to give her a few seconds to move out of the air lock and into the crew cabin before I could start up the ladder.

"Now, Mickey! Now!" came Trace's voice, sharp with fear.

"Don't stop!" I yelled. "I'll-make-it I'll-make-it I'll-make-it."

"*Six, five, four.*"

I don't think my feet touched the rungs of the ladder. I pushed off the ground and soared straight up into the air lock, grabbing the large metal handle and pulling the door closed behind me with one motion. My helmet cracked hard against the far wall of the cramped air lock.

"I'M IN! GO-GO-GO!" I yelled, as I was suddenly slammed backward sharply against the floor of the air lock and the hatch door.

At first I wondered why Trace had pushed me back so hard. But then I realized I hadn't been pushed back. The floor had been pushed up.

We had lifted off.

We had made it.

CHAPTER 22
Return

I lay there in the air lock, breathing heavily as I listened to the chatter of the radio.

Jonah's voice came through loud and clear. "Mission Control, we have power up and liftoff from the moon surface. We're coming home."

"Roger that, *Artemis 7.*" Dr. Yang's familiar voice squawked through the cabin's speakers. "Our instruments show a good liftoff. Um, we heard a lot of commotion and background noise before launch. Confirm your status, please. Do you have all four with you?"

"That's a negative, Mission Control, we're not four," replied Jonah.

"Roger that, *Artemis 7,*" came Yang's reply. "Who are you missing?"

"Nobody. We don't have four," repeated Jonah, looking back at the rest of us with a huge grin. "We have five. Mickey and Trace had the crazy idea of going to save Lance. They got him, and they all made it back.

As I said, we're coming home."

We could hear the sound of cheers and celebration erupting through the command center in the background, but Dr. Yang's voice remained calm, cool, and unflappable as ever. "Nice work, *Artemis 7*. Nice work. Over."

I imagined how Dr. Yang would react if he won the Megabucks lottery: calm, cool, and unflappable. The head of the lottery prize patrol would show up at the scientist's front door with cheerleaders holding balloons and a marching band and TV cameras. Yang would open the door, wearing his pajamas and holding a cup of coffee. The announcer would scream, "YOU'VE JUST WON ONE HUNDRED AND TWENTY MILLION DOLLARS!" Dr. Yang would slowly take another sip of coffee, blink, and say "Roger that, Megabucks lottery guy. One-two-zero million. Nice work. Over."

The next voice on the radio brought me back to reality. It wasn't Dr. Yang, but instead was the steely, sharp voice of Commander Riker. Director Riker, actually.

"*Artemis 7*, we will take a full report of your activities later. Nice . . . uh . . . nice job. Lance Marshall, are you there?"

"Yes, sir, here." Lance's shoulders slumped, and his voice lacked its usual cockiness.

"Lance," continued Riker, "did you get the sample?"

Lance's head sagged another few inches. He pressed the Talk switch. "Negative. I had it. I had the sample in my hand. But then it slipped out and I lost it. You see, we had to hurry back and—"

"That's enough, Lance," Director Riker cut in. "I heard you. You dropped it. You and I will talk when you get back. Mission Control out."

As I pulled myself up through the small door into the main cabin, I realized the air was filled with spinning brown, green, yellow, and red objects. It took me a few seconds to realize what they were. M&Ms. Hundreds of them. Maybe a thousand. Trace had emptied an entire bag into the weightless air of the crew cabin.

It was like confetti dropping on New Year's Eve or balloons at the end of the Super Bowl—or a swarm of fat, wingless, delicious bumble bees.

I started singing "We Are the Champions" at the top of my lungs. Trace, Cat, and Jonah joined in. Jonah was so far off-key, it was like he was singing a different song. But at that point, the tune didn't matter. It was all about the words. Without any question: We were the champions.

And then, out of nowhere, somebody joined in with an awesome, jamming imitation of a guitar solo. It was Lance, who had the first real, honest smile I had ever seen on his face. He then opened his mouth and grabbed about fifteen M&Ms in a single bite.

★ ★ ★ ★ ★

We zoomed through space at a nice speed of about five thousand miles per hour.

I did some quick math in my head. The Miami Dolphins football stadium was about 250 miles from my house in Orlando. Driving at fifty miles an hour, which was the fastest Sister Rinaldi was willing to drive, even on the highway, the one-way trip would take five hours. At five hundred miles an hour, you could drive the entire round trip in an hour . . . so that meant it would take only half an hour to get to Miami.

Five hundred miles an hour, thirty minutes to Miami. So at five thousand miles an hour, it would take three minutes to go from my house to the stadium.

Wow, three minutes. If only I could put this speed in a bottle and take it home with me. With that kind of speed, I could go to every game. I could even go to church in the morning, which Sister Rinaldi made sure we did every single Sunday, watch the pregame show, and make it to Miami during the commercial break right before kickoff!

Then I started thinking about the problems this would cause. With this kind of power, you'd step on the accelerator to back out of the driveway and end up two towns over before you realized it. If you saw a red light a mile away, you would have to stop in, um, um, how many seconds?

Ow. My head started to hurt. Any more math would require a calculator, so I abandoned the math daydream and stared out the window at the Earth, beautiful and blue and white and growing larger by the minute.

I was curled up in a back row seat between Jonah and Trace. I had traded seats for a while with Cat, who had moved up to the front row with Ziggy, buckled into her seat with her. She had wanted to spend some time looking out the front window, watching the European continent swing into view.

Every few minutes I looked out the front window at the Earth just to make sure it was still there. And every few minutes I tapped the object zipped into the right side pocket of my space suit.

"Pssst, Mick," whispered Jonah. He glanced over his shoulder at Lance, who had his eyes closed and his earphones on again. "Mick. You've never told me about The Glint. Did you actually see it? It was an alien spaceship, wasn't it?"

I pressed my finger to my lips in a *shhhh* gesture and tilted my eyes toward Lance. Then I shrugged my shoulders. What the heck, I thought. Lance was fast asleep, and Jonah looked like he might die if I didn't tell him the story. So I described it to him in every detail I could remember: the polished, shiny, perfectly smooth surface like a metal egg; the crumpled, torn section at the bottom, suggesting it had landed or crashed; the crack down the center revealing some sort of machinery inside.

"So," I concluded, "I guess it's a machine. Some sort of mining equipment, or satellite, or piece off a spaceship. But alien? I just don't know."

Jonah furrowed his brow, thinking hard. "And that 'sample' Riker asked Lance about? It wasn't a rock sample, was it? Riker ordered him to bring back something from The Glint, didn't he?"

I looked at Lance, who still hadn't moved. I nodded my head.

"I knew it!" whispered Jonah loudly. "I knew it. I knew it. So what was it? And why didn't he bring it back? He had it, but then, what, he lost it on the way back? Are you serious?"

I glanced up at Lance again. His mouth was open, and a little drool was spilling out of the corner, running down onto his coveralls as he slept.

"Okay," I said, leaning in, "Lance had something at first. He had pulled a piece off The Glint, or pulled something from the inside. His 'sample' was metal and was about, I don't know, maybe the size of a flat football. Or like a trumpet. Anyway, I didn't get a good look at it. There were other things to worry about at the time . . . like MAKING IT BACK ALIVE, remember? But I did see it. It was . . . I don't know . . . it's hard to describe. It had markings on it and bumps at one end. It was dusty, but under the dust it was shiny. A super-shiny silver color."

"Go on!" pleaded Jonah when I paused. "What else? What kind of markings? What kind of bumps on the end? What did it do? What else?"

"I don't know. Like I said, I didn't get a chance to really examine it. He had it in his lap when we were riding back in the zip buggy. And then, when we jumped over the canyon, it just slipped off his lap down into the darkness."

"Are you sure? You're sure it's gone?" Jonah said, disappointed and incredulous at the same time.

"Yes, I'm sure. Positive. I saw it slip off and fall into the million-foot-deep chasm we jumped over in the moon buggy. It's gone. That's it."

"That's *it?*" His whisper was curious but also angry. "That's IT? Oh, come on. He finds proof of alien life . . . finally, finally we have proof, after all this time . . . and then he goes and drops his alien souvenir into the first canyon he can find? And you come back empty handed? And all you can say is 'That's it'?"

He was breathing hard as he stared me down with a poisonous glare.

I couldn't help but crack a slight grin, which only seemed to make him madder. "Who said anything about empty-handed?" I asked.

The words hung there, like an M&M floating in the weightless air.

Jonah's eyes got huge. His mouth opened. He watched as I unzipped my hip pocket and pulled out, just for a peek, the small metal tube that had been hidden in my pocket since I left The Glint. Shiny. Silver. About the size of a flashlight, strange markings on one end and lines—like a little doorway compartment—on the other.

You see, I had grabbed a souvenir, too. Except I had enough sense to shove it in my pocket before we started the trip back in the zip buggy.

"WHAT THE—" yelled Jonah at the top of his lungs.

Everyone in the cabin jumped, including Lance, who lifted off his earphones and turned to face us.

"WHAT THE—" I repeated loudly, shoving the strange object back into my pocket. "What the . . . what's the . . . what's the first thing I'm going to do when we get back to Earth?" I asked quickly. "Great question, Jonah. You sure know how to ask the right question at the right time. What's the first thing I'm going to do? I think I have a trip to McDonalds in my future. Big Mac, fries, two chocolate shakes."

I looked up at Lance, who was eyeing me suspiciously. I kept my hand on my hip, hiding the strange, unidentified souvenir in my pocket.

"How about you, Lance?" I said with all the innocent

curiosity I could muster. "What's your first stop when you get home?"

"I dunno," said Lance, slumping back into his seat and facing forward. "Riker's gonna kill me. And my dad will probably ground me for a few years for disobeying orders. I might get to go to McDonalds again when I'm a senior in high school." He sighed heavily.

I almost felt sorry for him.

Almost.

✪ ✪ ✪ ✪ ✪

Lance was right about being grounded. His punishment started only a few hours later. When Dr. Yang announced it was time to begin our reentry procedure, he ordered Jonah and me up to the front row, with me in the flight commander's chair. Lance protested at first but then lurched sulkily to the back row.

Flight Commander Price, steering the *Artemis 7* through the Earth's outer atmosphere. Flight Commander Price, bringing the crew back home.

Things just keep getting better, I thought to myself.

"Price, I'll walk you through a few simple steps," Dr. Yang said. "There's not much for you to do."

Phew, I thought.

"Program 64 is the computer program that controls your reentry," Dr. Yang continued. "Once you start Program 64, the computer will do the rest. It knows when to fire the booster rockets and how much to fire them. It knows the correct direction and angle for the command module's reentry to put it on track for a perfect landing in the Pacific Ocean. You're familiar with this procedure. You practiced it in the simulation center before your mission."

I heard panting and barking from the back row. "Oh great, Captain Chihuahua strikes again," said Lance. "This time, make it the Sahara Desert for variety."

Boy, that guy was annoying. But he did have a point.

I clicked the talk switch. "Um, Mission Control, Program 64 and I didn't get along too well the first time we met. Remember? Can you say something to boost our confidence here?"

"The simulator is always harder than real life," came Dr. Yang's steady voice. "We threw you a few curveballs in the simulator. No curveballs this time. This is a baby pitch, right over home plate. And we fixed all the glitches, no crashes this time. You're on a perfect flight path. Program 64 will make a few adjustments, will handle your reentry, and will deploy your parachutes—all at exactly the right time. And we'll be watching your progress every step of the way."

"Cat," I called to the back row, "how confident are you about Program 64?"

"Not very. I'd feel better if I'd designed it," she said.

Cat lacked self-confidence about most things. But when it came to computers, she could take on the world.

"You know, Cat," I said, "I could use a little less honesty right now. Can you just tell me the thing's going to work?"

"Gonna work great, Mickey," she said with completely fake enthusiasm. "But next time, I'll write the program."

I heard an immediate hoot from Trace. "Next time? Mickey, I told you: if you get us back to Earth, it's all bicycles for me, all the time. For the rest of my life. I'm serious. Anything with an engine or a rocket . . . forget about it!"

Following a string of instructions, I reported back information on a series of dials and displays. Every time I called out a number, I got back a "Check" or "Copy that," which meant they agreed with me and everything was on track.

And then, on Dr. Yang's command and feeling the eyes of my fellow astronauts staring intently at me, I hit a green button marked "Go" on the right side of the main computer screen. Program 64 was now underway. I sat back for the ride.

"*Artemis 7*, we're 'go' for final reentry," came the words from Earth. "In T minus 60 seconds, LSR booster will fire for 17.5 seconds. Rotation adjustment into position 1-4-4-2-9 at angle 7.22 degrees. Service module will detach, pushing the command module into the outer atmosphere."

"Mick, did you follow all that?" asked Trace. "Could you please repeat the part after he said *Artemis 7*?" I couldn't see her face, but I could tell she was smiling.

"Trace," I said, "this is not the right time to tease the flight commander. Remember, I have the power to make you walk the plank."

"Aye, aye, Captain," came her immediate reply from the back row. "But, um, can we get a translation from Einstein here? What's happening now?" I could always count on Trace to ask the question I wanted to ask.

Jonah was happy to explain. "A translation for those of you who didn't pay the slightest bit of attention to Chapter 77B in the red binder they gave us when we arrived at Kennedy: The main thrusters will fire and put us into the desired position. Then the service module—the back half of our spacecraft—will detach, leaving just this little command module to fall through the atmosphere back to Earth. Oh, and, now a translation for Trace: Big rocket go boom, command module fall down."

A comment like that would have cost Lance two of his front teeth. But Jonah knew he could joke with Trace. A little.

"Watch it, Einstein, you can't run from me in here," Trace threatened without any actual malice.

I don't think Jonah was listening, though. I heard him muttering, "Coming . . . right . . . about . . ."

A sharp thrust pushed us forward as the main booster rockets kicked into overdrive.

"Now!" cried Jonah.

As the booster fired, I watched as the small sliver of Earth visible through the front window disappeared. The rockets had turned us so that the front window was pointed straight out into space. We were now backing our way home.

Then there was a loud boom and jolt that must have been the service module detaching. The big piece of our spacecraft containing our booster rockets, the air lock, and other equipment was now officially a piece of space junk.

"Service module has detached," said Jonah. "It's just us in this little command module now. All lights on the main panel are green. We're now like a brick, falling down into the exosphere toward home sweet home."

"*Artemis 7*, you should feel some light chop right now," came the warning through the radio.

Right on cue, our command module began to shake lightly as we entered the Earth's farthest outer atmosphere. Boy, this was happening fast. It was hard to believe we'd be floating in the Pacific Ocean in about fifteen minutes.

The Pacific Ocean.

I had lived near the Atlantic Ocean my entire life but had never seen the Pacific. I wondered if it would look the same.

"Mission Control, copy that," I said. "We're feeling light chop." Instinctively, I checked my seatbelt.

"*Artemis 7*, in thirty seconds you will enter the second layer of atmosphere, and you will lose radio contact for about four minutes."

"Which means some serious rock-and-roll," said Jonah from the copilot's seat. "Hang on to your underpants."

As I scanned the main display panel one more time, I noticed something change in the top right corner, followed by a rapid beeping.

"Mission Control, I have a flashing red light on the upper right. It reads 'Pitch Alert.'"

Dr. Yang's reply came right away. "Mickey, read me the numbers to the left of that light."

"Radio loss in ten seconds," said Jonah from my right.

"Eight-two-two, it says eight-two-two," I said.

"Eight-two-two? Should be seven-two-two," said Yang, a disturbing sense of urgency in his voice. The cabin had started to shake harder now, rattling my teeth along with it. The warning beep, which had been sharp and clear just a few seconds ago, was now almost drowned out by the rattling of every piece of metal inside the command module.

"Too steep! Too steep!" said another voice on the loudspeaker.

That was the last thing we heard from Mission Control.

The light chops had turned into full-blown thumps, like driving over a speed bump at seventy-five miles an hour. Backward.

The rattling sound in the cabin was now drowned out by a roaring noise, louder than the sound of the rocket at blastoff. A red glow appeared in the window ahead of me as we hurtled along at two thousand miles per hour. Flames. There were red, orange, yellow, and white flames shooting back from our module as we streaked down like a comet. It seemed for a moment that we were actually hurtling backward into the sun instead of returning to Earth.

With nothing left to do but ride it out, my mind raced. Pitch alert? Too steep? What did that mean? Hadn't the booster rockets set our course at the perfect angle? Too steep meant . . . what did it mean? Too steep meant too hot. Too hot meant we could flare out. Burst into flames like a marshmallow at a campfire. Oh, great.

And then I felt the heat. It was definitely getting hot inside the command module. I felt like I was being slow-roasted in my space suit. Through the bone-crunching shaking, I could see that the window in front of me had completely fogged up. I couldn't see the flames anymore but could still see the bright glow of the raw, angry heat.

And through all this I could still see the flashing red light: Pitch Alert.

I squeezed my eyes shut, blocking out the vision of searing heat through our front window and the view of the warning light alerting us to some uncertain danger. Up until that point in my life, I had loved roller coasters. The scarier the better. At that point, I vowed never to ride one again.

✪ ✪ ✪ ✪ ✪

And then, almost as quickly as it started, the worst of it was over. It was still a little choppy, but the command module was only skipping and wobbling instead of shaking insanely. And unlike the completely weightless sensation of outer space, I now had the stomach-tickling feeling we were falling. Falling hard and falling fast.

"Um, is anyone else alive?" Jonah called out. "Because I'm not completely sure if I am."

"That was *so* not fun," answered Trace. "Cat, seriously, tell me you didn't throw up."

The radio crackled.

"… respond . . . *Artemis 7*, please respond . . . *Artemis 7*, please respond." Yang's voice repeated over and over again. My hand jumped up to the Talk switch.

"Mission Control, *Artemis 7* here. Please tell us we're through the worst of it? Over."

We heard cheering and applause in the background as Yang replied, "Good to hear you, *Artemis 7*. We knew you'd make it. Yes, reentry is over. You only need to go through that part once. But listen carefully: There was a problem with Program 64. We don't know why, but you're off course, and you won't be landing at the Pacific Ocean landing site. We show you coming down much farther east. Much."

I glanced over at Jonah. He mouthed, "*Much?*"

"Um, Mission Control," I replied, "can you explain 'much'? Where exactly are we coming down?"

My heart sank when the answer didn't come immediately. They must have been debating what to tell us. I slapped the Talk switch again. "Hey, this little tidbit of information is pretty important to the five of us right now. Where are we coming down? Tell me we're hitting water."

It was Riker's voice that responded. Two words. "Dayton. Ohio."

CHAPTER 23
Destination Dayton

Now, I don't have anything against Dayton. Jimmy Jankowitz, who played shortstop on our baseball team the last season, had been adopted by a family in Dayton, so he moved out of our house. Jimmy and I had written a couple postcards back and forth, and he invited me to come visit sometime.

But crash-landing like a meteor in his back yard was *not* how I wanted to arrive.

I remembered my disastrous experience in the flight simulator. How could this be happening again?

"Mission Control, what do I do? How do I change course? What's the emergency plan? I've got all these controls, I've got a million buttons. There's got to be something I can do."

Silence. The only answer came from Jonah. "Mick, we don't have any booster rockets. Those were on the service module. We have no wings. We're falling like a rock. You can't steer a rock. We've played all our cards."

"The computer will deploy parachutes in sixty seconds," came Yang's flat, steady voice.

"Mission Control," I repeated. I must have been yelling. How can you *not* yell in a situation like that? "I've got to try something. What buttons should I hit? What should I do?"

"*Do nothing!*" Director Riker barked the reply back to me. "*Do absolutely nothing.* Program 64 is in control. You have to let it do its job and get you down to the ground. Prepare for ELCI. Emergency Land Crash Impact."

"So, what happens next?"

"The computer is in control," Riker's cold voice continued. "It will deploy your three parachutes. They will slow your fall. You will impact the ground at about forty miles per hour. You would rather land in water, but it *is* possible to survive an emergency land crash. After impact, if anybody is able to move, try to open the escape hatch. Don't bother trying to put out the fire. If you can, just try to save yourself. Crawl as far away as you can to escape the explosion. Ambulances will arrive within thirty minutes."

"Fire! Explosions? Great plan, Mission Control!" I yelled, trying to pump as much sarcasm into the radio transmission as possible, as though that would save us. "Way to go. You guys are awesome!"

"Price, do your crew a favor," barked Riker. "Don't do anything stupid. No other options."

"Parachutes in ten seconds," said Dr. Yang.

"Mick," came Trace's voice. "It's not your fault."

No other options? Oh yeah? Jonah was wrong, I

hadn't played all my cards. I still had one left. And I decided to play it.

Dr. Yang's calm voice came over the speaker. "Computer will deploy parachutes in four . . . three . . . two . . . ."

I reached up and slapped the large, circular orange button on the top-left side of the control panel. The one marked "Override."

I had just turned off Program 64.

"Parachutes have deployed," said Yang.

But the falling sensation continued, and the small command module kept whistling down toward land.

"Think again, Mission Control," I said to my crewmates without hitting the Talk switch.

"Um, Mick?" said Trace casually from the back. "I respect your protest here. But we kind of need those parachutes. Know what I mean?"

Lance wasn't quite as casual. "YOU TOTAL IDIOT!" he screamed. "YOU'VE RUINED EVERYTHING! We're not going to hit the ground at forty miles per hour. Without those parachutes, we're going to hit the ground at four hundred miles per hour!"

There was a sudden commotion from the back row. I heard the clicks of a seatbelt unbuckling and saw Lance start to climb toward the front row, a determined look on his face. "Mickey, move over. I'm taking command," Lance threatened as he advanced.

Quick as a ninja, Trace was on him. What she did next confirmed something I had thought in the back of my mind since the first time I met her: Never get into a fight with Trace Daniels.

With one hand, she grabbed Lance's jumpsuit and pulled him sharply backward. With her other hand, she put his head into a crazy wrestling move. And with still another hand—wait, how many hands did this girl have?—she yanked hard on his ear, causing him to yelp sharply. Meanwhile, with another crazy wrestling move, she looped her leg around his waist and slammed his head into the wall with a dull thud. Oh, I wish I had this on video.

Anyway, in about two seconds, Lance was back in his seat, facedown, whining, "Okay let go let go let go let go quit it! OW!"

Trace eased herself back into her seat. "Flight Commander Price, the mutiny has been defeated. Now, can you please tell us what the heck you're doing?"

Still amazed by her lightning quick ninja moves, all I could say was, "I'm playing my card."

"*Artemis 7*, your parachutes have not deployed," said Dr. Yang. "You're at 13,000 feet and falling. No problem. Push the manual parachute button. Top panel, right side, row two—it's marked 'PC-Master'—can't miss it. Push that button." His voice was calm as always. But insistent.

"You're doing what?" asked Trace, ignoring Yang.

"He's playing his last card," answered Jonah. He was gazing at me with a look of . . . what was that? I thought I saw a glimmer of understanding in his eyes. At least it wasn't a look of panic or disbelief, which I had expected to see.

"Let me explain this way," continued Jonah. "Let's say you have a long and complicated math problem.

You have all these numbers being added and subtracted and multiplied and divided. And the one thing you know is, you don't like the answer. You want a different answer. What do you do?"

"What do you do? You push the stupid parachute button, that's what you do!" squeaked Lance, defensively putting his hands up in case Trace didn't like his answer.

"Twelve thousand feet. You're falling fast. Deploy the parachute," said Dr. Yang.

"You want a different answer, what do you do?" repeated Jonah with a smile. "You change one of the numbers in the math problem, and you get a different answer. That's what you do."

"Ahhh," said Cat, "I get it. Mick, I'll use the term you taught me yesterday. This is a Hail Mary, right?"

"Guys," interrupted Trace, "you're talking about cards and math and football plays. Stop playing word games and explain the plan, okay? You do understand that we'll hit the ground in about a minute and turn into a big metal Frisbee pancake, don't you?"

"Roger that, Trace," I jumped in. "I'm waiting to pull the parachute at the last possible second. The computer projected that we would land in Dayton if we pulled the parachute at fifteen thousand feet. If we pull it later, then we'll land somewhere else. Right, Jonah?"

I looked at Jonah for confirmation, because honestly, I really had no idea if this would actually work.

"Mickey's right," said Jonah. "The computer calculated that we would land in Dayton based on how far the command module would float with the parachute, pushed by the wind. If we don't pull the chute until much later, we'll fall straight down for longer and we'll drift less. Meaning, we'll end up . . . well . . . we'll end up somewhere else."

"But where?" wailed Lance. "How do you know where?"

"I don't," I replied. "But it can't get any worse than Dayton. No offense to Dayton. And it just might get better. We might get lucky. Jonah—Einstein—just tell me one thing: When do I push the button?"

As we continued to plummet toward land, Jonah frantically scribbled numbers on a piece of paper. He had covered the front side of the page with numbers, so he flipped it over and started making more calculations on the back.

"Um, Jonah, we're kind of in a hurry here. Just give me your best guess. More or less. We're at ten thousand feet right now. When do I push the button? When we're at eight thousand feet? Three thousand feet?"

"*Artemis 7*," Director Riker's voice cut through the cabin like a knife. "You have disobeyed a direct order. You're below ten thousand feet. Deploy parachutes NOW! Respond NOW!"

"Mission Control, thanks for your suggestion," I said. "We're doing a little math problem up here and having a nice debate about wind speed. Meanwhile, can someone down there please tell us what's the last possible moment we can deploy our parachutes and still live?"

"DEPLOY NOW!" screamed Riker. "That's an order, you pip-squeak!"

"Forty-nine hundred feet," said Jonah. "That's my final answer. Pull it at 4,900 feet, and the three parachutes will have still be able to do their job and slow us down to about forty miles per hour. Any later, they won't have time to slow us down, and we'll be going faster when we smack into the ground, and that won't be good."

"Mission Control," I repeated, "the last possible moment we can deploy our parachutes?"

This time it wasn't Riker's voice on the radio, it was Dr. Yang. "*Artemis 7*, our engineers tell us five thousand feet. Don't go below that. Pull at five thousand."

"Eh," Jonah shrugged, glancing down at his complicated math work. "Close enough. They're being a little too cautious, but you'd expect that from grownups. Plus, they didn't have as much time to do the math as I did. Pull it at 4,900 feet."

The altitude dial was spinning like a clock racing backward. We were at six thousand feet. Through the front window, the bright blue sky had given way to some light clouds. I could almost feel the Earth looming behind us, like a big bully lurking over my shoulder, ready to wham me with something heavy.

"Mick, how about hitting that parachute button now?" suggested Cat. "To be safe. Not that we don't trust you, Jonah."

The numbers flew by: 5,500 feet from the ground and getting closer.

I reached up and placed my finger on the button.

"*Artemis 7*, push the dang button," snapped Yang. "YOU'RE GIVING ME A HEART ATTACK!"

Wow, we'd finally caused Mr. Cool Cucumber to crack!

The dial hit 5,000 and continued to race downward.

"All right, Mick," said Jonah. "I'd appreciate some parachute right about . . . now!"

I slammed the button marked "PC-Master" with all my might. There was an agonizing delay, which probably lasted only about one second. Then, with a tremendous lurch, we were all pressed down and backward into our seats as the parachutes engaged.

I could see the parachutes out the front window, a series of strong cords reaching up toward two enormous red-and-white parachutes that spread out and filled with air. They were glorious, straining hard to slow our command module and save our lives.

"Mission Control, parachutes have deployed," I reported. "Repeat, parachutes have deployed."

"Thank you for that, *Artemis 7*," said Dr. Yang. "You saved me from a heart attack. Barely. Prepare for impact in two minutes. We're tracking you on radar, recalculating your crash site. I mean landing site."

I breathed a heavy sigh. I had played the last card in a desperate attempt to change our landing location and find water—anything was better than central Ohio, smack in the middle of the continent. I watched as the two parachutes billowed in the air above us, several stray strings flapping on one side.

Stray strings.

Two parachutes.

"Um, Jonah. How many parachutes are we supposed to have?" I asked nervously.

"Yeah, you noticed?" he replied from the seat next to me. "The *Artemis'* master parachute array is designed to have three parachutes for maximum drag. It looks like parachute number three had different plans today."

"And what does that mean?" asked Trace from the back.

Jonah took a look at the complicated math equations on the paper in front of him and then crumpled the paper with his right hand. "It means you can throw my math out the window. Two parachutes won't slow us down as much as three parachutes."

"Which means prepare for impact," I said. "Really hard impact. Sorry guys."

"SORRY GUYS?" Lance shouted. "That's all you've got? Sorry guys! Let's get that on your tombstone: 'Here lies lousy Astronaut Mickey Price, 1964-1977. Famous last words: Sorry Guys.' I mean, really, what kind of . . ."

His voice trailed off at the sound of Trace cracking her knuckles.

"We might only have a minute left to live," said Trace threateningly. "But I can't think of a better way to spend it. . . ."

"Come on, guys, focus," I said. "You remember what Riker said. On impact, head for the escape hatch. First one there, try to open it. Second person, grab a fire extinguisher. We have three on board. After that, we try to get everyone out of here. Everyone. Nobody gets left behind."

The altitude dial was spinning a bit slower now, but still too quickly for comfort. We were below one thousand feet. But because we were heading backward and the only window was at the top, we still couldn't see where we were headed.

I was about to continue with my speech about "nobody gets left behind" when I was cut off.

"*Artemis 7*, listen closely. Impact in less than a minute. With two parachutes, your impact speed will be about fifty miles an hour. We are tracking your position on radar and have recalculated your landing spot. We checked it and checked it again. And we can't believe it. Your impact location is near Chicago, about one mile from downtown."

"Sweet!" said Jonah. "Maybe I can walk home."

I held my breath. I crossed my fingers. "Exactly where . . . near Chicago?" I asked. "Any chance—?"

"Yes, Mickey," said Dr. Yang. "You gambled and you hit the jackpot. Impact location: Lake Michigan."

CHAPTER 24
The Lucky Dollar

I have to admit, even after going to the moon and back, riding in an army helicopter over Chicago was even cooler. The police speedboat that picked us up from the broken command module headed south on Lake Michigan, away from Chicago, toward an industrial area with grimy docks and big, Great Lakes barges being loaded and unloaded.

As we pulled into a particularly dirty, empty dock, I saw a huge green helicopter streaking along the tops of the warehouse buildings, coming straight at us. It slowed when it reached our dock and touched down at exactly the same time as our boat arrived. The day was already windy, but the blast of air from the rotors made it almost impossible to stand upright.

The pilot didn't even turn off the engine, and we were rushed on board up a small ladder and into the back. Ziggy clung tight to Cat and buried his furry little head into her shoulder. I think the reentry, splashdown, boat ride, and now being rushed into this screaming beast of a helicopter was a bit much for a monkey—even a highly trained veteran of the space program like Ziggy.

Less than one minute after the boat pulled up to the dock, we were lifting off again into the sky.

There were several doctors wearing white coats, who were waiting for us in the helicopter. As soon as we lifted off, they started poking and prodding us, taking our temperature and pulse. They also peppered us with questions, but none of us felt much like answering, so we each just gave the thumbs-up sign and smiled. That seemed to do the trick.

Aside from feeling absolutely exhausted and wobbly-legged, none of us were hurt. Amazingly. The impact of hitting the water was bone jarring but surely not as bad as slamming into solid ground. The command module hadn't fared so well, though. It had started sinking almost as soon as we landed in the water. If the police boat hadn't arrived in those few seconds, we would have had a long swim. In space gear. Not a pleasant thought.

Jonah pointed out landmarks as the chopper raced back up the coastline toward Chicago. We saw the enormous Sears Tower in the distance, two giant radio antennae reaching up to the heavens.

"And look over there! Soldier's Field! Look, home of the Bears!" Jonah shouted into my ear. We passed directly over the stadium, then banked hard to the left. I could see cars backed up on the expressway heading into the city and even a few joggers in a park, looking at us with upturned faces. I realized I had no idea what time it was.

An arm came shooting over my shoulder from the left. It was Trace, giving me a big hug, leaning her face next to mine as we looked out the window at the city streaking past beneath us. Our breath steamed up the inside of the small, round window.

"Did that really just happen, Mick?" she asked, speaking quietly into my right ear.

"You better believe it," I said. "We just saved the moon. You, me, Jonah, Cat, and Ziggy." I smiled. "Oh yeah, I seem to remember some guy named Lance kicking around, too. We saved the moon. And lived to tell the tale."

✪ ✪ ✪ ✪ ✪

Director Marshall called each of us over, one at a time, to sit with him in the back row of the 10-seat Lear jet that was carrying us back to Florida. Back to Florida, where our families were gathering. Or for me, where the adventure would end, and I would return to the Orlando Home for Boys.

Not that there was anything wrong with that. At that moment, there was nowhere else I wanted to be. And to be honest, even though we were under strict instructions not to tell anybody about our secret mission, I didn't even feel like telling my friends back home, anyway. Except for Taco, who would make me tell him stories about the trip over and over again until my voice was hoarse.

I just wanted a heaping plate of normal . . . and my own bed.

But that would have to wait. At that moment, I was sitting in the back of the airplane next to Director Marshall, who had apparently reclaimed his job from Riker as soon as the command module touched down. He paused and looked at me expectantly.

I paused, too, hesitating with that uncertain feeling you get when you're deciding whether to jump into a cold pool. In the end, I knew I was going to jump. I just had to ask the question that had been haunting me for the past two weeks.

"Director Marshall," I said.

"Please," he drawled in his heavy Arkansas accent, leaning across the narrow airplane aisle toward me, "call me Bob."

"Um, with all due respect, I think I need to keep calling you Director Marshall if that's all right with you."

The big man nodded and raised his eyebrows. "Roger that. You were saying?"

"I need to know something," I said. "Why did you pick me? Out of everyone at the camp and out of every kid in the country, why me? I mean, I know why you picked the others: their special talents. And Lance. I mean, that's an obvious one. He's big, he's strong, he's your *son*—"

"Hold on right there, Mickey," said Marshall. He peered forward down the aisle, like he was making sure nobody else was listening. He lowered his voice. "I know it might look like I was playing favorites, but let me explain why I picked Lance." He sighed. "You don't understand how difficult it was to send you kids on such a dangerous mission. It was the hardest thing I've ever done, asking parents for permission to send their sons and daughters up into space. I sent Lance because . . . well . . . because I couldn't ask other parents to do something I wasn't willing to do myself. If I wasn't willing to send my own boy up to the moon and make sure he got back okay, how could I ask them to?"

As soon as he said that, it made sense. Perfect sense. Not just his decision to send Lance, but his decision to send me.

"Ohhhhhh," I said slowly, "that's why. I get it now. You sent me because I don't have any parents. That made it easy for you. You just picked me because you didn't have to convince a mom or a dad, or both. This was a dangerous mission, and you sent me because you knew nobody would miss me."

I saw a little smile at the corner of Marshall's mouth. "Mickey," he said, "you think you've got it all figured out, don't you?"

That must be it, then. He was about to confirm what I had suspected. But then, the director's smile grew broader before he pressed on.

"Mickey, I'm happy to say that you're totally wrong about that. True, getting permission from the parents before the trip was not easy. But if you think it's hard to get a green light from parents, you should try dealing with the Florida Department of Children's Services. And Sister Rinaldi. I almost gave up trying to get their approval. But as you might have figured, I'm a very stubborn man. And in the end, I got what I wanted."

He regarded me with his piercing slate-gray eyes. "No, you're wrong about why I picked you. If you really want to know, it's because I knew you kids would face some unexpected challenges up there. And I knew that you, Mickey—out of everyone up there—would be able to face those unexpected challenges and defeat them one by one. You—out of all those kids—wouldn't expect the adults down at Mission Control to have all the answers. You would figure things out for yourself. That's how it's been your whole life.

"Do you know how I know that?"

I shrugged.

"Because you remind me of myself forty years ago. My parents both died when I was a baby, and I was raised by . . . well . . . I don't know how many people in I don't know how many homes. I lived in an orphanage for a while, not unlike your Home over in Orlando. So when we were looking for a team of kids to send up to the moon, I knew just where to go. I went looking for someone just like me."

He paused to catch my reaction.

After a while I looked up. "But why me? Out of all the options in Florida, out of all the orphanages in the United States, why did you pick the Orlando Home for Boys? How did you pick me?"

"Well, that one's easy," said the director. "Your boys' home was the closest one to Kennedy Space Center, and we didn't have much time. As I've always said," he flipped a silver dollar coin in his hand, "sometimes in this business you've got to rely on luck. I took a chance on you. And I guess I got lucky."

"Wait a minute," I cut in. I had caught the great Director Marshall bending the truth. "On the night before launch, you said you didn't believe in luck. You said something like 'Luck is what saves you when you fail,' and 'Never rely on luck.' You said—"

Director Marshall winked and shook his head. "That was just a pep talk. I was trying to give y'all a little confidence. I didn't want y'all to know I had my fingers crossed, and my toes, too. I even carried this lucky silver dollar for seven straight days while you were up there.

"Here. I feel like I've used up all the luck in this one. Let's see how far it takes you." With that, he flipped the silver dollar into the air, and it sailed end over end across the center aisle of the airplane. My hand shot out before I could think, and I caught the heavy silver coin perfectly in midflight.

As I walked up the aisle toward my seat, I slipped the coin into my hip pocket. I smiled as I heard it clink against the small, heavy metal object I had been carrying in my pocket for the last three days. The one I had lifted from the fine, white, powdery surface of the moon. So now I had two souvenirs. One could buy me a large sundae at the Dairy Queen, though I decided I would never spend it. The other . . . well . . . I'd just have to wait and see.

CHAPTER 25
Sunrise

The faint but definite glow of morning spread across the waters of the still, glassy lake and crept into the campsite. Tom let out an emphatic moan as he stretched the night out of his joints. His sister stared disbelievingly at the dim light in the eastern sky, amazed that, yes indeed, her dad's story had lasted from bedtime all the way until dawn.

"So," said Tom, finally daring to inject his voice into the pause that was growing longer and longer. "Is that it? The end?"

"Well," said Dad, "I'm not sure I can go on." He faked a faint, bad-cold voice and rubbed a hand over his throat. Come to think of it, the twins realized that his voice had been getting a bit scratchy after talking for about eight hours straight.

"But anyway," Dad continued, "it does seem like an appropriate place to stop. We all got back safely. Mission accomplished."

Tom sat up and faced him. "Ooooo-kaaaaay," he said slowly. "So now, the moment of truth. The tire swing incident, the men with sunglasses, the space camp, the mystery metal, the trip to the moon. After all that, are you *still* telling us this was a true story?"

"Does it need to be true to be a good story?" asked Dad. "The old Greek myths are perhaps the greatest stories of all times. They have super-powered gods living on a magical mountaintop, half-human monster-creatures, fantastic battles, flying shoes, and all sorts of special effects. Or a gripping tale of wizards, dragons, flying broomsticks, and a school of magic? All of these, great stories, but do you need them to be true?"

"No, I suppose not," said Tom. "A story can be a total fib and still be enjoyable. But this one," he paused, "this one would be extra interesting if it was true, you know what I mean? With you, supposedly, as the real-life hero?" He stared at his dad with eyebrows raised. "Am I right?"

"Maybe," Dad shrugged. "What do you say, Tess? Truth or fib?"

Tess stared at him intently. "Dad, look at me right in the eye and tell me it's true."

"True, every word," said Dad without hesitation.

"Then, yes," Tess said with a glorious, instantaneous smile. "I've got a few questions for you, mister, but I believe you."

"And Tom?" asked Dad. "You know what, I won't make you vote. Let's just call it a 'good story,' and I can start up the campfire again and make us all some pancakes."

Tom frowned.

"Come on, Tom," said Tess. "Pancakes." She looked pleadingly at her brother.

"Okay, on the one hand, we have your statement that your story is true." Tom was talking deliberately, like a lawyer on TV. He extended his hands out in front of him like a set of scales, and tipped one hand down sharply. "And on the *other* hand, we have your history of telling wildly untrue stories. Like that one about the girl who jumped out of an airplane without a parachute and landed safely on a cactus. Well, not exactly safely, but she supposedly landed on the cactus and lived to play a starring role in more of your made-up stories."

Tom was on a roll.

"And on this same other hand," he tipped the low hand still lower, "we have the details of your story. Your tall tale. A bunch of kids who were practically kidnapped by NASA, prepared for a space mission that adults could not take due to some mystery metal we've never heard of, launched up into space, saved the moon from nuclear destruction, and found an alien device."

He paused and pointed at his dad. "Which, by the way, you haven't fully explained."

Dad shrugged and started to say "That's another story—" but Tom kept right on with his speech.

"And on top of all that, the hero overcomes a fatal error in the navigation system and manages to find . . . oh, miracle of miracles . . . he manages to find Lake Michigan by complete luck, rather than crashing and burning in a shopping mall parking lot outside Dayton. And all of this," he concluded grandly, "all of this, even landing a spaceship right in the middle of Chicago, without *anybody* finding out about it. No fame or fortune for the hero. No career as an astronaut. No parade or huge welcome home. The best-kept secret ever. No media coverage. No newspaper articles. Nothing."

The last part was said emphatically. Oh, he had his dad on the ropes.

"Well, Tom," said Dad, "if you describe it *that* way, I guess it sounds pretty incredible."

And that's when Tess saw the envelope.

She had actually noticed it in the faint firelight at some point earlier in the night. A regular white envelope, slightly worn and crumpled at the corners, sitting in the pine straw next to her dad. It hadn't seemed important at the time. But now . . .

"Dad?" asked Tess, pointing at the envelope. "What's that?"

"Oh, this? Hmmm. Yes, good point. We have this envelope here. Now, I'm trying to remember what you said, Tom. 'No media coverage. No newspaper articles.' Something like that?"

The words hung there in the air.

"Well," Tom finally answered, "I think I said it as kind of a question. Didn't I? Let me rephrase it. No media coverage? No newspaper articles?"

Dad leaned forward and prodded the smoldering embers with a long stick. The faint glow of dawn had now grown brighter, and the clearing around the campfire was starting to come into focus. Looking straight up, he stared at the moon, full and beautifully round, floating majestically in the sky far above the tall pines surrounding the campsite.

He scooped up the envelope and handed it to Tess.

"I'll see if I can figure out Mom's recipe for pancakes. Meanwhile, you go ahead and read what's in the envelope."

The Envelope

THE NEW YORK TIMES

Another NASA Success: *Artemis* Returns Safely

Honolulu Naval Station, November 2, 1977

At 7:15 A.M. Eastern Time Tuesday, the command capsule for NASA's *Artemis 7* mission splashed down in the Pacific Ocean 150 miles southeast of Honolulu. The U.S. Navy vessel *Durham* was nearby to collect the five-member crew.

"I cannot comment on the details of the mission other than to say it was a complete success and Commander Riker and his crew all returned safely," said NASA spokeswoman Amanda Collins.

The mission was shrouded in secrecy from the beginning, starting with its surprise launch on October 25th. The reason for the mission was not made public. One source inside NASA, who asked not to be named, told reporters that the crew was sent to the moon to repair a broken refrigerator in the moon base kitchen.

Reporters were not allowed to take their usual place on-board the *Durham* to watch the splashdown. No photos of the landing are available. NASA explained that the astronauts had endured a particularly difficult reentry procedure and were immediately hospitalized. The only member of the crew to speak publicly was Cmdr. Riker, a veteran astronaut who talked to reporters by telephone.

"The other members of my crew are extremely tired and asked me to speak on their behalf," said Cmdr. Riker. "They're tired, but I feel great, like I could go to the moon again tomorrow. Seriously. If NASA approves it, I'll go tomorrow."

NASA has not yet announced the date of the next Artemis mission.

The Weekly Tattler

NASA Space Craft Crash-Lands in Lake Michigan

By Lacy McKenzie   Chicago, November 2, 1977

An unidentified flying object plunged into Lake Michigan less than a mile from Chicago early yesterday morning, as witnessed by several citizens. A police boat was seen heading out to the landing spot shortly after the strange craft hit the surface of the lake.

Eyewitnesses described seeing a large object pulling red and white parachutes falling through the sky into the lake.

"The object was a shiny gold color, definitely metal. It was flat on the bottom and then narrower at the top, with windows on the side," said Ms. McKenzie, the beautiful, intelligent and reliable senior reporter for *The Weekly Tattler* magazine, who happened to be taking her dog for an early morning walk in Lakeshore Park.

Another eyewitness, Mr. Egbert Winzel, offered an identical description. "It looked exactly like an Artemis command module," reported Mr. Winzel. "It had those huge red-and-white parachutes. Except all those pictures in the papers show three parachutes. Strange, because this one had only two."

At the time this article was printed, no photographs of the spectacular event were available. Anyone who witnessed this strange sight, and especially anyone with a photograph, is urged to contact this magazine immediately.

An eyewitnesses reported one more odd twist. Using binoculars belonging to Mr. Winzel, the eyewitness spotted a police boat removing what appeared to be five very short people, quite possibly CHIL-DREN, from the strange craft. The five seemed to be wearing matching astronaut suits.

And, even more odd, one of the female astronauts was seen carrying what appeared to be a small baby, also wearing an astronaut suit.

Officials at NASA refused to confirm that this was the *Artemis 7* spacecraft. Instead, they claimed that the command module had landed, at approximately the same time, in the Pacific Ocean. NASA's claim cannot be confirmed because reporters were not allowed anywhere near the recovery area and were not allowed to photograph or interview the astronauts when they returned.

The Weekly Tattler contacted NASA for a comment about whether the *Artemis 7* module had actually landed in Lake Michigan. NASA spokeswoman Amanda Collins said, "Oh my gosh, how did you find out . . . I mean . . . how did you find out my telephone number?"

Pressed for a formal response, Ms. Collins said, "Look, the *Artemis 7* mission was led by Commander Frank Riker. Everything he does is strictly by the book. Trust me, with Frank Riker at the controls, that spacecraft would never have landed in Lake Michigan."

Author's Note

The space program and the race to land astronauts on the moon was one of the greatest seat-of-your-pants adventures in human history. Figuring out how to get humans to the moon and back took years of teamwork by dreamers, metalworkers, professors, mathematicians, computer programmers, daredevil test pilots, chefs (who do you think invented freeze-dried ice cream?), and, of course, rocket scientists. There were terrible setbacks, including unmanned rockets blasting off at strange angles and, tragically, astronauts losing their lives on the launchpad and in space. But there were also amazing successes, including Yuri Gagarin's historic first trip into space and Neil Armstrong's famous stroll on the surface of the moon in 1969. And there will be others.

If you want to learn more about the history and science of the space program, ask the librarian at your school or local public library. Hopefully, you already know that librarians are an excellent source of information—even better than the Internet, because they can help filter out the junk and lead you to what you're looking for. Or ask at your local bookstore, because they can help you find any book on the planet. Try it.

If you read more about the space program, you will recognize a lot of events from this book. The parts about the early Mercury, Gemini, and Apollo missions are true. I wasn't kidding: the average distance from the Earth to the moon really is 238,000 miles, although it varies by a few thousand miles depending on the moon's orbit. Also, I didn't make up the top speed of a rocket leaving the Earth's atmosphere: a scalding 25,000 miles per hour.

There are, however, a few things you won't find in other books. You won't find any mention of an astronaut named Mickey Price, or anything about the Artemis program, or about a mining center built on the moon, or a special metal called pleurinium. Neither will you find any description of any NASA command module making a "direct descent," landing straight on the moon, and then blasting off again for the trip home. In the Apollo program, NASA scientists figured out that taking the entire command module down to the surface of the moon and then back up again used way too much fuel. Instead, they decided to send the command module almost all the way, putting it into orbit around the moon. From this position, the Apollo astronauts rode in a small, lightweight landing craft to the moon's surface and then back again to their orbiting command module for the return trip home. Much more fuel efficient.

Does that mean it's impossible to build a spacecraft that lands directly on the moon? Impossible to erect buildings on the moon? Inconceivable that a group of young astronauts could have led a glorious mission to save the moon?

Just because none of this can be found in any of the excellent books your librarian shows you, does it mean that it can't happen? Or that it didn't happen?

Mickey Price and a handful of others know the secret of what happened at that space camp back in 1977. And now you do, too.

Acknowledgements

There are a number of people whom I need to thank profusely for their help on this book. Sara for helping conceive the idea and for encouragement at every step of the way. Freddy and Joey for laughing out loud when I first read the book to them and for not complaining when I changed the names of their characters. Ryan Kirschner, Willie King, Alex Hoffman, Jack Stanley, Josh Leffler, Maggie and David Hacker, and the other test readers in Garrett Farms and Duke School. All the Dellingers for their unwavering support. Aviva Goldfarb, Suzy Yalof-Schwartz, Brad Meltzer, and Dan Abrams for expert advice and strategy. Paul Forsyth for bringing the characters and scenes to life with inspired drawings. The Furman family for taking the manuscript to the beach. And finally, to Peggy Tierney and Tanglewood Press for, like Tess, believing in Mickey.

About the Author

John Stanley lives in Durham, NC. At night when the moon is clear and full in the Carolina sky, you might catch him staring upward, wondering what it would be like to stand on the lunar surface and look back at a small, blue earth swirled with white clouds. He and his wife, both lawyers, hope their twin boys will grow up to be explorers or scientists or historians or teachers but will still love them if they become lawyers, too. *Mickey Price: Journey to Oblivion* is his first published book.